"I do not wish you to enter into an arrangement that is distasteful to you."

Distasteful? It ought to be distasteful, given all it would mean. She ought to be snatching up the papers and running for her life. And yet something in his eyes froze her in place. Raw hunger swirled in the dark brown depths. Not the heat of desire, although that was there too, but a bleak, deep-seated loneliness as he waited to bid her farewell.

Her foolish heart ached to ease his hurt. A wild desire to dispel that look from his eyes pulled at her soul. She'd made a bargain.

"Go," he said.

The harshness in his voice said if she accepted his generous offer she would never see him again. Torn in two, she stared at the documents.

Go now, the voice of sanity whispered. She didn't want to go.

Reckless Ellie, always too impulsive by half, crossed the room behind him and laid a hand on his arm. "My lord, I would not have suggested it if I did not wish it."

He lowered his gaze to meet hers, then he pulled her close and brushed her lips with his—a hesitant, questioning kiss, as if he doubted her words.

A rush of pleasure heated her body. Two days ago had been the first time she had felt a man's body, hard and strong against her own. And she'd liked it. She'd had no idea, until then, that kisses crea░░░░░░░░░░░░░░░░░░░░░now she wanted more.

Mistress
░2—May 2010

Author Note

The moonlight meeting between Eleanor, a lady highwayman, and the brooding Marquess of Beauworth played out in my mind like the opening scene of a movie one quiet summer evening. Why would a woman take to the High Toby? And why did Garrick so obviously hate the idea of going home? These were puzzles I had to solve. By the early nineteenth century, highwaymen were a rarity. And it was a time when a man's home was his castle.

I hope you enjoy unravelling the answers and learning their story as much as I did. If you would like to know more about my writing and my books, visit my Web site at www.annlethbridge.com. I always love to hear from readers, and can be reached at ann@annlethbridge.com.

WICKED RAKE, DEFIANT

Mistress

ANN LETHBRIDGE

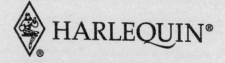

HARLEQUIN®

TORONTO • NEW YORK • LONDON
AMSTERDAM • PARIS • SYDNEY • HAMBURG
STOCKHOLM • ATHENS • TOKYO • MILAN • MADRID
PRAGUE • WARSAW • BUDAPEST • AUCKLAND

Recycling programs
for this product may
not exist in your area.

ISBN-13: 978-0-373-29592-0

WICKED RAKE, DEFIANT MISTRESS

Copyright © 2009 by Michèle Ann Young

First North American Publication 2010

Available from Harlequin® Historical and
ANN LETHBRIDGE

The Rake's Inherited Courtesan #941
Wicked Rake, Defiant Mistress #992

Other works include:

Harlequin Historical Undone eBooks

The Rake's Intimate Encounter

I would like to dedicate this book to my husband, Keith, and my wonderful critique partners, Molly, Maureen, Mary, Sinead, Teresa and Jude. My special thanks go to my editor Joanne Grant, whose skill and patience is gratefully acknowledged.

Chapter One

Sussex, England—May 1811

The anger burning in the Marquess of Beauworth's throat tasted of bile and bitter regret. While the horses thundered through shadows and moonlit tracts of rolling Sussex landscape, Garrick fought the urge to turn back for London.

He swallowed his ire and the carriage raced on. Home to Beauworth. The place he hated most in the world.

Not even the person closest to him, Duncan Le Clere, understood his hatred of the place. Sometimes he didn't understand it himself, but lack of knowledge didn't lessen the tension in his shoulders or the foreboding.

The pain of bruised tendon and bone reminded him of the reason for his return. One by one, he unclenched his fingers, forcibly relaxing his hands in his lap, breathing deeply and slowly, regaining control. He lounged deeper in the corner, stretching his legs along the gap between the seats, a picture of insouciance.

After all, the Marquess of Beauworth, idle rake, reckless gambler and bored dandy, had a reputation to uphold.

The carriage swayed violently. He grabbed for the strap beside his head. The vehicle slowed, then stopped.

'*Mon Dieu!* What now?' He let down the window and stuck his head out.

The carriage horses tossed their heads uneasily, their shapes indistinct in the shadow of the high hedges lining the road. The sound of their hard breathing and jingling harnesses cut through the warm stillness. Garrick narrowed his eyes, staring ahead into the dark. 'What do you see, Johnson?' Probably a puddle. The poor old fellow should have retired years ago.

Something white gleamed eerily in the shadows ahead. A white horse walking in the centre of the road, moonlight slipping luminescent over a dappled coat. At first he saw only the horse. Then another dark shape, a slight figure clutching the bridle. A woman in a black riding habit. Walking alone? Bloody hell. She must be in trouble.

He wrenched open the carriage door, leapt down and started forwards with an offer of help on his lips. The sight of a pair of long-barrelled pistols in her hands, one aimed at his forehead and the other at his servants, stopped him short.

Cold moonlight revealed a black mask covering all but her mouth, while a point-edge cocked hat adorned a curled and powdered peruke. Black lace frothed at her wrists and throat.

'Good God.' The exclamation exploded from his lips as recognition struck. Lady Moonlight, the daring cavalier's lady from Cromwell's time, forced to take to the High Toby to feed her family. Her exploits were legendary in this part of Sussex as were the sightings of her spirit after she'd hanged.

'Stand and deliver!' Her husky voice, tinged with the accent of the dregs of London, echoed off the overarching trees. The grey minced sideways and she checked it with a low murmur.

No ghost this. Merely a common criminal.

Garrick glanced up at the box where Johnson and Dan sat wide-eyed and motionless, apparently taken in by the clever ruse.

'Hand over yer valuables or the boy is dead meat,' she called out.

There was a desperate edge to the coarse voice he didn't like, but the pistols remained steady enough and both were cocked and ready. Damnation, but he wasn't in the mood for this tonight. A rush of anger roared through his veins, a red haze blurring his vision, his fingers curling into fists.

He inhaled long and slowly.

Control. Anything else and someone less innocent than he would die. Behind her mask her eyes glittered. Courage or fear? Would she shoot an unarmed man?

Dan, fear bleaching his cheeks, rose in his seat. One pistol tracked his movement.

'Curse it, lad,' the thief said. 'Yer want to die?'

Nom d'un nom. Garrick might be prepared to take a chance with his own life, but he would not risk the boy. He, more than anyone, deserved better. 'Sit down, Dan,' he ordered.

Scared eyes found Garrick's face. He nodded encouragement. The boy subsided on to his seat beside the rigid Johnson. Garrick shook his head. 'Be still, both of you.'

Clearly realising Garrick's dilemma, the little witch

kept one pistol fixed on Dan as she slipped the other into a saddle-holster beside a cunningly wrought sword sling. The intricate hilt protruding from the scabbard fitted her costume well enough. His lip curled. He'd like to see her try to best him with a sword.

She tossed her hat on the ground near his feet. 'Throw yer trinkets in there.'

A shimmer of light surrounded her face and body as she moved. A ghostly light. Was he going mad? Then he saw the sequins. They covered her mask and reflected moonlight from her coat and waistcoat. The little wretch looked like a reveller at a masquerade, and for such a deadly purpose.

An elegant twist of wrist and flutter of black lace drew his attention to the upturned hat. 'I ain't got all day.'

Garrick bowed with a flourish, acknowledging her impatience with charm and grace. 'Your wish is my command, milady.'

As he straightened, her full lips curved in a quick smile. She bobbed a curtsy. 'Yer too gracious, sir.'

'Ah, a polite Lady Moonlight.' He raised a brow. 'I'm waiting, *chérie*.'

Her smile fled and oddly he found himself regretting its loss. 'For what?' she asked. 'A bullet in yer brain?'

'For my kiss. Lady Moonlight always kisses the men she robs if she thinks them handsome.'

'Just put yer valuables in the 'at, milord.' A hint of laughter coloured her nasal voice.

Aware of the astonished gazes of those on the box, he spread his arms in a mock gesture of appeal. 'Are you saying you find me lacking? How cutting. You break my heart.'

She chuckled, soft and low and very feminine, but

the pistol steadied in the region of his chest. 'Now, milord.'

He put a hand to his pocket as if seeking his watch and cursed silently. He had left his travelling pistol in the coat lying on the carriage seat. Perhaps it was as well. He had no wish to harm the wench. He kept his voice calm and soft. 'This is dangerous work for a woman. If you get caught you'll hang, whereas I could offer you gainful employment.'

'Hah. I know yer sort's idea of work. Enough gabbing or you'll be joining yer ancestors.' Underneath the bravado, her voice shook with the tremor of tightly stretched nerves.

Much as he didn't care if he joined his ancestors, he didn't want her nervous and threatening the servants again. He pulled out his fob and dangled his watch between them. Slowly, he twisted the gold links in his fingers. The diamond-encrusted case winked and glittered like moonbeams on water.

The pistol trembled. She wouldn't use it. He was certain.

She reached for the prize, her head no higher than his shoulder as she snatched at the watch with her leather-gloved hand. Garrick caught her fine-boned wrist in one hand and restrained her pistol arm tight against her side with the other. He crushed her slender body hard against him, encircling her waist.

Her exhale of shock was warm, sweet and moist on his neck. Soft breasts compressed against his ribs. She smelled of vanilla with undertones of leather and horses. An oddly heady combination. He lowered his head and planted his lips firmly against her mouth, pleased when her lips drifted open in surprise.

The air around him warmed and swirled, sending his

blood pounding and his senses alert to her response. Her delicate lithe body, at first inflexible, softened just enough to let him know she was not unwilling. Indeed, her body moulded most deliciously to his. He ran his hand down her slender back and savoured the soft curves of her buttocks.

Somewhere in this exchange, his earlier fury had softened to the heat of desire. Another passion requiring control. And control it he would. He deepened the kiss and inched his fingers towards her hand, feeling for the pistol.

The little hellion broke free and leapt back, breathing hard, her eyes in the slits in the mask sparkling with reflected sequins or some deeper, hotter fire. Chest rising and falling in quick succession, she levelled the barrel at his chest. A point-blank shot. 'Stay back.' Her glance darted to the servants. 'All of ye.'

Laughing, he reached for her. 'Surely we can find a more amenable way for you to earn a living? One we would both enjoy.'

She stilled, those rosy just-kissed lips curving in a saucy grin. She curtsied, full and deep. 'I think not.'

'Look out, my lord,' Johnson called.

Garrick caught a blur of movement at the corner of his eye. With a curse, he whirled around. A large masked man, a pistol clutched in his fist, raised his arm high. Garrick dodged. The blow hammered against the side of his head. A blinding light flashed. He fought descending darkness. The ground hit his knees as he fell into black.

Blood rushed in Lady Eleanor Hadley's ears. Her head swam. Her heart raced. At any moment she would measure her length beside the man at her feet.

She took a deep breath, crouched at her victim's side and found a strong steady pulse in his wrist. She stood upright, glaring at Martin. 'Did you have to hit him so hard?' she muttered.

'What the devil are ye doing, letting him get so near?' Martin's deep, low mutter rang harsh with anger. He levelled his pistol at the men on the box.

Panting, she stared at the inert body on the ground. What had she been thinking? That he was tall and im-possibly handsome under the soft light of the moon? That the easy smile on his lean, dark face held no danger? If not for Martin, she might have fallen into his trap like a wasp in a jam pot. He had to be cocksure of his abilities as a lover if he thought to overpower her with a kiss. A laugh bubbled up. Hysterical, born of nerves and the strange sensations he'd sparked in her body. Never had she felt so horridly wonderfully weak, as if her bones were liquid and her mind was mush. Not her normal self at all.

If it wasn't for his grab for the pistol, he might have swept her off her feet.

'Where were you, Martin?' she muttered. 'Weren't you supposed to be covering the driver?'

'I never saw you start forrard. The plan was for me to give the signal.'

Even in the dim light, she saw his skin darken. Poor Martin. The best man to lead a charge, according to her father, but he made a terrible highwayman. She'd tried to send him away after their first foray. He'd refused point blank. Dear loyal Martin.

'Never mind.' She pointed to her victim and raised her voice. 'See wot 'e's got on 'im before 'e wakes.'

As Martin bent to do her bidding, the coachman fumbled under his seat. Oh God, this could get out of hand very quickly. She jerked her pistol in his direction. 'Don't try it.'

He straightened and raised his hands again. The angelic-looking boy beside him sat rigid, his shoulders shaking, his teeth biting down on his bottom lip. No heroics there, thank heavens.

Martin rolled the man on the ground on to his back. He moaned, his head lolling against his shoulder, his brow furrowed as if, even unconscious, he was aware of pain. The strong column of neck disappeared into a crisp, elegantly tied neckcloth and merged with powerful shoulders encased in a snug-fitting dark coat. Dark hair and olive skin gave his strong features a foreign cast.

Her heart pounded a little too hard. He was beautiful. Not an adjective she normally used about a man. They were usually either rough, or gentlemanly, or they were simply men she saw every day and gave no thought to at all. This one was beautiful in the way of a bronze sculpture: a perfectly moulded jaw, smooth plane of cheek, straight dark brows above a noble nose. Her fingers itched to trace his features, to feel the texture of bone and skin, much like one might run a hand over a fine statue. The line of his full bottom lip echoed the feel of his mouth on hers, warm and unbelievably exciting. And his voice, with its faint French accent, had brushed across her nape like the touch of velvet.

Madness.

He moaned again. She jumped back. To her relief, he did not open his eyes. Martin had struck him hard. She swallowed. Hopefully not a fateful blow. She didn't want him badly hurt, for all he'd seemed so careless with his life. Nor did she want to face him again. 'Time to go. Into the coach with him. You,' she said, pointing at the coachman, 'get down and lend a 'and. And no tricks.'

The coachman heaved his portly frame over the side.

Martin went to his head. 'Pick up his feet,' he ordered the coachman, who bent with a grunt and grasped the man under the knees above black Hessians polished to an impossibly glossy shine.

'Hold,' she said.

'What now?' Martin said in a growl.

'Take his boots.'

Stiff with anger, he dropped the man to the ground. He pushed the coachman aside with a grunt of disapproval and heaved off the tight-fitting footwear. He returned to his post at the man's head.

Eleanor opened the door of the carriage and stood back. The two men hoisted their burden on to the floor of the coach. Martin slammed the door.

'Be off with you,' she said to the panting coachman. 'As fast as you can before I change me mind.'

The coachman wasted no time in climbing up and a moment later the carriage sped down the road. Its swaying lamp disappeared around the corner.

Martin bent and cupped his hands and boosted her on to Mist, her steady little gelding, who had waited so patiently all this time.

Eleanor struggled awkwardly with her skirts as she settled into the saddle. 'Next time I'll wear William's breeches.'

'There ain't going to be no next time.' Martin stuffed their booty into his saddlebags and climbed aboard the chestnut. 'Mark my words, you'll end up like her, my lady. On Tyburn tree.'

Eleanor's stomach twisted at the worry in his voice. 'Do you have a better idea?' She dug her heel into

Mist's flank and they galloped swiftly into the protection of the woods. Eleanor used to love the freedom of riding at night. Many times, she and William, her twin, had slipped out to roam the countryside around their Hampshire estate after midnight. They'd been best friends in those days. She'd borrowed his clothes. And why not? She'd ridden as well as, if not better than, her brothers, shot as well as they did. And that was her downfall. She thought she knew better than them.

Look at tonight. This victim had been wonderfully rich, but the night had almost ended in disaster. Everything she touched went horribly wrong. William was on his way home, his ship due in Portsmouth any day now, and he'd come home to find himself ruined.

All because she couldn't leave well enough alone. Heat flooded her body. He'd think her such an impetuous fool.

Unless she could put things right before he arrived.

It didn't take long to reach the barn where they hid their horses. Eleanor slid out of the saddle and led Mist inside. She swept off the mask, wig and hat, casting them to the floor, scrubbing at her itchy scalp as her hair cascaded around her shoulders.

'Do you know who he was?' Martin asked, following her in.

'A dandy with gold in his pocket and jewellery to spare.'

'It was Beauworth. I recognised the coach.'

'What?' A cold, hard lump settled in her stomach. Beauworth? The man bent on destroying her family. She'd flirted with him, let him kiss him. Her face warmed at the memory. How demeaning. She yanked the leading rein through the metal ring in the wall. 'You should have told me.'

'Weren't much time for talking,' Martin said, turning

from the task of lighting a lantern hanging from a beam. His voice sounded disapproving. 'He's a gambler and a libertine. Cuts a swathe through the ladies like a scythe through hay, I'm told. The way he took hold of you fair makes my blood boil. We should never have held him up, neither. His uncle is the magistrate. We'll be knee deep in Bow Street Runners in a day or so.'

Eleanor grimaced. 'Without money, we'll starve and what will I tell William? That I carelessly lost his home and fortune?' Her stomach dropped away, her skin turning clammy, the way it did every time she remembered. William had trusted her to look after his interests until he returned. By forging his signature, she'd spent every penny in the bank. And then, out of nowhere Beauworth had demanded repayment of a mortgage she'd known nothing about. Damn him.

When he realised they couldn't pay, he'd sent in the bailiffs, forcing her and Sissy to seek refuge where they could.

If only the ship into which she'd sunk all William's money would return from the Orient, everything would be all right. The stupid thing seemed to have disappeared without a trace. Her heart picked up speed. What if it never returned?

And she needed money so they could eat. Blast it all. She had thought she was so dashed clever. Instead, she'd brought them all to the brink of ruin.

Miserably, she pulled a carrot from the pocket of her coat. Mist's warm breath moistened her palm as he nuzzled it free.

'Perhaps if I went to speak to the Marquess, he would listen to reason,' she said.

'Take pity on a helpless woman, you mean?'

Phrased in such bald terms, it sounded thoroughly

dishonourable. William would never approve. But then he wouldn't approve of her taking to the High Toby, either. A career that she'd discovered all too quickly, lacked the romance and adventure of legends. If they were caught, the authorities would respond without mercy. 'Ask for more time.'

'Jarvis said he needs the money. Got debts of his own.'

They always did, these fashionable men. Michael, her eldest brother, had had huge debts when he died. They were what made her invest in the ship.

There had to be some other way out. 'We need something to trade for the mortgage.'

'Too bad you didn't think of that an hour ago. We could have traded his lordship.'

Jaw slack, her eyes wide, she gazed at Martin's broad back. 'Blast. I walked away from the perfect solution.'

Martin swung around. 'Oh, no. I was jesting, my lady, and badly. I promised your father my loyalty to his children and I've kept my word, but I'll not be party to abduction.'

'You are right. It is far too dangerous.' She tossed an old blanket over Mist's back. Martin did the same for his mount.

'Why didn't you tell me the rest of that stupid legend?' she asked. 'The kissing business?' A kiss as sweet as sugar and as dark as the brandy on his breath. Not to mention strange delicious shivers deep in places she never knew existed. His body, where he pressed her close, had felt satisfyingly hard. She had wanted to touch him. All over. At the thought of her fingertips on his skin, her stomach tumbled in a strangely pleasant dance.

Blankly she stared at the plank wall with limbs the

consistency of honey. She clapped a hand to her mouth. How could she feel this way knowing what this man had done?

Martin scratched his chin. 'My brother never mentioned no kiss, my lady.' Which meant it probably wasn't true. She felt the heat rise in her face as Martin turned to look at her. 'Why did you take his boots?'

Eleanor still didn't understand the sudden teasing urge she'd felt and she certainly wouldn't tell Martin about the way his wicked smile and brush of his lips had turned her insides to porridge. 'They were new and he's a dandy.' She shrugged. 'It will annoy him. You know how ridiculous William is about his boots.' Besides, he'd been too bold, too reckless for his own good. A real criminal might have killed him. A lesson in humility would do him good. 'Throw them in the pond.'

She picked up her hat, tucking the wig and mask inside it. She stripped off the coat and waistcoat and handed them to Martin, who hauled the bundle up to the rafters in a net by way of an old block and tackle they'd found in the hayloft. 'We will have to ride out again.'

'Please, my lady. You are risking your neck for naught but a few baubles and a handful of guineas.'

She winced. As her father's sergeant in the army and later his steward, Martin would have given his life for her father. Now he held doggedly to his promise to serve his children, but she couldn't ask him to take any more risks. Not when everything she touched went wrong. 'It would serve William best if you returned to Castlefield. Keep an eye on the house. Make sure the bailiffs don't steal anything.'

'And let you risk your neck alone?' Martin glowered and shook his shaggy head. 'Your father always said you was a handful.'

A tomboy, he meant. Too competitive for a girl. Too impetuous, Father had said, when Mother defended her. And she'd been so sure she'd show William how well she could handle things in his absence. Pride had definitely ended in a fall. And if she didn't do something soon, she'd drag the rest of the family into the pit.

Garrick groaned and sat up on the floor of the carriage. Cursing, he pulled himself on to the seat and investigated the bump behind his ear with his fingertips. A knot as big as an egg. Blast the woman.

A comely female at that, if he hadn't been mistaken. He recalled the spiralling heat between them and her delicate trembles beneath his touch with a searing jolt of desire. For one heady moment, he'd thought he'd wooed her out of her villainous purpose. He might have, too, if she'd been alone. His luck was definitely out. First he'd taken the bit between his teeth to tell Uncle Duncan the bad news, and then he'd been robbed.

Head aching, he probed the tender spot on his scalp. Brandy might help. He fumbled in his cloak pocket and pulled out his flask. He rubbed some of the alcohol on the lump, hissing at the sting, then took a swig. The servants must have been terrified.

The abominable pounding in his head increased. He closed his eyes and leaned back against the squabs, uttering a sigh when, some twenty minutes later, the carriage crunched on gravel to a gentle stop.

Beauworth Court.

Johnson pulled open the door and let down the steps. 'My lord? Are you all right? I darsen't stop on the road.'

'I'm perfectly all right,' Garrick said, forcing a smile.

He allowed the coachman to help him out of the carriage and glanced at the house. Stone lions guarded

the wide granite steps to the front door. Columns, illu-
minated by torches, rose up to the first floor with Pal-
ladian grace and the lower windows blazed with light.
Uncle Duncan must be entertaining. Garrick bit back a
groan. *Merde.* He really did not want to be here.

'Dan,' he called out. 'Bring my coat, please.'

Dan jumped down with alacrity and dived into the
coach for the garment. ''Ere, my lord.'

'Good. Stay close to me.'

The gravel stabbed into the soles of his feet as he
hobbled up to the front door. 'Damn, blasted wench.' Why
the hell she had stolen his boots he could not imagine.

On cue, the door opened. The butler, a slick-looking
fellow Garrick didn't recognise, stared down his nose.
Recovering swiftly, he stepped back with a bow.
'Welcome home, my lord.'

Hah. 'Thank you.' He handed over his greatcoat and
headed for the arching sweep of staircase leading to the
first-floor chambers.

A door opened. Light spilled from the dining room.
A heavily built figure, his military bearing obvious,
strode purposefully across the black and white tiled
floor. Duncan Le Clere, his father's cousin, and
Garrick's trustee for twelve more months.

Dan ducked behind Garrick as Le Clere's stern gaze
took in the scene. 'The devil. What is the meaning of
this?'

'Got held up.' His uncle stiffened. 'By highwaymen.' Garrick chuckled at his pathetic humour.

Le Clere quickened his pace. 'Are you injured?' He
must have caught a whiff of the brandy because he
recoiled. 'Or drunk? Is this one of your pranks?'
Nothing slipped past Uncle Duncan with regard to
Beauworth and its heir.

'I might be a trifle foxed, but I am fully in possession of my faculties, I assure you. The damned rogues relieved me of my valuables and my boots.'

Two more men hurried into the vestibule: Matthews, the Beauworth steward, and Nidd, his father's ancient valet who did for Garrick on the rare occasions he came home.

'Johnson told us what happened,' Matthews said. 'These villains need teaching a lesson.'

And the beefy Matthews was ready to mete out the punishment. The thought of the saucy little wench in his hands did not sit well in Garrick's stomach.

'Send for the constable,' Uncle Duncan said, taking in Garrick's stockinged feet with raised brows.

'Not tonight.' Garrick put a hand to his head and winced. 'The morning will be soon enough. Right now, I'm for bed.'

Uncle Duncan's lips flattened. He glanced toward the dining-room door. 'I expected you for dinner. It takes more than a contretemps with the lower orders to keep a man from his duty.'

'Johnson said they struck his lordship on the head,' Matthews said.

The hard expression on Le Clere's face dissolved into concern. 'I'm sending for the doctor.'

The doctor who would poke and prod and wonder. Garrick put up a hand. 'A small lump, nothing more. I'll be well by morning.'

The broad back stiffened. 'A knock on the head, Garrick... I'm only thinking of your welfare.'

'Don't fuss.'

Le Clere recoiled. 'But your head, Garrick...'

A black emptiness rolled out from the centre of Garrick's chest. He knew what Le Clere was thinking, knew from the wary look in his eyes what he feared, and Garrick honestly couldn't bear it.

Garrick rubbed his sore knuckles. Le Clere hadn't yet heard of the latest débâcle. 'I'm sorry, Uncle. I know you mean for the best, but I do not need bleeding or quacking tonight.'

His uncle blew out a breath. 'As you wish. But if there is any sign…' He had no need to finish the sentence; his gentle smile said it all.

Garrick nodded. 'I'll see the doctor.'

'So be it,' Le Clere said. 'I cannot tell you how good it is to see you come home. There is much to be done, much to learn in the next twelve months, my boy.'

Hardly a boy. And the rest of it would wait for the morning. 'Good night, Uncle. Oh, and I brought my tiger.' He gestured to Dan, who moved closer to Garrick.

Uncle Duncan glanced at Dan with pursed lips. 'He belongs in the stables.' He waved off Garrick's response. 'We will talk tomorrow when you feel better. I must attend my guests. Take good care of him, Nidd. Matthews, I'll see you in the library later.' He hurried back to the dining room. The stolid Matthews bowed and wandered off.

Nidd's cadaverous face was anxious. 'He worries about you, my lord. You know how he is.'

Garrick sighed. 'Yes, I know. But I wish to God my father hadn't tied up my affairs so tightly.'

'You were but a babe then, my lord. He never dreamed he and your mother would go so early.'

A regretful silence filled the empty hall. It pressed down on Garrick's shoulders with the weight of a granite mountain. He started up the stairs.

In Garrick's chamber, Nidd eased him out of his

coat and went to work on his waistcoat. Garrick gestured at the boy hovering by the door. 'My wits were begging. I should have sent him to the stables with Johnson.'

'Leave him to me, my lord. I'll see he gets there. Johnson was only saying the other day as how he could use more help.'

That was another thing. Why so few servants in the house? In the old days there had been a footman stationed in every corridor. Was something wrong? Did he care?

Sometimes he did, and then the old anger he worked hard to contain erupted.

He leaned back in the chair and closed his eyes, seeking distance. 'Take him now, Nidd. I can manage the rest.' Since he had no boots to be pulled, undressing presented no difficulty. He opened his eyes as Nidd headed out of the door with his hand on Dan's bony shoulder. 'Tell Johnson to treat him gently. He's had a rough go of things.'

Eyes closed, he unbuttoned his waistcoat. His fingers sought his fob. Gone. He stared down at his right hand in horror. His signet ring, a family heirloom handed to him by his dying father, had also been stolen. Rage surged in his veins like a racing tide. This time he let it flow unchecked.

To lose the family signet ring now, when he'd finally made his decision. Damn the woman to hell. Damn him for falling under the spell of her kiss.

He pulled off his shirt and glared at the tester bed with its carved insignia of the Beauworth arms, the shield and white swan, a motif repeated on the moulded ceilings here and in the dining room. The same as the insignia engraved on his ring. He would have it back if he had to search the length and breadth of England. And when he found the woman, she'd rue the day she'd crossed his path.

Chapter Two

The next morning after an early breakfast, Garrick traversed the second-floor gallery and made his way down the sweeping staircase. Marble pillars rose gracefully to support the high carved ceiling above a chequerboard floor he couldn't look at without cringing. He took a deep breath, determined to keep his composure. He was twenty-four, not a scared child. Nor would he allow his uncle's cautious solicitude to get under his skin.

He knocked on the library door out of courtesy and entered. A polished oak desk dominated one end of the long room. Immersed in the papers before him, Uncle Duncan did not look up.

While Garrick waited, memories curled around him like comforting arms. He could almost hear the sound of his father's voice, the feel of his arm heavy on Garrick's young shoulders as they poured over maps or Father told him stories of military engagements.

On a warm spring day like today, the bank of French windows leading to the balcony would have been thrown open, a breeze heavy with the scent of roses from the garden beyond billowing the heavy blue curtains into the room.

He hated the smell of roses.

Garrick blinked, but the recollections remained imprinted in his mind like a flame watched too long: a young boy wide-eyed with imagination, his father, jabbing at the air with his cigar to emphasise some important point of strategy, until Mother chased them out into the fresh air. How his father's face lit up at the sight of her as she swept in, her powdered black hair piled high, her hands moving as she talked in her mix of French and broken English.

Mother. Like an icy blast from a carelessly opened door in mid-winter, the warmth fled, leaving only a cold, empty space in his chest. Hell. He would have sent Le Clere a note if it had not been cowardly.

It seemed to require every muscle in his body, but somehow Garrick slammed the door on his memories. He locked them away in the same way his father's old maps were locked behind the panelled doors of the library bookcases and focused his attention on Le Clere instead. Uncle Duncan, as Garrick had called him since boyhood, had grown heavier in the past four years. His ruddy jowls merged with his thick neck. His hair was greyer, but still thick on top and he looked older than his fifty years, no doubt dragged down by responsibility. As if sensing Garrick's perusal, he raised his flat black eyes. Garrick resisted a desire to straighten his cravat. Damn that the old man could still have that effect on him.

'Well, Garrick.' The deep voice that had once reached to the far reaches of a parade ground boomed in the normally proportioned library. Garrick winced as the harsh tone reverberated in his still-sensitive skull.

'What can you tell me about these villains that set upon you last night? This is the second time they've robbed a neighbourhood coach.'

Le Clere took his responsibilities as local magistrate seriously, but Garrick was not going to let the morons who stood for local law and order frighten off the cheeky rogues before he recovered his property.

He shrugged. 'They were masked. I barely caught a glimpse of them before I was struck.' He was certainly not going to admit being bested by a woman and he trusted Johnson to say nothing about that kiss. Damnation. Was he smiling at the memory?

A sour expression crossed his uncle's face. 'I had hoped you would be of more help. The last man robbed babbled on about a ghost.' He inhaled deeply. Garrick recognised the sign. Control. Uncle Duncan hated it when things did not go according to plan. Apparently in command of himself once more, Le Clere smiled. 'No matter. I am simply glad you are here, ready to devote yourself to duty at last.'

The old man's hopeful expression twisted the knife of guilt in his gut. He didn't like to tell him that the command to come back to Beauworth and take up his responsibilities had tipped the scales on his decision.

'I've decided to join the army.'

Le Clere sat bolt upright in his chair. 'You can't mean it.'

The anger, always a slow simmer in his blood, rolled swiftly to a boil. He let it show in his face. 'I certainly do.'

Bushy brows snapped together. Red travelled up his uncle's neck and stained his cheeks, the same signs of anger he experienced himself. The old man opened his mouth and Garrick awaited the parade-ground roar that had cowed him as a boy, but now left him cold. Le Clere inhaled a deep breath and when he finally spoke, his voice rasped, but remained at a reasonable pitch. 'What brought about this sudden decision?'

'I found one of Father's campaign diaries in the library in town. I'd forgotten how much he loved serving his country. I want to follow in his footsteps.'

Le Clere slammed a fist on the table. 'I should have burned them. Your father should never have risked his life in that manner, neither should you.'

'Father never got a scratch.' Only to come home and die in a hunting accident. Garrick rose to his feet. 'I have made up my mind. There is nothing you can say to convince me otherwise.'

Le Clere sagged against the chair back. 'All these years I've worked to safeguard your inheritance and you treat it as if it is nothing.' He pressed his fingers against his temple.

More guilt. As if he didn't have enough on his conscience. 'I have to go.'

'Why?'

'You know why.'

'Nothing has occurred since that incident at school. You've been all right. Got it in hand.'

It. The Le Clere curse. Something they'd never spoken of since the day Garrick had learned what it meant.

'No.' He stared at his bruised knuckles. If his cousin Harry hadn't pulled him off the bullying bastard beating Dan with a pitchfork, Garrick might have been facing charges of murder instead of spending every penny of his allowance to pay the man off.

'I see,' Le Clere murmured, his brow furrowing. 'Then you've wasted these past few years. Learned nothing of the estate. The war cannot continue much longer, surely, and when you come home I may not be here. I'm getting old, Garrick.'

Garrick tugged at his collar. 'I'm going.'

'Wait until my trusteeship is over. Twelve months is not such a long time. Learn all you can. Set up your nursery, get an heir, then go with my blessing.'

The older man's anxiety hung in the air like a sour London fog. If it hadn't been impossible, Garrick would have sworn he smelled fear. He could not let his uncle sway his purpose. Staying in England as he was, a short-fused powder keg waiting to go off at a stray spark, was asking for trouble.

'I've made up my mind.'

Le Clere ran a hand through his hair. 'What if you are killed? What will happen to Beauworth?'

'Cousin Harry is the heir.'

His uncle stilled. He seemed to have turned to a block of granite. His face reddened. The veins in his neck stood out above his neckcloth. Dear God, was he going to have an apoplexy? 'Uncle, please. Don't upset yourself.' Garrick strode for the table beside the hearth and poured a glass of brandy from a decanter. He took it back to Le Clere. 'Drink this.'

His uncle accepted the brandy with a shaking hand. It hurt Garrick to see the liquid splash over the side. Le Clere took a long swallow. He stared into the bottom of his glass. 'How long will this visit last?'

He'd planned only to collect his mare and bid his uncle farewell. The loss of the signet ring meant a delay. It must be there for Harry. At least his cousin didn't carry the Le Clere taint in his blood.

'A week.' Plenty of time to run the little vixen to earth.

Uncle Duncan straightened. 'Then we will use what little time we have to good purpose.'

Inwardly Garrick grimaced. If the old man hoped to use the time to change his mind, he was in for more disappointment. More guilt. Ah, well, if he was going to be here anyway… 'All right.'

Le Clere beamed. 'Good. Very good. Let us get started right away. After all, we don't have much time.'

Garrick hid his sigh of impatience. What he really wanted to do was question the local people about the thieves. It would be hours before he could make his escape. 'I'm looking forward to it.'

Eleanor bore most of the weight of the basket swinging between her and her twelve-year-old sister, Sissy, as they trudged through Boxted toward their cottage. After the hour's walk from Standerstead on a fine spring day, a trickle of sweat coursed down between her shoulder blades.

Her stomach tightened. Time was running out and here she was having to spend it buying supplies instead of doing something about her predicament.

As they passed the Wheat Sheaf across from the village green, a tall man with broad shoulders in snug burgundy velvet stepped into their path. The Marquess of Beauworth. No one but the local lord of the manor would cut such an elegant figure in the humble village of Boxted. And he looked lovelier in bright sunshine than he had beneath the moon.

Eleanor's heart skipped and her breath caught in her throat as she fought not to stare at him, tried to pretend he wasn't there. But when he bowed with elegance and a charming smile, she could pretend no longer. She halted.

'Good day, ladies.' His deep voice sounded intimate, seductive.

A disturbing surge of exhilaration heated her cheeks and sent shivers tingling from her chest to her toes. The man was downright dangerous if he could do all that with a smile. And she did not like the puzzlement lurking in his amber-lit brown eyes. Please, don't let it be recognition.

She bobbed a small curtsy. 'Good day, my lord.'

'May I help you with that heavy basket, miss?' he asked.

Before Eleanor could respond that he need not trouble, Sissy piped up with a cheeky grin and a look of relief in her dark brown eyes. 'You can help me.'

Eleanor groaned inwardly. Why couldn't the child hold her tongue for once? 'Sissy, please. You must excuse my sister, my lord, she is too forward.'

'Why, I believe she is just truthful. It would not be at all out of my way, you know.' With a smile warm enough to melt an icicle in mid-winter, he grasped the handle of the basket.

Fate in the shape of a black-haired imp had taken the decision out of Eleanor's hands. 'Thank you, my lord.' She released the handle and he hefted the basket as if it weighed nothing at all.

'It is a remarkably fine day, is it not, Miss...?'

'Brown. Ellie Brown, sir, and this is my sister, Sissy.'

'Miss Brown, Miss Sissy Brown.'

He bowed politely to each of them in turn as if they were gentry and not simple village misses. If it was possible, her heart beat a little faster. For the first time in weeks, she felt valued. Her cheeks flared hotter than before. Lord, what would he think?

'You have just come from the market?' he asked.

'Yes, my lord. For baking supplies.'

'Ellie makes the best biscuits in the whole world.' Sissy added, 'I think she should sell them.'

Eleanor wanted to put a hand over her sister's mouth. She was far too ready to confide anything to anyone. She quelled her irritation as the Marquess smiled winsomely at the vivacious child peeping admiringly up at him. Clearly he applied his charm to any female who crossed his path. She resented the pang of something unpleasant in her chest as he directed his lovely smile at Sissy.

'I hope I might try some one day,' he said.

Outwardly polite and ineffably charming, while inside there lurked the worst sort of rake. A man who had done untold damage to her family. The strangely weak feelings she had around him were inexcusable. She scowled at Sissy behind his back.

Seemingly impervious to Eleanor's stare, Sissy gave a little skip. 'Perhaps you would like to buy some.'

Now the child sounded like a merchant. Access to Beauworth Court might solve their problems, but not at the cost of involving her innocent sister. 'Silly girl. The Marquess will not be in the habit of purchasing food.'

'Very true, Miss Brown, but I will mention your talents to Mrs Briddle, our cook.' His dark gaze searched her face. Against her will, her gaze roved over the elegant lines of his bronzed features. Definitely foreign looking. And that French accent made her toes curl. Mortification dipped her stomach. This must stop.

'Miss Brown, I have the strangest feeling we have met,' he said. 'Before I went away to school, perhaps?'

Surely he would not recognise her as Lady Moonlight. 'It is not possible, my lord.' How breathless she sounded. She inhaled deeply, willing her pulse to stop its gallop. 'We only moved here recently.'

'In London, then?'

'I've never been to London.' Fortunately she hadn't. With the deaths in her family, her come-out had been postponed for three years in a row and if she didn't sort things out soon, would probably never occur. Not that she minded. Primping and simpering had never suited her temperament.

'We lived in Hampshire—' Sissy announced.

Eleanor gave her a little pinch to stop the flow of words.

'Ouch,' Sissy cried. She rubbed her arm and glared balefully at Eleanor.

Eleanor bent over her. 'Oh dear, have you hurt yourself?'

'No. You—'

'Good.' She straightened 'This is our cottage, my lord.' She pointed at the last dwelling in the row of five. Beyond it, fields of hay and ripening corn spread as far as the eye could see. 'Thank you so much for your help.' She took the basket from his grasp. 'Come, Sissy.'

Uncomfortably aware of his gaze on her back, Eleanor kept her shoulders straight and her eyes firmly focused on her front door. She would not look back. Next time they met, she would be ready for him and his winsome smile.

Like a connoisseur of fine wine, Garrick savoured the gentle sway of Miss Brown's hips and her proud carriage as she negotiated the wooden plank across the sluggish stream running alongside the road. As if she'd forgotten him completely, she opened the gate and walked up the short path through the unkempt patch of garden.

With guinea-gold hair pulled back beneath her plain straw bonnet and her serious expression, she presented a delicious picture of demure English womanhood. Somehow she put the sophisticated ladies of London in the shade. Prim and proper as she seemed, the confused blushes on the creamy skin of her face indicated an interest. None of his former loves had ever coloured so divinely. Although her wide-set, dove-grey eyes set in an oval face observed him coolly enough, they warmed to burnished pewter when she smiled with a heart-stopping curve of two eminently kissable lips.

How extraordinary to find such a beauty in sleepy Boxted.

The feeling that he knew her remained. He combed his memory without success. Eventually he would remember. Miss Ellie Brown was not a female a man would easily forget. Not when the mere sight of her had pulled him away from his purpose at the inn. An instant attraction that was not plain old-fashioned lust, so swift to rouse when he'd kissed Lady Moonlight. Rather, the purity shining in her face had evoked a different kind of admiration. Not one he'd had much experience with. And yet the spark of innocent passion he'd sensed running beneath the modest appearance offered an ir-resistible challenge, even if it could result in no more than harmless dalliance for a day or two.

He returned Miss Sissy's cheery wave as she fol-lowed her sister inside.

He frowned. The cottage, like the others in the row, sagged like an ancient crone. Mortar crumbled around the windows and patches of stone showed through the rendering. Nesting birds had pitted the moss-covered thatch, while the stench of stagnant water hung thick in the air. He narrowed his eyes. He hadn't noticed any problems with the estate's finances during his session with his uncle this morning, but in his father's day, these cottages had been well-kept abodes. Perhaps he needed to look a little closer.

He turned his steps for the Wheat Sheaf where he'd abandoned his horse and his tankard of ale for a pretty face and a well-turned ankle. The local men must know something about the highway robbers. A glass of heavy wet should loosen their tongues.

Her heart having settled into its normal rhythm after her encounter with the Marquess, Eleanor set a batch of cakes to cool in the pantry. The sweet smell of baking reminded her of helping her mother in the medieval kitchen at Castlefield. The servants had grown accustomed to the sight of their Countess, the daughter of an impoverished gentleman parson, in a starched white apron over her gown and flour up to her elbows. As soon as Eleanor had been old enough to stand on a stool, she had loved helping Mother, breaking the eggs into a little cream-and-brown china bowl, learning the art of baking the lightest of confections, creating something from nothing. It was the only thing she and William had not done together, though he wolfed down the results of her efforts cheerfully enough.

Sweet memories. Best not to let them intrude. She shivered and rubbed her arms briskly against the chill. The fire, the bane of her existence, had gone out again. It seemed to have a mind of its own. A mean mind. Every time she turned her back, it died. Or it smoked.

She opened the outside door. Cuddling Miss Boots, a tabby cat of questionable heritage, Sissy sat reading in the shade of a straggly rosebush.

'Fetch some wood, please, Sissy,' Eleanor called out.

The child glanced up with a pout. 'Why do I always have to fetch the wood?'

'Please, don't whine. I need your help. It's not too much to ask.'

Sissy grumbled her way to her feet. Eleanor returned to her nemesis. This time she would make it behave.

For once, the paper spills caught with the first spark of the flint and the slivers of kindling flared to light with a puff of eye-stinging smoke. Where was Sissy?

Eleanor ran to the front door. Her jaw dropped. Sissy had her head beneath the bush apparently trying to rescue Miss Boots.

'How could you?' Eleanor cried. 'You know I need firewood.'

Sissy jumped guiltily and dashed for the pathetic pile of logs against the wall. 'Coming.'

'Really, Sissy. I had it lit. Now the spills and the kindling are burned and I have to start over.' Eleanor wanted to cry. She snatched the logs from her sister's hands and hurried back inside while Sissy ran back for more.

Jaw gritted, she laid the fire once more. The tinder-box shook in her hand. She struck and it failed to spark. Calm down. She took a deep breath and struck it again. A tiny glow dropped on to the tight twist of paper.

'Please light,' she begged. The fire flared. 'Hah.' She nodded in triumph and balanced the logs on top. Now for tea. She marched to the pantry. Hearing Sissy's steps behind her, she called out, 'Put the rest of the wood on the hearth and then set the table.' She tucked a loaf of bread under her arm and grabbed a pat of butter and a jar of jam.

Sissy screeched. Eleanor whirled around. A lump of soot lay on the floor, a black monster writhing with red

glow-worm sparks. The rug at Sissy's feet smouldered.
At any moment it might burst into flame.

'Sissy, move.' Panic sent her voice up an octave.

The child remained glued to the spot, coughing as
choking black smoke rose around her.

Heart pounding, Eleanor dropped everything and
ran. She caught Sissy by the arm and thrust her out of
the front door. She flew back inside.

Rubbing her eyes, Sissy poked her head in. 'The rug
is on fire.'

'Stay there.' Flames played among the ragged ends
of the rug. Glowing soot took flight in the draught from
the door and landed on the tablecloth. It flared up. Oh
God, soon the whole place would be alight. She glanced
wildly around. Her father's calm voice echoed in her
ears. *Smother a fire.*

She ran to the bedroom, pulled a blanket off the bed
and ran back to toss it over the flames. Smoke billowed
up. Vaguely, she heard Sissy screaming, 'Fire!'

The door burst open. A tall figure loomed through
the rolling smoke like a warrior wreathed in mist. He
wrenched the blanket from the floor and beat the
flames into submission. The burning tablecloth went
out of the window. Water from the bucket by the sink
sluiced over the rug.

Eleanor peered at her rescuer through streaming
eyes.

The Marquess of Beauworth flapped the singed
blanket, chasing the last of the smoke out through the
open window. 'Good thing I was riding by. It looks like
the day King Alfred burned the cakes.'

She stiffened. 'It was the chimney, not my baking.'

He grinned. He was teasing. She tried to smile back,
but as her gaze roved around the disaster, her shoulders

sagged. The rug was naught but a charred ruin. A few minutes more and the house might well have burned to the ground. Sissy might have been hurt. Her legs turned to water. Heart racing, she dropped down on the sooty sofa. 'Thank you, my lord. I dread to think what might have happened had you not been on hand.'

He shrugged. 'You seemed to have things under control.'

She hadn't, but she was grateful for his kind words. Her heart slowly returned to normal and she looked around at the mess.

Sissy's head appeared around the door. 'Is it out?'

'Yes,' Eleanor said. 'But don't come in. There's soot and water all over the place.'

'Your horse is loose on the other side of the stream,' Sissy said. 'Won't she run away?'

'She won't go anywhere without me,' the Marquess replied with a smile.

Sissy's head disappeared.

Eleanor pulled herself to her feet, her knees shaking and her hands trembling. She began to roll up the remains of the evil-smelling carpet.

'Let me.' The Marquess took the rug from her hands. It followed the tablecloth into the front garden, as did the blanket.

He glanced curiously around the room. How he must scorn their poverty, whitewashed plaster bellying from the damp stone walls, sticks of furniture acquired by Martin from who knew where. Lit by a lattice window, the room looked positively dreary. She hoped the shame did not show on her face.

'I'm sorry I couldn't save the rug.' He sounded sorry. She hadn't expected that and she smiled.

He grinned, his eyes crinkling at the corners, his

teeth flashing white against his soot-grimed face. He looked nothing like the elegant Marquess she'd met earlier. She giggled. 'You look like a sweep.'

He dragged a sleeve across his brow. 'No doubt.'

Taking the bucket to the door, she called out, 'Sissy, fetch water from the well. Bring it back and then come inside.'

She turned back to her rescuer. 'Will you take tea with us?'

He hesitated. What was she thinking, inviting someone like him to take tea? In her present circumstances, she was far beneath his touch. She tried to hide her chagrin with a diffident shrug.

He smiled and her heart did a back flip. 'Yes, thank you.'

She knew she was beaming at him, but she couldn't help it. She dashed for her pitcher of water in the bedroom. She filled a small bowl, setting a cloth, soap and towel alongside it.

'Please,' she said. 'Use this to wash. There is a mirror above the sink.'

The Marquess stared at his blackened hands. 'Good idea.' He took off his jacket, something no gentleman would do in the presence of a lady, but she couldn't hold it against him. Not when he'd saved them. He rolled up his shirtsleeves and she saw that his forearms were strong, corded with sinew that shifted beneath his tanned skin as he scrubbed. A shimmer of heat rose up her neck. A little squeeze in her chest made her gasp.

She shouldn't be looking. She shifted her gaze to his back. It didn't help. The way his broad shoulders moved beneath the fine cambric of his shirt created more little thrills. Her heart gave a jolt at the weird sensation. What on earth was wrong with her? This man was her enemy.

Do something else. Tea. She'd offered him tea. Set the table. That was it. Gaze averted, she hurried for the dresser. Where was Sissy with the water?

'Miss Brown?'

'Yes, my lord?' She turned.

As he wiped his jaw with the damp cloth, his gaze travelled over her face in a long, slow, appraising glance. Heat rushed to her cheeks.

'You look quite smutty yourself,' he said with a smile. He reached out with the cloth and dabbed at her nose. She couldn't breathe. She snatched at the cloth.

Laughing, he caught her hands in his large warm one and wiped them clean. Such strong hands. She seemed bereft of the will to move.

He stepped back, his head cocked to one side. 'You know, you have a streak on your chin. If you will allow me?'

Her heart thundered in her chest. Her body clenched with another delicious thrill as the tips of his fingers, feather light on her jaw, tilted her chin towards the light. She held perfectly still, afraid she might do something rash like place her hands on his shoulders for support. Her pulse raced unmercifully as gently, softly, he dabbed her chin, her cheek, her nose, the water delightfully cold on her heated skin.

Long dark lashes hid his eyes as he lowered his gaze to his task. The scent of sandalwood cologne and smoke filled her nostrils. His expression softened, then his glance flicked up and caught her watching.

Amber glowed like sunbeams in the depths of his warm brown eyes. He bent his head and his parted lips hovered above hers. Heat radiated from his body and her heart skipped and thudded.

She struggled to catch a breath, as if something tight

restricted her ribs, and feared he would hear the soft pants for air she couldn't control.

His cheekbone filled her vision, clearly defined above a lean suntanned cheek. A whisper away from her skin, his dark brown hair curled at his temple. She held her breath, while her heart raced wildly. For the life of her she couldn't move. Didn't want to.

He brushed his lips across her mouth, warm and dry and soft. A mere whisper of the kiss he'd given her in the dark on a moonlit road.

A lightning bolt seemed to shoot through her body, hot yet pleasurable. She stiffened in shock.

'I've been wanting to do that since the moment I saw you,' he said, his voice carrying on a warm puff of breath against her chin.

She shivered, her mind a blank to everything except trembling anticipation.

A smile dawned slowly, lazy and sensuous. She could not tear her gaze from his mouth. He slid one hand behind her neck. 'You are very pretty, Ellie.'

His husky voice seduced her ears. He was the sun and she the moon, pulled inexorably into his orbit. She leaned closer. He dropped the cloth and enfolded her in his arms, his hand spanning the arch of her back, his breath warming her lips.

What was she doing? It felt so right, but was very, very wrong.

The door crashed back on its hinges.

Eleanor jumped back. The Marquess turned away, but not before she saw a glimmer of rueful amusement in those warm brown eyes.

'Here you are,' Sissy announced. Water from the bucket slopped over her shoes. She glanced around. 'Gracious, and after you spent all day yesterday cleaning.'

Eleanor busied herself clearing the table and wiping away the soot, praying that Sissy would not notice her heated face or agitated breathing. 'Put some water in the kettle and the rest in the sink.' Her voice sounded different, throaty, rough.

The Marquess grabbed the bucket. 'Let me. That is far too heavy a load for such a small person.' He poured water in the kettle and hung it over the traitorously merry fire.

Eleanor laid the table and, while the water boiled, she covered the old wooden table with another thread-bare cloth, dusted off the bread and pot of jam she'd dropped unceremoniously on the floor and brought cakes from the pantry. The Marquess helped Sissy move the chair and two stools to the table. Somehow he didn't fit with Eleanor's idea of a rake. He seemed no different than her brothers. Well, not quite like a brother, but nice, friendly and fun.

'Goody,' Sissy said, 'cakes. We never have cakes unless Martin comes, and not always then.'

'Martin?' The Marquess looked enquiringly at Eleanor, but it was Sissy who replied.

'Mr Martin Brown, he's—' began Sissy.

'A relative of ours,' Eleanor put in swiftly. Sissy knew the story they'd woven, but sometimes she forgot. 'He works nearby on his cousin's farm.'

'Please sit down, my lord.' Eleanor bobbed a curtsy and gestured to the chair. She and Sissy took the stools. Eleanor poured tea and Sissy passed him the plate of cakes.

'Special cakes,' Sissy said.

He popped one in his mouth. 'They are delicious.' He took another and Eleanor smiled. It was nice to have a compliment from someone like the Marquess.

'How long have you lived here, Miss Brown?' he asked in formal conversational tones.

'Almost one month.'

'I see.' He glowered at the hearth. 'That chimney should be cleaned.' His gaze roamed the room. 'The walls are damp.'

'The roof leaks a little,' Eleanor admitted.

'And the stream outside overflows,' Sissy said, placing her cup in its saucer with a decisive clink. 'We had water running right through the kitchen. And frogs.'

'Please don't think I am complaining,' Eleanor hurried to say. 'We were lucky to find a place we could afford so close to the village.'

He looked at her curiously. 'Miss Brown, you are not from around here. Your accent is not from Sussex. Indeed, you both sound almost…'

What had he been about to say. Educated? Noble? She'd made no attempt to change her or Sissy's speech. Not in this particular role. Once more he'd surprised her, this time with his perception. She tried to keep the guilt from her voice and face while the lies she and Martin had concocted tripped glibly from her tongue. 'We were brought up on a great estate, similar to your own. Our mistress was fond of my mother and allowed Sissy and me to be taught with her children. I plan to become a governess, but have as yet to find a suitable position.'

'I like it here,' Sissy said. 'I found Miss Boots in the garden.'

'Miss Boots?' the Marquess asked with a raised eyebrow.

'My cat,' Sissy said. She ducked under the table and pulled out the kitten. 'See, she has little white boots.' She pointed to the cat's tiny white feet and legs.

'So she does,' he said. He pulled out his watch, a

plain silver thing. Nothing like the glittering piece she'd stolen. 'You will forgive me,' he said. 'I have another engagement this afternoon.'

And here he was listening to a child's artless chatter. Eleanor tried not to let the chagrin show on her face. 'Please, do not let us keep you. Thank you for allowing me to pay my debt in some small measure.'

He shook his head. 'The pleasure is mine, I assure you.'

And she believed him. Despite their apparently different stations, he showed not a smidgen of condescension. Why could she not have met him in her old life?

Oh, Lord, what was she thinking? This man had ruined her life. But somehow she no longer felt any hatred. After all, he'd saved them from a fiery fate. Her change of heart had absolutely nothing to do with all those other hot sensations. Or his kisses.

He shrugged himself into his jacket and picked up the hat and cane he had dropped on his way in. 'I will certainly tell Mrs Briddle that Boxted village boasts one of the finest bakers in all of Sussex. I am sure you will hear from her very soon. Good day, Miss Brown, Miss Sissy.' He bowed and, with a touch of the head of his cane to his forehead, departed.

Eleanor, with Sissy at her side, watched him stroll down the path from the doorway. He paused briefly on the wormy plank across the stream, looking down into the water for a moment, before mounting his horse.

'Eleanor, that's it,' Sissy said. 'You can bake cakes for Beauworth Court and we will be rich again.'

The hope in Sissy's voice brought Eleanor down to earth with a painful jolt. If she didn't find a way out of this morass soon, things were going to get a great deal worse. 'He's a dangerous man.'

'I liked him,' Sissy said. 'He has nice brown eyes.'

'You only like brown eyes because you have them, too.'

Sissy laughed. 'Well, he likes you. He looked like he wanted to eat you instead of the cakes.'

Eleanor put a hand to her lips as she recalled the way she had melted at the brush of his mouth. The man was a practised seducer. How many other young women had he brought to ruin?

Not to mention that if he hadn't called in the mortgage, they would not be in such desperate straits. Perhaps Martin's ransom idea had merit after all.

Chapter Three

Arriving back at the stables, Garrick found Johnson in the barn mending tack. 'Where's Dan? I want him to come with me on a small errand.'

'I sent him to the kitchen for summat to eat. Got hollow legs, that lad 'as. Needs feeding up.'

Garrick nodded. 'Saddle the quietest thing we've got for him, would you? I'll look after Bess.'

They worked in the side-by-side stalls in silence for a few minutes.

'Bright that lad 'e is,' Johnson said to the jingle of a bit.

Garrick knew he meant Dan. He grunted agreement as he lifted his saddle on to the mare.

'Good with the horses,' Johnson continued. 'You don't have to tell him a thing more than once. 'Ad some rough treatment somewhere, I reckon.'

No point in keeping it a secret. 'Apprenticed to a bad master. I convinced him to let him go.'

'With your fists, I hear, my lord. Served the bastard right.'

A sick feeling roiled through Garrick's gut. When

he'd caught the bully laying a stick across the boy's back, he'd seen red. The blood red of terrible rage. If Harry hadn't separated them, the man might have cocked up his toes.

When it was over, he'd paid handsomely, both for Dan and for the damage he'd wrought, yet his gut still churned when he recalled his desire to spill blood. After years without incident, he'd lost control, let the inner beast slip off its chain. He'd been a fool to think he could beat the Le Clere curse. He wasn't fit for civilised society.

If it wasn't for his lost signet ring, he'd have left for Lisbon today.

'Dan should not have said anything,' Garrick muttered.

'I winkled it out of him, my lord. I couldn't understand why he flinched every time I raised me arm. Won't do him any good around your uncle.'

Garrick patted Bess's neck. 'Keep the boy busy and he'll do well enough. I'm surprised you don't have more help.'

Johnson shrugged. 'Mr Le Clere don't like to spend a shilling when a groat will do.'

At that moment, Dan entered the stable whistling. Garrick leaned out of the stall. 'Give Mr Johnson a hand, lad. You are riding out with me.'

Dan's angelic face lit up. 'Yes, my lord.'

From his side of the stable wall, Garrick listened to Johnson giving instructions. He'd been right to bring the lad here to Beauworth. He'd learn a useful trade as well as grow strong away from the foul London air. Today, he'd explain his plan for the boy's future.

He finished saddling Bess and led her out into the sunshine. Dan followed a moment later, the old nag Johnson had found for him chewing on its bit.

'Ready, boy?' he asked.

'Aye, my lord.'

They mounted and rode out of the stable yard towards the place where they'd been held up the previous night. If luck was with him, he'd find some trace of his attacker. Attackers, he amended. Damn it. He should have expected an accomplice. Her husband, perhaps? Or was she his doxy? A repulsive thought. Just thinking about the man with his hands on the saucy wench made him go cold.

What the hell was the matter with him? To be attracted to two women in one week seemed overly debauched even for him. Two very different females, too. One sweet, innocent, barely aware of her feminine appeal. The other, coarse and brash, a lure to the brute every civilised man held at bay.

What a base cur he was, to look forward to meeting the lady highwayman again.

Leaving the lane, they entered the woods. Ancient oaks and elms rose above their heads, the cool air smelling of leaf mould. A breeze stirred the branches and gold-dappled shadows shifted on the track. Here and there the damp soil revealed the passage of two horses travelling fast, one large and one smaller.

When they emerged into open country again, Garrick lost the tracks. Forced to dismount, he cast around.

Dan slid warily from his horse a short distance off. 'There are hoof prints in the dried mud over here, my lord, leading that way.'

Garrick inspected the prints. They were the same as those he'd seen in the woods. 'Well done, Dan. Let's see where they lead.'

Walking their horses, they continued on. In the

distance, hedgerows seemed to stitch the patchwork of green-and-gold fields together, and the dipping sun gilded the tops of emerald trees. Once in a while, a patch of soft earth, or dried mud, revealed evidence of their quarry.

Tucked in a valley near a copse of trees they came across an ancient-looking barn hunkered beside a stream-fed pond. 'This looks promising,' Garrick said.

Dan shifted in his saddle. 'Do you think they are in there?'

'Doubtful. But in case, I want you to remain here out of sight with our horses. Ride back to Beauworth if anything goes wrong.'

Straightening his thin shoulders, Dan dismounted and grabbed the bridles with a determined expression. The lad was tougher than he looked. He had to be, or he wouldn't have survived.

Garrick cautiously crossed the clearing to the sound of twittering birds in the nearby trees. He peered through a crack in a wooden door barred and padlocked from the outside. He made clicking noises with his tongue and listened with satisfaction to the sound of stirring feet and the huffing breath of animals tethered inside. The faint gleam of a white coat in the shadowy interior confirmed what he had hoped. He had found their hiding place. And if they were keeping their horses in the neighbourhood, they no doubt expected to strike again.

He returned to Dan, his mind busy forming a plan. If this worked, he'd be leaving in a day or so. He looked into the face of the anxious boy and remembered why he'd brought him along. 'I have some bad news for you, lad.'

The day after the fire, Martin's bulk overflowed the wooden chair at Eleanor's kitchen table.

'Beauworth has been making enquiries,' he said, glancing out of the window to where Sissy was sitting reading to Miss Boots. He lowered his voice.

'Really,' she said, hoping he wouldn't hear the sudden increase of her heartbeat in her voice.

He nodded. 'According to my cousin, he was worried they might try to steal the gold expected from London tonight.'

Eleanor straightened.

Martin's eyes narrowed. 'It's a trap, my lady. Stands to reason.'

Traps sometimes closed in more than one way. 'I think you are right.' She crossed her fingers in the folds of her skirt. 'And besides, I wouldn't dream of trying a robbery while you are gone.'

A sceptical expression passed across Martin's rugged features, but he said no more. He flung a small leather pouch into her lap. It landed with a soft clink. 'This is all the money I got from the first robbery. Not much, considering the danger.'

She nodded and gestured to the valise on the floor. 'We need to make sure Lady Sissy is safe before we think of doing anything else.'

'Did I hear my name?' Sissy wandered in with Miss Boots draped across her shoulders. She rubbed her cheek against the cat's soft fur.

'Martin is going to take you to Aunt Marjory,' Ellie said.

Tears pooled in Sissy's eyes. She dropped to her knees by Eleanor's feet. 'No. You said I could stay with you.'

With a wince, Eleanor looked at Martin. He shook his head. He didn't like this any more than Sissy did, but Eleanor could not let the little one stay any longer.

She ruffled the dark curls on the bowed head at her knee. 'You like Aunt Marjory. She has cats. Miss Boots will have company.'

Sissy clutched Eleanor's skirts. 'Please don't send me away, Len. Everyone else has gone. I'll fetch the wood every day, I promise.'

Not even the loss of her parents to influenza or Michael's freakish carriage accident had caused Eleanor so much pain in her heart as Sissy's tears did now. Until William returned to take up his title, she and Sissy were all that were left of their once close-knit family. 'This is just a visit, dearest. You always visit Aunt Marjory in the summer.'

A hiccup emerged from the face buried against her lap. 'You won't leave me there forever, will you? Cross your heart and hope to die.'

'I promise.' When Sissy looked up, she made the obligatory sign over her chest.

'All right.'

The tone was grudging, but Eleanor breathed a sigh of relief. She kissed the top of her sister's head, stroked the glossy dark brown curls into some sort of order and blinked back her own tears. 'William will be home soon, don't forget.' Anguished, she looked at Martin. 'Time to go.'

He swung Sissy up into his strong arms. Eleanor handed up Miss Boots and followed them outside to the waiting gig. Martin lifted the child, her kitten and her bag into the carriage and climbed up beside her. He touched his hat. 'I'll return tomorrow.' He set the horse in motion.

'Give my regards to Aunt Marjory.'

Sissy stared at her mournfully. 'I will.' The child looked over her shoulder all the way down the road and

Eleanor waved cheerfully until the gig was out of sight. Eyes burning, she closed her front door. If things went wrong, she might never see her family again. But she had to try to put things right.

Moisture trickled down her cheeks, hot at first, then cold little trails. Crying? She never cried.

She wiped her eyes and lifted her chin. This would be her last chance to make amends. She must not fail.

After pushing the bolt home in the door, she drew the curtains across the windows in the parlour and the bedroom. She pulled the trunk from beneath the bed she shared with Sissy and placed the pouch of money among the articles they'd stolen. Items she'd rejected for sale as too distinctive. One such sparkled in her hand. The Marquess had tried to seduce her in order to keep it. And she was a numbskull to be swayed by the charm of a man who had ruined so many lives.

She sat back on her heels, staring at her ill-gotten gains. She would do well to keep that in mind.

Dinner over, Garrick sauntered out of the house with his father's sword under his arm. After a full morning going over the estate's ledgers in his uncle's absence, he now had an inkling of why Beauworth seemed less than healthy. Over the last decade, rents had declined. Why, he wasn't sure. Le Clere would no doubt have the answer, but would he have a solution?

Modernisation might be the key. He'd heard others talking about new farming methods. He'd mention it to Uncle Duncan when next they met. Right now, he had to deal with the robbers.

In the stables, Johnson had Bess ready to go.

'Some lucky lady you're keeping warm tonight, my lord?' Johnson said with a leer. 'Not that nice Miss

Ellie in the village, I hope. I heard as how you'd been showing an interest in that quarter.'

Garrick frowned. Blasted gossipmongers. In a small place like Boxted, it didn't take much for rumours to fly. 'Quite a different sort of entertainment.' He showed the old man his sword. 'Going to pay a call on Appleby. I've been promising him a return match since the last time I was home.'

Johnson nodded his head. 'No doubt 'e'll regret it.'

Garrick grinned. He had no intention of letting his coachman guess what he was about. He buttoned up his coat and pulled his beaver hat down low. 'You know how Appleby is, so don't worry if I'm gone for a day or two.' It might take some time to track down the ring. If they'd sold it, he might have to follow it as far as London. Heaven forefend that they'd melted it down.

Dan must have heard his voice, for the boy came galloping down the ladder to the loft. 'Can I come with you, my lord?'

'Not this time, Dan.'

The boy's face fell. 'But you'll be gone soon and—'

'Don't argue with his lordship,' Johnson said. The boy flinched.

It only took one sharp word and the old fear resurfaced. Garrick's ire rose, curling his hands into fists. The boy stepped back. Afraid of him, too. And rightly so, yet it cut him to the quick. 'Lead the horse out to the yard, lad,' he said quietly.

Dan hurried to comply. Garrick followed him outside.

With only the lamp above the stable door to light the courtyard, Garrick took the reins from a miserable-looking Dan. The lad was all alone and clearly worried about Garrick's departure. 'Can you keep a secret?'

The boy nodded.

'I've laid a trap for our highwaymen.'

'At the barn?'

He'd decided against laying in wait at their hideout. Things might get ugly if he cornered them both. He wanted to separate them. Catch one of them out in the open. Divide and conquer. Not something he had time to explain to the lad, so he nodded agreement. 'Not a word to anyone, if you please.'

The boy's face brightened. 'And you're takin' yer sword, too. I'd like to see a sword fight.' He lunged, with one arm straight. 'Stick her with it.'

Bloodthirsty little wretch. 'Perhaps,' Garrick said, holding back the urge to laugh. 'Be a good lad and obey Mr Johnson as you would me.'

Dan stepped back and bowed with an innate dignity that seemed at odds with his rough upbringing. He'd miss the lad when he left for the army, he realised. Enough maudlin thoughts. He had work to do.

With a nod he mounted and urged Bess into a canter. Beyond Boxted he found a rise not far from where Lady Moonlight had held him up two nights before. From this vantage, he would see the villains when they set up their ambush for the non-existent Beauworth coach. They were in for a nasty surprise.

Clouds fled from the moon and Mist stood out like a patch of snow on a bare mountain. Eleanor edged deeper into the shadows. As usual, her stomach tightened like a windlass and her mouth dried to dust, but tonight her nervousness was pitched far higher than normal. She missed the stalwart Martin. She tightened her grip on Mist's reins.

The horse pricked his ears, flicking them in the direction of the field on the other side of the hedge. She held her breath, listening. A rustle of leaves, barely noticeable above the sound of the wind in the trees. A crack of a twig. It had to be him.

A rider broke through a gap in the hedge at the same moment the pitiless moon chose to reappear. Bad luck for him. 'Now, Mist. Fly.' She crouched over his neck and they galloped for the woods.

After a few minutes of dodging trees and bushes, she reined in. The pursuit crashed through the undergrowth behind her. She smiled. He'd taken the bait. A heady rush of excitement filled her veins, buzzing in her ears. He'd come alone, too, so she didn't have to worry about leading more than him astray.

She guided the horse off the well-worn path and into the tangled bushes. Low branches kept her ducking, but Mist required only the lightest touch as he followed the path she'd mapped out earlier in the day.

The clearing came up fast. She stopped and glanced back. Nothing. No sound or sight of anyone. Dash it. She'd been too clever and managed to lose him. She started to turn back.

'Hold.' The harsh word came from in front, not behind.

She whipped her head around. There, across the moon-drenched space, pistol drawn, he waited, his horse breathing hard. He'd circled around instead of following. Her heart thundered, her mind scrambled with the alteration to her plan. She gulped a breath. Things would go very ill if she made a mistake.

'You may observe,' the Marquess said coolly, 'that I have my pistol trained on you. So I suggest it is your turn to stand and deliver.'

She walked Mist into the middle of the clearing.

'Throw down your pistols,' he demanded.

No fool, then. She pulled them from their holsters one at a time and tossed them at his horse's front hoofs. The animal rolled its eyes, but remained still. Damn.

'Dismount,' he said, his voice cold, his hand steady.

A chill ran down her spine. He looked dangerously angry. She turned, preparing to dismount with Mist between them.

'Oh, no, you don't. Get off on this side or I'll shoot the horse.'

Blast. He obviously knew that old cavalry trick. She bit her lip. She had no choice but to obey. Cautiously, she slipped out of the saddle, retaining her hold on Mist's bridle.

Still mounted, the Marquess walked his horse to stand directly before her. The big-boned mare towered over her and Mist. Raising her gaze, Eleanor watched his eyes, ready to drop to the ground if he decided to fire. You didn't grow up with older brothers and a soldier father without learning something useful.

Atop his horse, his face stern, he looked like some avenging god of war. Beautiful in the way of a cold marble statue.

'Well, wench, we meet again.' His gazed raked her from her head to her heels. 'An interesting costume. You don't expect me to believe you are a boy, do you?'

She'd opted for the freedom of breeches for the work she had to do tonight. She cast him the saucy half-smile she'd copied from Lizzie, the upstairs maid at Castlefield. A lass with an eye for the lads. 'Well, well, if it ain't the Markiss Boworthy. So we meets agin', milord. Come for another kiss, 'ave yer?'

Casually, he gathered his reins in one hand and prepared to dismount. The nodcock. Underestimating her because she was female. She tensed. As his foot touched the ground, his body turned and his pistol moved off target. She tore her sword from the scabbard on her saddle and clutched the blade in her left hand. As he squared up, she lunged. A swift arc with the hilt knocked his pistol up. It exploded harmlessly into the air. A flick and she tossed the sword into her right hand, ready to run him through.

'Stand back,' she ordered.

Steel hissed as he drew a sword from the scabbard at his side. He was carrying a sword? Only the military carried them these days, or those with nefarious intent. He must have noticed hers on her saddle the other evening. Damn it. Now what?

He must have seen her surprise, because he laughed. 'Nice move, wench, but I am an expert swordsman. You might as well give up now.'

The way he said swordsman, almost like a caress, sent a shiver down her spine. Arrogant man. She would dashed well show him a thing or two before she presented her nice little surprise. 'Damn yer eyes, Markiss.' She slashed at him, testing his skill.

He stumbled back, yet parried the unexpected thrust. He chuckled softly. Was he enjoying this? He had the reach, without question, but he was nothing but an idle rake, whereas she had practised for hours with William every day before he left for his regiment. She hacked at him in a flurry of blows.

At first, Beauworth gave ground to her attack. He fought lazily, his tip dropping time and time again. Always managing to recover before she broke through. He kept glancing around. 'Where's your accomplice?' he asked in insultingly conversational tones as he parried a particularly tricky thrust with seeming ease.

'Takin' care of business in Lunnon.'

'So you thought you'd try thieving on your own?'

'Like taking lollipops from a baby it is.' In spite of her bravado, her heavy breathing meant she found engaging in a conversation difficult. She'd tried every trick she knew. Sweat trickled into her eyes. She dashed it away on her sleeve, circling her opponent and taking advantage of a brief reprieve.

'Had enough, wench?' he jibed.

Enough? She'd almost pinked him twice. She had the upper hand, despite her tiring arm. She gulped air into her desperate lungs. 'Not 'til I have yer 'ead on me spit.'

His husky chuckle drifted maddeningly into the night. Damn him. She was wilting and he seemed not the slightest bit discomposed.

Without warning, he changed his stance, attacked her hard and fast, lunging and stabbing. No more did his sword point waver, it flashed in a quicksilver blur. The grate of steel on steel screeched into the silence. Forced back by his superior strength, she retreated toward the great oak tree, which had stood guard over this clearing for centuries. She bit her lip. Had she been too confident?

His sword tip closed in on her throat. She defended and recovered. Again, he forced her back. She tripped on a root, staggering back, her arms wide.

He flicked his wrist and her coatsleeve was cut from elbow to shoulder. They both knew it could just as easily have been her flesh. She could see it in his eyes and the arrogant tilt of his head.

Air scraped her throat dry. Trembles shook her hand. Her wrist ached. The point of her blade wavered badly. *Tip up. Tip up.* Her father's laughing voice rang in her ears. Her wrist refused to comply. This man was dangerous and she was running out of time. She glanced over her shoulder, lined herself up.

The Marquess's grin exuded arrogance. At any moment, he would have her. He knew it. She knew it. He was far better than he'd let her believe. She should have been more wary right from the beginning, more focused on what she needed to do.

The tree trunk loomed behind her. She thrust at him one last time. He twisted his wrist. Her sword spun free. He caught it neatly and effortlessly in his left hand and crossed both blades at her throat.

Her heart beat wildly. Her stomach pitched. She swallowed dust. This was not supposed to happen.

His teeth flashed white and his eyes gleamed. While her ribs ached with the need for air, his chest barely rose and fell. 'Now, Lady Moonlight, we need to talk. But first, let's see your face.' He tossed her blade aside.

Eleanor's knees shook so hard, she feared she might stumble on to his point, yet somehow she dodged his hand. 'Put up…I concede.'

He gave a little ground, but his sword point did not waver from the base of her neck. 'So, you thought you would have my head on a spit, did you? I wonder how yours will look stretched on the gallows. Give me the mask.'

She lifted her hands away from her sides in an extravagant gesture of defeat, felt the dagger slide into her palm. She flicked it free of her sleeve. The blade flashed wickedly.

His jaw dropped, then he laughed. 'You think to defeat a sword with a hat pin?'

God, she hoped so. She cast it underhand at the branch behind his head. He dodged. The net dropped, tangling his sword in the mesh. He cursed. Sawed at the ropes to no effect. She ran for the coil of rope behind the tree, hauled it through the block and tackle she'd nailed above his head. The mouth of the net tightened, trapping him and his sword inside.

She ran for her pistols and spun around. 'Me-thinks…yer took o'er long, Markiss,' she gasped. She wrapped the length of rope around his torso, while he glared at her through the mesh. 'You should 'ave finished it when you had the chance.'

A net. The little hellion. Garrick's face heated. She'd caught him like a cod fish. No matter how he twisted, he couldn't break free and could get no leverage with his blade.

'Drop yer sword,' she said, pointing her pistol at his head. With his legs free, he could try a flying leap and no doubt one of them would get shot. Trouble was it was more likely to be he with his arms trapped against his body. He released the hilt of his sword, and she extracted it from the net, kindly not slicing him in the process.

He tried stretching the ropes with his shoulders and elbows.

'Save yer strength,' she advised, tying the free end of the rope to her horse. 'You've a long walk ahead of yer.'

'Like hell.'

'Yer choice. Walk or be dragged.' She mounted the grey and gathered up Bess's reins.

Bloody hell. He was going to see her hang for this.

It was a long walk back to the barn he'd found the day before, but she took it nice and easy, and if he hadn't been bundled like a sack of washing, he might not have minded the exercise.

Inside the barn, she bade him sit.

'What now?' he asked as she tied his ankles and fastened the rope about his waist to a metal ring on the wall.

'I would think a Markiss ought to be worth a guinea or two.'

That he hadn't expected. He forced a laugh. 'So it's a ransom you're seeking, is it?' He tried to ease the pressure of the ropes, but there was no give. 'My uncle won't fall for it. 'Tis well known that once the ransom is paid, abductors kill the victim. He will, however, hunt you down like dogs.'

She kicked at his boot. 'Looks like yer the dead man, then.'

She left him in the dark with his thoughts, his growing anger and the scent of hay and horse manure in his nostrils.

He struggled inside his bindings. Nothing he did made them any looser and he found nothing within reach to serve as a blade.

The more time passed, the more fury filled his heart until his head ached. He imagined his captor swinging from a gibbet, or hanging by her arms in some dark dungeon. But each time he got to the point of murdering her, he found himself kissing her instead. More frustration.

What would Uncle Duncan do when he received their ransom note? He'd be worried mindless. He'd probably pay the damned ransom, too. Something the estate could ill afford, apparently.

She'd have to set him loose at some point and then he'd find a way to break free. In the meantime, it would be better to think of something other than his captor if he wanted to remain sane.

The delightful vision of Ellie Brown floated across his mind's eye. Now there was a maid worth thinking about. She reminded him of untouched spring mornings and pristine golden beaches—all that was good in the world—whereas Lady Moonlight was dark nights and silk sheets and the heat of lust—pure wickedness.

Given the choice, which one did he want? Both. Together in one bed. He groaned as his body expressed approval of the image then let his mind take him where it would. Better to be driven mad by sexual frustration than rage.

Garrick opened his eyes to the sound of raised voices. Two voices, one male, one female, outside the barn. A falling out of thieves? He blinked to clear his vision. He must have slept. His neck and back were sore and his hands and feet were numb. The barn door swung open and sunlight streamed into his prison. He squinted at the large figure outlined in the doorway. Her accomplice had returned. He looked furious.

Pistol in one hand, knife in the other, the masked man slashed through the net and then the ropes. He yanked Garrick to his feet. Blood rushed into his extremities. He bit back a protest. 'Outside,' his captor said.

Struggling to regain his wits, Garrick shuffled out on feet pricked by a thousand pins, and every joint in his body complaining. Outside in the dazzle of a fine morning, the woman, also masked, bent over a pan on the fire. The blankets piled nearby suggested she'd camped there.

As usual, her hair was covered with her peruke. She looked up as Garrick sat down cross-legged against the wall of the barn. 'You walk like an old man.'

He glared at her. 'So would you if you'd been tied like a parcel all night.'

She collected more wood for the fire from a pile at the

side of the barn. On the way back she sniffed as she passed him. 'You stinks. Ben, take 'im to the pond to wash.'

So her partner's name was Ben.

'On your feet, my lord,' the man said.

'Why bother?' he said, glowering at Ben. 'You're just going to murder me.'

Ben picked up his rifle, grabbed Garrick by the upper arm and marched him down to the pond where he untied the ropes at his wrists.

'Strip.'

Garrick glanced at the woman. 'No.'

'Then I'll do it fer ye while she holds the rifle. Leave your damned breeches on if ye must.'

Garrick huffed out a breath. No point in arguing for the sake of it.

He removed his coat and dropped it at his feet. His shirt followed, and he sat to remove his boots and stockings. Retaining his breeches, he stood. With a wary eye on Ben, he backed into the water.

'You'll see my bullet coming,' Ben said.

Garrick didn't trust either of them and let disbelief show in his face. When the water was deep enough, he sluiced the water over his arms and face. The woman strolled to the water's edge and tossed him a bar of soap, then she picked up his shirt and stockings, rinsed them and hung them to dry over the fence.

'I'll have those back, wench,' Garrick called. She ignored him.

Although the mud on the bottom oozed between his toes, the water was cool and reasonably clear. Garrick could not help but enjoy the freshness after his ghastly night. He kept an eye on Ben who, while he held his rifle casually, held it with the assurance of a man prac-

tised in its use. Garrick was sure the man had seen
military service from his disciplined movements and
ramrod carriage. A hard man, who would not make
escape easy.

He soaped his hair and sank beneath the water to
rinse. When he came to the surface he saw Ben alert,
his rifle cocked. He stood up slowly, aware of the wench
watching from the bank, her gaze travelling over his
torso, her lips parting slightly as if she'd never seen a
man without his shirt.

Heat pooled instantly in his loins. Damn her. She'd
done it on purpose. He splashed more water over his
face, forcing his body under control before he could
think of leaving the water. Fortunately, she returned to
her cooking.

So Garrick made his way out of the pond and headed
for his clothes.

'No need to be shy,' the woman said. 'Put them on
when they are dry.'

Ben looked scandalised. He muttered something
under his breath, but gestured for Garrick to go ahead.

The scent of bacon assaulted his nostrils. Whether
because it was being cooked outside, or because he was
ravenously hungry, his mouth watered. He kept his face
impassive and returned to his place against the barn
wall.

'Sit by the fire,' she ordered. 'We don't want yer
catching a chill.'

He curled his lip. 'Not before you get my money, at
least.'

Ben jerked the rifle. 'Sit near the fire.'

Garrick cursed and sat as directed.

The woman slapped the eggs and bacon on to a slab
of bread and handed it to him. She did the same for Ben.

It tasted as good as it smelled. It would do no good to starve himself. He'd need every ounce of strength to escape these two.

She stood up. 'We need fresh water.' She walked away.

Moments later, he heard her gasp behind him.

Ben looked up from his food. 'What is it?'

Garrick knew what had caught her attention. It was the reason he never removed his shirt in public. He glowered, but said nothing as she placed a cup of water beside him, her gaze still fixed on his back.

'Look at this,' she said to Ben.

Unfolding his brawny body with a grunt, Ben stood up and joined her at Garrick's shoulder. He whistled softly through his teeth.

'Who did this?' she asked.

Garrick heard the pity in her voice and cringed. He did not need her sympathy, damn her. 'An accident, years ago.' Uncle Duncan had lost his temper. He'd expressed his regret as Garrick lay on his stomach, bandaged and medicated. Le Clere had never lost control like that again but it always served to remind Garrick what lay beneath the surface.

'An accident?' She stared at Ben, her face full of incredulity. 'Have you ever seen…?'

'In the army, I have. An officer's cane can do that kind of damage.'

She reached out and pressed a finger on his back. Garrick jumped with a curse.

'Sorry,' she said, whipping her hand away.

'Forget it,' he ground out through clenched teeth. 'Just give me my shirt if the sight troubles you.'

But once again she touched him, gently now, tracing the three straight diagonal lines across his back. His skin jumped and flickered, although her touch was as gentle as a butterfly, as light as a whispering breeze, almost a caress. He felt his chest constrict. The women he had known in London were interested in only one thing and it did not involve tenderness. No woman had ever touched him so softly, not since his mother…

Garrick squeezed his eyes tight, forcing down the memories. He pulled away from her questing fingers.

Ben shook his head. 'They're old, but no accident.'

She paced away. 'If he's to spend another night here, you will need to find a better way to make him secure.'

He glared at the woman. How long did they expect to keep him here? 'Le Clere won't pay you. He is not such a fool.' He hoped.

'I'll find something.' Ben's voice sounded kindly, less harsh. 'Up you get, lad. Sit over by the fence.'

Garrick rose to his feet. Silent and grim, Ben tied him to the fence with enough rope to shift his position. Tied up like a wild animal. Like one of his nightmares. He clenched and unclenched his hands, forcing himself to hold back the anger rising in his gullet. He took a deep breath. Then another. Control. Sooner or later they'd make a mistake.

Ben left them on foot, meaning he was headed for somewhere nearby. Were they in league with one of the local farmers? One of his tenants? An interesting and disturbing thought.

Forced into idleness, he watched the wench groom all three horses. The skin-tight breeches hugged the flair of her hips, and her slender thighs above riding boots were the stuff of pleasurable dreams. The full shirt and open waistcoat didn't hide her narrow waist, but gave no impression of the size of her breasts. Those he'd felt, small and firm, when he'd kissed her.

He shifted, furious and uncomfortable at his body's arousal. No doubt she knew how incredibly sensual she looked in her boy's garb. He wouldn't give her the satisfaction of knowing he'd noticed. Instead, he closed his eyes to picture her face behind the mask, light eyes, certainly. But what colour hair lay beneath her ridiculous old-fashioned wig? Her eyebrows were fair. But her hair could be anything from red to gold. The sun warmed his skin. A bee bumbled by in a soft drone on air scented with grass and sweet clover.

Having finished with the horses, Eleanor decided to feed her prisoner before Martin returned and they left for the night. A platter of bread, cheese and pickles seemed a somewhat meagre offering for a man who must be used to the finest dining. On the way, she gathered up his now-dry clothes. The Marquess needed to get dressed. The sight of him sprawled on the grass like some Adonis really was too much, especially since he had fallen asleep, leaving her free to peek all she wanted. The way he had watched her from beneath half-lowered lids, while she groomed the horses, had made her feel hot and awkward. She'd been glad when he'd drifted off to sleep.

He looked so peaceful propped against the fence, his head lolling against a naked broad shoulder. Like an angel. A fallen one, with that sensual cast of his lips and the body of a heathen god. And there was just so much of him. Even stretched out on the grass, his male virility was overpowering.

Her breath became shallow as she stood just looking at the rogue. What would they have thought of each other if they had met under different circumstances? In London, perhaps? Would they have met? A proper young lady wouldn't be introduced to a rake with his reputation.

Whereas a real lady highwayman might well take advantage of a handsome prisoner tied up at her mercy. A little thrill shot through her insides at the image. Dash it. How could she be so wicked? She really wished she'd never started along this path.

She set the plate beside him and the pile of clothes. He must have sensed her presence because he opened one eye, then the other and stretched. 'You'll forgive me for not getting up.'

Polite to a fault, even if there was an edge of sarcasm in his voice. 'I'll forgive ye. Eat. It's all you'll get today.' She flopped down against the fence. 'So you thought to trap us with yer talk of gold at the inn?' she asked as he munched on the bread.

He swallowed and she watched the rise and fall of his Adam's apple in the strong column of his throat with utter fascination. 'I wanted my signet ring back,' he said.

'Not the watch?'

A glimmer of a smile curved his lips. 'A gift from a lady with rather flamboyant tastes. You are welcome to it.' His face sobered. 'The ring was my father's.'

The hollow note in his voice made her cringe—she knew how awful she'd feel if she lost her mother's locket. But he only had himself to blame. If he'd not proved so intractable about the repayment of the mortgage, none of this would have happened.

Something moved at the edge of her vision. By her knee. A spider. Big and black and hairy. Walking up her leg.

She froze. A shudder ran down her spine. Held her rigid.

'Looks like you've made a new friend,' he said, grinning.

'Get it off,' she gasped.

He laughed. 'It's only a spider.'

'Get it off me,' she said through stiff lips, afraid to breath in case it moved. 'Please.' Her voice shrilled.

With a muttered curse, he leaned forward and brushed the horrid thing away with his bound hands. It scuttled into the grass. 'There. It's gone.'

Her skin prickled as if it was crawling all over her. Trembles shook her body. Her teeth chattered. 'I hate them.'

'It's gone.' He tipped her chin with the back of his hand, smiling. 'I promise you.' He lifted his arms, dropped them over her head, around her shoulders and drew her on to his lap. 'You are all right.' He pressed his lips to her jaw below her mask, let her nuzzle into his shoulder where she drew on his calm, comforted by the steady sound of his heartbeat.

Slowly her trembles dissipated. She felt safe, protected, for the first time in many months. And being held in his arms seemed like the most natural thing in the world. The chills of revulsion lessened. Heat rushed to her face. 'I'm such an idiot,' she muttered against silken skin smelling of soap and smoke from the fire, and another scent. Him.

'We all have our fears,' he said gently, as if he really understood. He tipped her chin with the back of his bound hands, the sight of the rope making her cringe. And when she met his gaze, his warm brown eyes showed concern. 'All right now?' he asked, then frowned. 'Tears?' He smoothed her cheek below the mask with his thumb, then bent his head and pressed his lips to the place he had rubbed as if to kiss away her fear. Like an adult with a child. Sweet. Kind.

An ache squeezed her chest. Guilt. And something else she didn't dare name.

She dropped a kiss of gratitude on his cheek, missed and landed on the corner of his mouth. He angled his head and captured her lips full on, licking and tasting, while his forearm supported her nape. Tingles raced across her breasts. Her insides clenched.

Oh, heavens. At any moment, Martin would return. Yet she didn't want to stop. Couldn't stop. Not yet. Soon. She opened her mouth to his questing tongue. And she was lost. Lost in pleasure. Dizzy with the rapid beat of her heart. The lack of air. Sensations rippled though her body, pleasurable little thrills, warmth, and languid melting.

Her hands clung to his sun-warmed shoulders. Satin skin, firm muscles rippled beneath her fingers. Pure strength. Lovely wicked flutters deep between her thighs held her enthralled.

She lay her hand flat against the haze of beard on his jaw. He broke the kiss, turned his head, the roughened skin grazing her palm, and licked the base of her thumb, hot and wet, followed instantly by cool. A shiver of delight danced across her breasts.

She moaned at the sensual onslaught.

This is wrong, a little voice whispered. You will never be the same again. Get up now.

He shifted his weight and eased her on to the ground, cushioning her shoulders with his forearm. She opened her thighs at the nudge of his knee and a sweet burst of pleasure fired in her core.

'Untie me, *chérie. Vite.* Quickly. Free my hands.'

Eleanor stared at him blankly.

'Cut the rope,' he pleaded, his breathing ragged and shallow, his voice hoarse. 'Set me free. I'll do nothing to hurt you.' His soft, accented voice was an urgent enticing whisper in her ear. His thigh ground against her, pushing between her legs, creating hot surges of sweet agony.

'A promise you will keep, my lord.'

Ah, no. Martin. Face scalding, she slipped under the loop of the Marquess's arms and rose to her feet, breathing hard. What had she been thinking?

Martin cocked his rifle with a loud threatening click and the Marquess struggled to a sitting position.

Bewilderingly, her mind seemed to be full of molasses, thick and syrupy and deadly. He'd comforted her and she'd dissolved like butter in hot milk. Mute with embarrassment, she stared at Martin weighed down by a necklace of iron chain and shackles. He levelled his rifle.

The Marquess stiffened, as if bracing for… Oh God. Martin was going to fire. 'Put the gun down,' she yelled. 'He is unarmed and bound. No harm was done.'

Martin held her stare for a long moment, then grimaced. He let the rifle fall to his side, but his body remained stiff, his movements jerky as he set the rifle against the fence. He pulled the Marquess to his feet. 'Back to the barn for yer lordship.'

'Take your hands off me,' the Marquess said, steadying himself on his feet, his face as flushed as hers felt.

Was he ashamed of their kiss? And why did it matter? Once this was over, she'd never see him again. A pain she couldn't fathom filled her heart. Oh, God, what was wrong with her? Kissing him like a wanton, all the while knowing Martin would return at any moment. She had lost her mind.

He'd been so kind about the spider, not laughing the way her brothers always had at her stupid female fear, that she'd forgotten they were enemies. And now Martin looked ready to commit murder. Something she would not allow. She picked up the Marquess's clothes and the rest of the food and followed them into the cool depths of the barn.

Martin fixed the iron chain to the ring in the wall and fastened the shackle to the Marquess's ankle before cutting the ropes free.

'That'll hold you,' Martin said.

The Marquess glanced up from inspecting his chain. 'Your accommodations leave much to be desired.' The lazy drawl seemed at odds with the revulsion she glimpsed in his eyes. 'Why not shoot me and have done? I'll be damned if you'll get any money.'

Bravado, she thought. And yet…

'We'll see,' Martin said, stepping back.

'Leave me alive and I'll hunt you down like dogs,' the Marquess said, in matter-of-fact tones.

He meant it. Was he taunting Martin deliberately so he'd shoot? Did he hate those chains so much? Bile rose in her throat, a sour taste of guilt. Her heart sank. She couldn't see it through. She could not keep him chained here day after day, thinking they were going to kill him and watching his hatred grow.

She gazed down at him. He winked. More bravado.

Martin growled a curse.

In her heart she knew the Marquess would try again to charm her into setting him free. And she wasn't sure how long she could resist, unless she kept away from him completely. It would be best if she left him to Martin. Best for her. Not for him, given Martin's present mood.

Coward.

And what if his uncle wouldn't pay the ransom? What would they do then? Not only would they not have the money they needed, they'd have the Marquess bent on revenge. If only she had something he wanted in exchange for the mortgage.

There was one thing he seemed to want. Her. And that was out of the question. Wasn't it? Was it really too high a price to pay for what she'd done?

She inhaled a deep breath. 'Bring 'is horse inside,' she said to Martin. 'We needs to talk.'

They did very little talking on the way back to her cottage after leaving their horses at Martin's cousin's farm. Anger surrounded Martin like a wall Eleanor could almost touch; while she regretted causing him upset, his grim silence left her free to mull over her options.

The Marquess did like her. He kissed her when she was Ellie. And he kissed her when she was Lady Moonlight. And instead of kissing her, he could easily have overpowered her before Martin came back. He'd been too busy kissing her to save his own neck, the rake, and she'd thanked him by chaining him to a wall. She winced.

But if she took this step, she'd be well and truly ruined. Wasn't she already far beyond the pale of what was acceptable? A thief, and, if this afternoon was anything to go by, a wanton. Her stomach gave a horrid little lurch, the kind that stops your breath at the knowledge of the inevitable. It didn't matter. She was the one who'd created the mess, she should be the one to pay the price. Not the Marquess. Certainly not Sissy and William. And definitely not Martin. It also would not lead to prison.

But she'd have to get Martin out of the way.

Once inside the cottage, Martin put his hands on his hips and glowered. She braced herself for a lecture. She was actually surprised he'd lasted this long before taking her to task.

'What is it you want to say, Martin?'

'I'd like to know what you thought you were doing

with that lordling. Don't you understand? He could…'
He took a breath. 'You don't know what these men of
the world are like.'

A flash of heat scalded her cheeks. Martin thought
of her as an innocent, but what had happened out at the
barn wasn't all one-sided by any means. Where the
Marquess was concerned, it seemed she didn't have an
iota of control.

'It wasn't what you think,' she muttered. 'There
was a spider.' Martin knew how she hated the horrid
crawly things.

'Well, if you hadn't been rolling around the grass
you wouldn't have seen a spider. I know what I saw, and
he had his hands on you.'

And she hadn't resisted. Not for a minute. Shame
flooded through her at the look of disgust in his eyes,
even though she knew he was trying to hide it.

'Give up this nonsense, my lady,' he pleaded.
'Before you end up on the gallows, or worse.'

Unfortunately, worse seemed to be the only alterna-
tive. She avoided his gaze, fearing he would sense
something amiss. 'You are right. This is not going to
work.'

Martin let go a long breath. 'Thank God. I'll go and
set him free.'

'No. I'll do that first thing in the morning.' She took
a deep breath. 'I need you to take a message to William.
Right away. Then go to Lady Sissy and wait.'

'You will be there when I get back?'

'No.'

He looked startled, then worried. He opened his
mouth to argue.

She forestalled him. 'It is all in the note to William.
I'm going to Scotland to visit Molly MacDonald—you

know she's been begging to see me for weeks. I can't risk the Marquess discovering my whereabouts.'

The worry on his face didn't ease. 'I suppose you're right.'

'I know I am.'

She pulled out paper and a quill and sat down at the kitchen table while Martin paced back and forth, as if he couldn't quite make up his mind. She ignored him. First she wrote a short note to Mr Jarvis, telling him the money was on the way. Next a note to Molly, asking her to forward her letters on to William when they arrived and promising to explain the whole when she arrived in a few weeks' time. 'I want you to post these for me in the morning.'

Martin halted and nodded.

The next letter was to William. Explaining the mess she'd caused and begging him to wait with Sissy until he heard from her that all was resolved. She sanded and sealed the note. 'You will take this to Portsmouth and leave it with the harbour master. Stress that it must be put into William's hands the moment his ship arrives.'

'Don't worry. I'll make sure he understands. You will take care, my lady? Setting him free and all?'

'Yes, Martin. I know exactly what I have to do. Give me the key.'

She handed him the letters and he gave her the key to the Marquess's shackles.

'I'll wait until you have time to get well on the road,' she said. 'Tell William not to worry when you see him. And, Martin, whatever you do, do not bring him here. The Marquess is not to blame for this.'

He narrowed his eyes. 'Something tells me you are keeping something back. You should go to your brother yourself. Tell him the whole story to his face.'

No fool, Martin Brown. 'Martin, do this and I promise I will never ask you for aught else. Now make haste. You don't want to miss William's arrival.'

He sighed. 'Very well, my lady. But I will keep you to your word.'

Chapter Four

Another night in the pitch black with only his mare's soft breathing for company. Instead of kissing the wench, he should have forced her to untie him. Used her as a hostage. Instead he'd let his lust overcome reason.

That and her tears. He hated to see any woman cry. Something that had cost him dear over the years in farewell trinkets.

Where the hell was Le Clere? Surely a ransom note would have had him scouring the countryside? And Dan knew of this place. He would have told Johnson where to look.

An owl hooted. Had something disturbed it? Garrick listened. Nothing. He returned to his fingertip exploration of every board in the wall behind him, every crevice within reach on the floor. One little nail to poke in the padlock was all he asked.

A splinter drove under his fingernail, sharp and agonising. He cursed.

'Is that you, my lord?' The whisper came from the direction of the door.

Puzzled, Garrick peered into the impenetrable darkness. 'Who is it?'

'It's me. Dan.'

Thank God. 'Have Johnson or someone break open the door, boy.'

'There's only me, my lord. You told me it was a secret.'

Not what he wanted to hear. 'Go for help. Hurry up.'

The sound of splintering wood drowned out his words. Would the lad never listen?

'Where are you, my lord? 'Tis so dark, I see naught.'

'Over here.' Garrick kept talking until Dan stumbled into him. He grasped the boy by the arm. 'Has there been no hue and cry at Beauworth? No one out searching?'

'No, my lord. Everyone thinks you are visiting friends.'

No ransom note? How bloody odd. 'Very well. Take my horse and ride back to the Court. Tell Le Clere he will need a hammer, a chisel, tools.' Garrick rattled his chain.

'Nay, not so much, my lord.' Pride filled the boy's voice. He fumbled with the chain, his breathing a dry rasp in Garrick's ear. 'Gimme a tick,' he muttered. The sound of metal against metal, scratching, a click. The padlock fell with a clunk, followed by a rattle of iron.

'Good God. I had no idea you were so accomplished.'

'No, my lord.'

Garrick got to his feet. 'Come on, show me where you got in.' He followed as Dan felt his way along the walls to the broken plank. By widening it, Garrick was able to crawl out.

'What on earth brought you?' Garrick asked, looking around for signs of his captors. The waning moon lit a silver path across the pond and stars winked a greeting.

The boy shuffled his feet. 'I was afeared you was

goin' to tip the old fellow a double. I thought you'd gone off and left me.' He wiped his nose on his sleeve. 'I weren't goin' to stay there on me own. So I followed. I didn't know where else to start.'

Garrick ruffled his hair. 'Well, I'm bloody glad you did.'

'I brought this.' Metal glinted as Dan handed Garrick a pistol. 'I *borrowed* it from Mr Johnson. If yer joining the army, I wants to go, too.'

The weapon dated from the last century, but looked serviceable and clean. 'Did you ask Mr Johnson?'

He shrugged. 'He would've said no.'

Incorrigible. 'I don't suppose you thought to bring bullets and powder?'

Dan's teeth flashed white. 'That I did.'

'Damn me, boy, you are a marvel.'

'I got a blade, too.' The boy pulled forth a knife. A sliver of steel with a bone handle. A deadly weapon in the right hands, and also useful in opening padlocks.

'Where did that come from?'

'It's mine.' Dan caressed the blade with a fingertip. 'A friend gave it me. I were going to use it on *him* if you 'adn't come along.'

'Then I saved you from hanging. May I borrow it for a while?' The more he thought about it, the more he wanted to teach his captors a lesson they wouldn't forget. And with surprise on his side, they were in for a nasty shock.

The boy handed over the knife and Garrick tucked it inside his boot.

'What are you going to do?'

'I'm going to ambush them inside the barn. Wait for me in the trees yonder,' Garrick said. 'Watch carefully. If anything goes wrong, ride for help. Can you do that?'

'I'd sooner hide in the barn with you.'

'I need you to stand watch. It's an important job.'

Dan looked unconvinced, but he finally agreed and Garrick squeezed back into his prison. Dan replaced the broken plank behind him. 'Be careful, my lord,' he whispered.

'I will. Try to stay awake.'

A snort greeted his words, then he heard the boy move off. Once back in his corner, he lay down in the straw with the manacle loose about his ankle. He was going to enjoy giving these rogues a taste of their own medicine. They deserved a little bit of terror, before he got his property back.

Dawn lightened the eastern sky, but it was still dark in the valley as Eleanor pulled back the barn door with shaking hands. If she had any sense she'd send Le Clere a note, tell him where to find his missing nephew and flee.

And they'd be out on the streets with no money and deeply in debt. No. Taking advantage of his attraction was the last arrow in her quiver. The fact that she found him equally attractive wasn't a bad thing either. It would make playing her part easier, perhaps even enjoyable, although thoroughly disgraceful. She shivered.

She touched her mask. If only she could keep it on. But she couldn't. He would have to know she was both Lady Moonlight and Ellie Brown. She'd have to tell him as much of the truth as she dared without actually admitting to her real identity. Once it was over, she'd disappear.

She took a deep breath and perched her hat on top of her boy's wig. It must look strange with her blue dimity gown, but she wanted to break the news gently.

Dust motes danced in the fingers of light poking through the knots and gaps in the walls. The Marquess lay on his back in the straw, his chest rising and falling as if he hadn't a care in the world. His lashes lay like dark fans above high olive cheekbones. So peaceful. His horse blew out a breath, a snort of disgust no doubt.

She shook his arm. 'My lord.'

He mumbled and opened his eyes, slowly gazing around.

'What is it? It's still the middle of the night,' he grumbled. 'The deuce.' He stared at up her, rather warily, she thought.

'My lord, you must listen, I—'

He sprang to his feet and grabbed her by the arm. She felt something cold and hard against her neck. A pistol.

'Cry out and you are dead,' he whispered.

The breath left her body in a terrified rush. He sounded angry enough to shoot her. Disaster. Her plan made no provision for this. She opened her mouth to speak and found her mouth drier than the well beside the barn. Her knees seemed to have lost all their strength.

'Where is he? Ben?' he asked.

His warm breath was hot in her ear, his arm a steel band around her waist. He brought the muzzle around to her face. 'Answer me, wench.'

She swallowed hard, managing to salvage some moisture for speech. 'He's gone.'

He squeezed her harder, crushing her ribs with his steely grip. 'When will he be back?'

'He left for good this time.'

She made no struggle as he propelled her towards the door.

'Let's hope he values your life,' he said with the pistol still pointed at her head. His body partly shielded by hers, he eased her out of the door. His heart knocked against her ribs, slow and steady, unlike hers, which seemed ready to leap from her chest. One false move on her part and she would find herself with a bullet to the brain. Not a preferred solution to her problems.

After a long pause, he thrust her away from him with such force she fell to her knees. Unmoving, she watched him check the vicinity of the barn.

Apparently satisfied, he returned to where she knelt, close to the spot where they had kissed the day before. He cast her a look of suspicion. 'He won't get far. When I catch him you'll both be up before the beak.'

He was going to cart her off to prison. She reached into the pocket of her skirt.

He levelled his pistol. 'Careful, wench.'

She froze. Her heart seemed to forget how to beat. 'I brought you something.'

One eyebrow went up. 'How sweet of you, my dear. A token of appreciation for helping you yesterday, no doubt.'

She opened her fingers. They shook and she steadied her wrist with her other hand. Beside the key in her palm lay his signet ring, a large solid circlet of gold mounted with heavy claws grasping the Beauworth shield. 'I was going to set you free. I hid the ring from Ben after you told me you wanted it back.'

The Marquess's lip curled. 'Admit it. You lost your nerve. Very clever of you to realise I would come after you for the ring. I suppose you expected me to forget the whole thing in exchange?'

This was not going according to plan. He clearly hadn't needed her to set him free and he accorded her only the worst of motives for returning his property. Even as it hurt, she acknowledged his right to think her despicable. She swallowed. What a fool she had been to risk everything on his seeming attraction, when a nobleman of his rank and physical beauty could have any woman he wanted.

She'd failed. Again. Moisture burned at the backs of her eyes. She sniffed. Whatever he decided now would be her punishment for letting William and Sissy down.

'Tears?' he said. 'You don't expect me to believe those are real, surely?' He sighed and took the ring from her hand. 'First, let's see who you are. Then we'll decide what comes next.' He grasped the edge of the mask and whipped it over her head in one swift movement. Her hat and wig fell to the ground. Her hair cascaded around her shoulders. Now he would know everything. Hot-faced, she lowered her head, hiding behind her hair's silky screen.

'No,' he said. 'It cannot be.'

A cool hand cupped her chin. He lifted her face, swept back the hair.

'Bloody hell. Ellie Brown?' He could not have looked more appalled to see Satan himself. 'There must be some mistake. This is some sort of trick.'

The disappointment in his expression took her aback. It was almost worse than his earlier disgust. Confused, she lowered her gaze, searching for the strength to follow through with her plan. 'It is me. I'm sorry, my lord.'

He reached out to touch her face as if he couldn't believe what he saw. 'Hell's teeth. You certainly fooled me finely. What game are you playing?'

For one mad moment she felt the urge to tell him the whole sordid story, to throw herself on his mercy. But she'd done that before, written to him asking him for more time to pay the mortgage without effect. No, far better to stick to her plan to bargain than beg for kindness. She dashed away tears that had somehow spilled over and took a deep breath. 'Ben was angry about what happened yesterday. He took all the money. Whatever will happen to Master William now?'

He blinked. 'Master William?'

'Lord Castlefield. He got into debt. The bailiffs came and threw us all out, because of the mortgage due on the estate. I was trying to raise money to help him, but it got out of hand.'

His glowered. 'More than out of hand, I would say, you little idiot. Why isn't this man taking care of his own debts?'

'He's away. Fighting in Spain.'

He cursed softly. 'Who holds the mortgage?'

She stared at him. How could he not know? Perhaps he just wanted to make her suffer. 'You do.'

His jaw dropped. 'Me?' He gave a harsh laugh. 'Don't tell me. You were going to use my money to pay me back? You really are one brazen hussy.'

If she didn't know better, she might have thought the glint in his eye was admiration. The straight line of his firm mouth and the hard set of his jaw said otherwise.

He looked down at the toe of his riding boots, scuffed and dirty, his thoughts hidden. 'Why come here today? Why didn't you cut your losses and run?' He frowned. 'Why not simply ask me for help without all this nonsense?'

'His lordship's lawyer wrote to you. You insisted the debt be paid or the house would be forfeit. When you said your uncle wouldn't pay the ransom, I thought of something else.' She winced as he narrowed his gaze on her face, his fingers playing with the strings of her mask.

'Well?' he prompted.

'I was going to offer to…' Heat spread from her face all the way to her feet. It had sounded so easy when she had gone over it in her mind. Now it sounded horrid. She swallowed what felt like a feather pillow stuck in her throat. 'To do whatever you wanted in exchange for the mortgage.' The words came out in a rush.

The thin black ribbons stilled. The silence lengthened. 'This Lord Castlefield must be very important to you.'

'Yes, he's—'

'Enough.' He squeezed his eyes shut briefly. 'I really don't want to hear the sordid details.' He stared down at the ring. 'I really have been seven kinds of a fool about you. I respected you, Ellie. Thought you were a very different kind of woman.' He shook his head. 'You and Ben must have enjoyed your little jokes at my expense.'

'I was desperate.'

He stilled. 'Desperate enough to offer yourself to me in exchange for this Lord Castlefield's debts.'

Spoken so softly, without emotion, it sounded dreadful. Her heart contracted, it grew small, and tight, all the joy and hope squeezed out of it as he laid out what she had become. 'Yes.'

'I'm not sure it's a compliment. How much does he owe?'

Her chest felt tight. 'A thousand pounds.' Her voice came out in a very small whisper.

'An expensive roll in the hay.' His gaze reflected some kind of cynical amusement. 'And for how long am I to receive the benefit of your services?'

Shame emblazoned her face. She closed her eyes briefly. What was one more nail in the coffin of her pride? In a panic, she picked a number at random. 'Three months. More if you want.'

Too much? Too little? She couldn't tell from his wooden expression.

'High priced indeed,' he said, his face bleak. He made a faint sound of disgust, then strode impatiently to the remains of the fire and stirred the ashes with the toe of his boot, clearly trying to make up his mind. The acrid smell of wood ash filled her nostrils as fine dust puffed up. 'I will let you know my decision tomorrow,' he said finally, without looking at her.

Clearly, he wasn't at all thrilled by her offer. No doubt he had plenty of beautiful women from whom to choose. Perhaps he wasn't as interested in her as she had thought. And that made her feel just a little...hurt. Which was ridiculous. At least he hadn't turned her down flat. Yet. 'Yes, my lord.'

He dropped the mask into the dead embers. 'How did you get here?'

'I walked.'

'Then I will take you home.' He put his fingers in his mouth and gave a shrill whistle. She jumped, her heart pounding. Who was he calling? Had he been playing some sort of cruel game? Toying with her the way he had during their duel? And now the constable would ride out to cart her off to prison.

Approaching hoof-beats had her spinning around in time to see a gawky blond lad emerge from the woods. The lad who'd been up on the box of the carriage the night of the robbery. He rode across the meadow in an ungainly gallop. So this was how her prisoner had escaped.

'Do you have any weapons on you?' the Marquess asked softly in her ear. She jerked away from him. 'No.'

'You won't mind if I check?'

She minded very much as his fingertips ran over her body. And even more when his large hands gently outlined the curve of her hip. She minded because her body responded with longing, whereas he looked completely unaffected, dispassionate. When he knelt before her, the tousled dark hair close to her stomach, and stroked between her thighs—gently, true, but missing not one inch of sensitised flesh—she minded so much that she felt dizzy and hot. Her breathing shortened, while her mind tried to assimilate the unnerving sensations on her skin.

He glanced up, an odd half-smile on his lips. 'I am glad you told the truth this once, wench.'

Her heart gave a painful squeeze. She wished she could tell him the truth about everything.

The boy drew his mount up close to the Marquess, staring at her open-mouthed.

'It's all right, lad,' the Marquess said. 'Return home and let Johnson know I will follow shortly.'

Knowing her face burned scarlet, Eleanor avoided the boy's curious glances by staring off into the distance. It wasn't until he had departed that she dared steal a glance at the grim man at her side.

He had said he would take her home. Did he mean that?

'Come. We will use my horse.'

He gestured her into the barn and readied his mare in silence. The ripple of muscle beneath his shirt as he worked reminded her of the strength she had seen in his arms on the previous day. Sculpted and bronzed, they'd been lovely. And his back had been broad and strong… and horribly scarred. She wished she hadn't seen that. It made her feel pity, when she wanted to feel practical, businesslike, unmoved by what would happen next.

With her wrist in a firm grip, he walked her and the horse outside and placed his hands about her waist.

They were warm and large, filling the hollow between her ribs and hips. He tossed her up on to his horse and climbed up behind her, pulling her on to his lap so she sat sideways across his thighs. She sat within the circle of his arms, wedged against his chest. Almost hysterical, still unable to believe how awry everything had gone, she held herself stiff and straight.

She ought to be flirting with him. Batting her eyelashes, charming him to do her bidding, but he seemed so remote, she couldn't bring herself to try. He had his arms around her; she could feel the heat of his body against her back and yet she felt chilled. She'd hurt his pride. He'd as good as admitted it. After all, she was a woman and she had duped him finely. Not a good thing. Having grown up with two brothers, she knew how sensitive men were about those sorts of things.

Unable to bear the heavy silence any longer, she glanced up at his grim face. 'I truly am sorry for what I did. It was meant for the best. It was all I could think of to save my...lord.'

'Where is your sister?' he asked abruptly.

'I sent her to a relative.'

'I wish to hell you'd gone with her.'

She wished she'd seen it as an option. She shrugged. 'I needed the money.'

He leaned forwards, the hard wall of his chest pressing against her back, his warm breath tickling her ear, starting a series of tingles in other places she tried to ignore.

'Miss Brown,' he said, 'you are a reckless wench. Someone needs to curb your wild behaviour.'

'Someone like you?' she asked, and gasped at the hiss of his indrawn breath.

Silence was obviously the better part of valour, so she held her tongue for the rest of the way.

* * *

When they arrived at her door, the early morning sun was casting long shadows in the lane outside her cottage. Soon the rest of the village would be up and about. The Marquess set her down in the road and walked her up the path.

What to say under such awkward circumstances? 'Can I offer you tea, my lord?'

He hesitated, his brown eyes searching her face. He raised his hand and tipped up her chin. Her skin scorched where his fingers touched and she could not raise her gaze from his full mouth, as if her body yearned for the wicked sensations he engendered with his kisses. She held her breath. A delicious feeling of anticipation coursed through her veins. Her pulse raced. A shadow passed over his face. Regret? Longing? Or was it anger? It disappeared too fast to be sure.

He grasped her by the shoulders, turning her towards him, drawing her close. He touched his lips to hers. Her arms went around his neck. Her fingers twined in his silken hair. An instant surrender she could not control as he tasted her lips with infinite sweetness. A languor overtook her limbs.

He put her from him with an almost forced gentleness, as if he also fought some inner battle. Her arms felt bereft, her legs not exactly steady.

'I will come and see you tomorrow afternoon,' he said. He left without looking back. Eleanor went inside and bolted the door. She leaned against the old rough wood, a hand to her mouth. What had she done? She shivered. There had been no kindness in his face just now, no tenderness in his eyes. Just the heat of desire.

An answering heat flared in her body.

* * *

After bathing and changing his clothes, Garrick went down for breakfast and found his uncle already seated at the table with his usual two slices of toast.

Le Clere half-rose in his seat, relief warring with irritation for supremacy in his expression. 'Is it your idea to cause me an apoplexy, Garrick? I was ready to send out a search party if you hadn't returned this morning.'

The irony made Garrick want to smile. 'I rode over to Appleby's. Did you not get my message?'

His uncle cleared his throat. 'You did not say you'd be away so long.'

The sensation of being smothered returned to Garrick in full force. Memories of his boyhood. 'Well, here I am now,' he said cheerfully.

'You missed our meeting yesterday. I thought we had an agreement.'

'I apologise for that. I did look at the ledgers before I went. I wanted to ask you if I could look at the rent books when next we met.'

'Rent books?' Le Clere's eyes narrowed.

'Revenues have fallen. I wanted to see if the rent books gave any clue as to why. See which tenants are in trouble.'

His uncle frowned. 'They won't tell you much.' Garrick opened his mouth to argue. 'But why not?' his uncle said swiftly with a shrug. 'Matthews collects the rents. I'll ask him to bring them along, when he's finished making this month's rounds. How did you find the Applebys? All well?'

A rather swift change of topic, given how badly Le Clere had wanted him to take an interest in the estate. 'All in the pink of health, Uncle.' Fortunately for Garrick, they lived far enough away so that Le Clere was unlikely to run into them. Garrick pulled out a chair and sat down. 'They sent their regards.'

The butler bustled in with a freshly filled toast rack, poured coffee in Garrick's cup and left.

'I have a rather unusual request,' Garrick said, feeling a trickle of sweat run down the centre of his back.

Le Clere put down his paper with a genial smile. 'What can I do for you?'

'I understand that you…er, rather that we, have called in the mortgage on a property in Hampshire? Castlefield Place.'

Le Clere stiffened, his eyes narrowed, the expression in them piercing. 'What do you know about Castlefield?'

An oddly defensive response? Garrick maintained a relaxed expression. 'Not a great deal, although the name sounds vaguely familiar. You must know of it.'

Le Clere grunted.

'Ellie told me the son is unable to pay.'

'Ellie Brown?' An odd expression flickered across his face.

Blast. He hadn't meant to mention her by name, but since Le Clere made it his business to know every tenant on the estate, he would soon work it out. 'Yes, she was his servant.'

His uncle's eyes narrowed to slits. 'A servant, eh. Well, it's a straightforward foreclosure. What else did you want to know?'

Garrick's jaw tightened under his uncle's unblinking contemplation. 'I want you to forgive the mortgage and put the man back in dibs.'

'Is this some sort of jest?' Le Clere's laugh sounded incredulous. 'Do you know the size of the debt? The estate needs those funds to maintain your extravagant lifestyle.'

Garrick leaned forwards and locked eyes with his uncle. 'Are you telling me we are facing ruin? Is that why the servants have dwindled and Boxted is going to seed? You've never mentioned it before.'

Le Clere reared back. 'Damn it, Garrick. Is that all the gratitude I get for looking after your welfare? It's this bloody war of which you are so fond ruining everything. If you think you can do better, I encourage you to try.'

Struck with remorse at Le Clere's obvious distress, Garrick softened his voice. 'I didn't mean to criticise. You've worked harder than anyone for the estate, but my father would never have called in a loan if it meant throwing a friend's family out on the street and you know it.'

Le Clere sat silently for a moment, his expression pained, thoughts Garrick couldn't read racing over his usually bland face. A smile dawned and he visibly relaxed. Unaccountably, Garrick's hackles rose.

'Finally,' Le Clere said. 'I suppose I have Miss Brown to thank for you taking a real interest in Beauworth. While it is not exactly as I hoped, it is an interest none the less.' He leaned back, his lips pursed. 'I have a proposition for you. I will do exactly as you ask, against my better judgement, I might add. As your trustee, I could refuse, you know. In return, do something for me. Remain here at Beauworth. Devote yourself. Dally with this young hussy, if you must, but get yourself married and produce an heir.'

Garrick felt the room rock around him. 'I hadn't planned to marry for years.' If at all.

'Garrick, be reasonable. I must see you settled

before I relinquish control of the estate. It will ease my mind to know I did my duty, left everything properly ordered. It is what your father would have wished.'

He fought the guilt Le Clere invoked. 'It isn't what I want. Let Cousin Harry produce the next heir.'

Le Clere's eyes had a suspiciously moist glint. 'You are Beauworth. If you won't do it for me, do it for the family name.'

How could he fight such devotion? 'And the money?'

'It goes against the grain, my boy. The estate is owed that money.' He sighed. 'But Beauworth needs its Marquess far more. Do your duty and, if you still want it when the title is secure, you'll have your captaincy.'

Until he was of age, he could not access his funds without Le Clere's cooperation. And, damn it all, what was being asked of him was not unreasonable. 'I'll give you three months. That should be quite enough time to learn all I need to know about the estate. But no more talk of betrothals.'

Le Clere narrowed his eyes. 'What did Miss Brown offer in exchange? Her favours? Your women don't usually last more than three weeks.'

His skin crawled. How did Le Clere know so much? 'That is my business. I need a thousand pounds to pay off some of her pressing debts.'

His uncle blinked, clearly thunderstruck, but when he spoke his tone was soft and businesslike. 'Very well. Come back in two hours and I'll have it ready.'

Garrick supposed it could have been worse. And three months would be more than enough time for Ellie Brown. 'Thank you for being so understanding.'

'Dear boy, you forget, I, too, was young once.'

The oddly triumphant look on Le Clere's face dis-

turbed something low in his gut. He pushed the feeling
aside. Why would he quibble? His uncle had given him
everything he requested. Although at a price.

The bigger question in his mind was what Ellie wanted.

Nervous and restless, Eleanor spent her morning
tidying up the cottage and baking. Then she washed her
hair and coiled it neatly at her nape. She dressed in her
finest gown, a sprigged muslin, one of the few she'd
brought from home. Whatever the outcome of his visit,
she would behave with dignity.

A rap at the door. Her heart pounded. He was here.
She smoothed her hair, took a deep, calming breath
and opened the door.

He looked wonderful. Clean shaven, his hair carefully
ordered *à la Brutus,* his dark blue coat snug on his
powerful shoulders. Wonderful yet stern, his jaw set hard,
his dark eyes watchful, as if he suspected her of treachery.

'My lord.' She curtsied low and gestured for him to
enter.

'Good day, Miss Brown.'

His demeanour was so serious, her heart beat a
warning of impending disaster. 'Please sit down, my
lord. May I offer you some tea?'

'Thank you.' He took the wooden chair.

She felt his gaze upon her as she moved around the
tiny kitchen, setting out teacups and a plate of cakes on
the cloth-covered table. He appeared stiff and ill-at-
ease. It must be bad news. She handed him his cup and
perched on a stool.

He cleared his throat. 'Miss Brown, yesterday you
made a proposal with respect to the relief of your
employer's financial difficulties.'

'Yes, my lord.' Her voice sounded strained and tight. From the heat in her face she felt sure it must be crimson all the way to her hairline. She managed a smile. 'My lord, I believe that we discovered some warmer feelings for each other than mere acquaintance. Even though you did not recognise me in my other calling, I very much appreciated your kindness to me and my sister these past few days.' She was pleased to note that her voice barely shook.

He reached across and took her hand. Warmth travelled up her arm. His charming smile made an appearance and she knew everything would be all right.

'Ellie, I think you know that I found you enchanting the first day I met you in the village. I have continued to feel admiration for you since that day.' His serious expression returned. He placed a rolled document tied with a red ribbon and a package on the table between them. 'I was shocked when I realised your deception. I was rude. I honour you for your loyalty to your employer. I am returning the mortgage without further obligation. There is also enough money to help with the debts. You can choose to stay, or you can leave without recrimination.'

She gasped, not quite able to believe what she'd heard. He was letting her leave?

He rose, prowling to the window to gaze outside. Against the light, the profile of his cheekbone seemed to be cut from something harder than mere bone and flesh.

The hairs on the back of her neck prickled. This was a test. A trap. He was seeing if she would keep her word. If she didn't, he'd snatch up the papers and call their bargain off. Or was it something else? Something that made her stomach sink to her feet. She'd managed to disgust even a rake such as him. 'You don't want me.'

He swung around, his expression pained. 'Not true. I do not wish you to enter into an arrangement that is distasteful to you.'

Distasteful? It ought to be distasteful, given all it would mean. She ought to be snatching up the papers and running for her life. And yet something in his eyes froze her in place. Raw hunger swirled in the dark brown depths, tightly controlled, yes, but there all the same. Not the heat of desire, although that was there, too, but a bleak deep-seated loneliness as he waited to bid her farewell.

Her foolish heart ached to ease his hurt. A wild desire to dispel that look from his eyes pulled at her soul. She'd made a bargain. Arranged it so no one would know. It was only for three months, but perhaps given time…

'Go,' he said.

The harshness in his voice said if she accepted his generous offer, she would never see him again. Torn in two, she stared at the documents.

He turned away, clearly expecting her to leave.

Go now, the voice of sanity whispered. She didn't want to go.

Reckless Ellie, always too impulsive by half, crossed the room behind him and laid a hand on his arm. 'My lord, I would not have suggested it, if I did not wish it.'

He lowered his gaze to meet hers, and in those dark depths she saw a lightening of his spirit and felt glad. Then he pulled her close and brushed her lips with his, a hesitant questioning kiss as if he doubted her words. A sweet kiss. Her body thrilled to his touch, her traitorous heart picked up speed.

She leaned close and teased his lips with the tip of her tongue, something she had imagined doing in her dreams.

He groaned against her mouth

A rush of pleasure heated her body. Two days ago had been the first time she had felt a man's body, hard and strong against her own. And she'd liked it. She'd no idea, until then, that kisses created such internal conflagrations. And now she wanted more. He seemed equally inflamed by her bold responses. Crackling heat flickered between them like the electricity in the air before a storm.

He placed one hand behind her knees and one around her shoulders. He picked her up seemingly without effort and carried her into the bedroom, setting her on the edge of the small bed so that she faced him, her feet just off the floor, her knees touching his thigh. The intimacy sent heat to her cheeks.

He bent and kissed her mouth, a soft brush of his lips, back and forth, while his fingers worked on the fastenings of her gown. Little kisses rained down on her face, her lips and her neck. She shivered with pleasure. Her skin tingled wherever his lips touched. He pulled the pins from her hair. It fell around her shoulders, brushing against her cheeks, her neck. He ran his fingers through it, carrying it to his face and inhaling deeply.

'Lovely,' he murmured.

How easily she slipped down this path to dishonour, she thought as she reached for the buttons of his waistcoat. Was she really this wanton, or was it he only who tempted her into wickedness?

His sharp breath offered a reward for her boldness in the way her stomach clenched, as did the way he tore off his coat and helped her slip the waistcoat over his shoulders. He knelt and slipped her gown down to her waist, baring her stays and shift. He dipped his head to the exposed rise of her breasts and trailed butterfly kisses across skin so sensitive it shivered under his lips. Delicious torment. She moaned.

'You are beautiful.' The dark murmur as he gazed into her eyes sent waves of heat rushing to her core. There was more. She knew it in the way she wanted to touch and kiss and explore. Her fingers fumbled with the snowy white cravat at his throat and he chuckled. 'In a hurry, are you?' He dropped a kiss on her forehead, then untied the knot at his throat and she pulled the muslin free. The buttons of his shirt came next. Finally she had her prize. Feeling exceedingly brave and very naughty, she placed her hand on his bare chest. His skin was soft, sprinkled with crisp brown curls and warm. Her fingers tasted his flesh, marvelling at the underlying muscle beneath the satiny softness. She leaned forwards to kiss him on his breast the way he had kissed her. Again she heard his indrawn breath and her own little thrill. He liked her touch.

She drew back to see his expression. His eyes were dark, almost black, his mouth curved in a sensual smile, his breathing as rapid her own. She rejoiced in her powers of seduction even as she trembled at the knowledge of her ruin.

He pulled her to her feet and turned her around. His movements were gentle, but swift and sure and very male. He pushed her gown to the floor and pulled impatiently at the ties of her undergarments until they, too, slid to her feet.

Oh, God. She was naked. She was a fallen woman. Heat consumed her. Embarrassment? Desire. She no longer knew as he parted her hair and kissed a delicious spot beneath her ear, one hand around her waist and his hips tight against her buttocks. His other hand caressed her breasts. The skin tingled, tightened. His thumb brushed across her nipples. They furled into tight little buds, an achingly irresistible sensation. Weakness invaded her bones. Only his grip prevented her from falling. He played with her breasts, stroking, kneading, teasing her nipples, till she thought she would go mad with the need to touch him.

Being married must be like this. The freedom to touch one's man. She'd never thought about that part of it. Exciting. Wonderful.

She leaned against his chest and reached up with her hands and stroked the back of his neck. She pulled his head down so she could kiss the side of his face. The stubble on his jaw rasped against her cheek. His musky cologne filled her senses. An intoxicating brew.

After this, she would not be the same person. All she had been taught in life to value would be gone. Another of her risky adventures. The last one.

She had never felt so alive or so scared.

Chapter Five

Her kiss, so tender on his cheek, cut through Garrick's lust. It hinted at affection. That she desired him was obvious. Her arousal was as strong as his, he could smell it, taste it on her skin, feel it in her physical responses. But there was unselfishness in her hesitant gentleness. The women he had known demanded satiation, as he had. It had always been about *taking* pleasure.

Ellie seemed to want to give. The intensity of tenderness she evoked in him threatened his defences, threatened his control. Pleasure. He had nothing else to give.

'Ellie, sweetheart,' he whispered. 'Turn around.'

She twisted in his arms, maintaining the contact of her lips with his face. Her breasts, nipples hard with desire, brushed against his arm, his ribs. Piercing longing ripped at his resolve. He bent his head and ravaged her mouth, plunged his tongue into the warm heat. He could taste her sweetness and smell her clean fresh fragrance, the hint of vanilla. She leaned against him, winding her arms around his neck, her fingers tracing a path through his hair.

He picked her up and laid her on the bed and her half-closed eyes watched him shyly. Her peeping gaze as he stripped off his shirt was more erotic than any bold stare. He wanted her so much his body trembled deep inside, as if every bone, muscle and sinew needed her for survival. He stopped undressing to kiss her, claimed her mouth, while her hands wandered his back in a light exploration that drove him wild with a need to make her forget her other man. Hands shaking, he rose and pulled off his boots and pantaloons. Her eyes widened as she took in his naked body. She looked away quickly, blushing. So she would play the maid to the end. God, how it inflamed him.

Golden hair spilling in abandon on to her shoulders and breasts, a small silver cross on a blue ribbon at her neck. He bent over her, kissing her cheek as chastely as a boy and she smiled. His chest ached sweetly as she draped her arms across his shoulders, encouraging him closer, but he held himself away, intent on his own exploration. His hands slid across her ribs, then around her waist, measuring the span. So fine, so tiny. He traced her navel with a fingertip, shaped the curve of her belly with his palm, until his hand reached her most private place. He combed through the crisp fair curls. She shivered and his shaft pulsed in response.

Garrick eased his hand between her elegant thighs, nudging them apart. A faint murmur of protest escaped her lips. The way she played the innocent was so unbelievably erotic. A delightfully sensual act designed to trap him in her web. His need surged rampant and urgent.

He stroked the velvet softness of her inner thighs, caressed her cleft and found it slippery with her moisture. For him. It felt like a gift from the gods. A treasure beyond compare. Her eyes drifted open on a moan. He smiled down into her passion-filled face, seeking the tiny nub of flesh, desiring her pleasure above all else. He circled his thumb. Her expression softened and her eyes glazed over, then she arched her back and cried out deep and guttural in her throat.

No virtuous games now, just her body responding to his touch in mindless ecstasy.

Her hands stroked his chest, his arms, his back. His skin tingled and his blood flared wherever her hands caressed. Sweet heavens, he needed to be inside her. He lowered his head and kissed her, tasting, plundering her soft welcoming mouth, sucking at her lips, drawing her tongue into his mouth as he kneed her legs wider. Slowly, he dipped the tip of his finger inside her wet, hot passage and found her ready. Hot blood roared through his veins.

Cradled by her body, her inner thighs a soft support for his hips, he lowered his mouth to her wonderful breasts. Tightly furled, her nipple rubbed against his lips as he kissed and licked the soft, tender flesh. Then he suckled. She moaned. His groin tightened. He lifted her hips, reached down and guided his rigid shaft to her entrance.

She stilled beneath him, her eyes wide in wonder and the pretence of fear. It drove him to the edge of madness and beyond. He eased into her warm wet flesh, rejoicing in her heat tight around him. So damned small. Almost too small. Deliciously resistant. He thought he would die of pleasure. He moved slowly. He knew how to prolong his partner's enjoyment, but now she struggled, deliberately exciting him beyond control, fuelling his masculine need for ascendancy.

He thrust his tongue into her mouth, gathered up her wrists and held them above her head, her breasts lifting.

He kissed and sucked each nipple while she squirmed beneath him. So damned sexy. He thrust his hips forwards and she cried out in genuine pain.

He froze. 'Bloody hell.' He stared down at her. 'Ellie?' She shook her head, her face shocked. His arms and body shuddered with the effort of holding still.

'Sweet Lord. Tell me this is not your first time.' His body screamed a furious protest. His mind refused to grapple with the truth.

She nodded and swallowed, obviously scared to death. He groaned. What was done was done. He stayed still inside her, gasping for air, summoning control. If he left her now, hurting and afraid, she might never recover. He had to bring her more than pain, but she was rigid beneath him. No longer aroused, just afraid and tight and tense. She wasn't pretending. He'd deflowered an innocent.

Hell and damnation. The realisation cut through him like terrible blades. He'd known. Deep down, he'd known. God damn it. The urge to strike out balled his fists.

He fought his rage, trembled with its force, beat it down until he could finally speak. 'I'm sorry,' he whispered. 'Trust me. I will try not to hurt you more. Sweetheart, kiss me.'

Her lovely mouth trembled. Tears welled in her eyes. Damn, they were joined together and he needed to gain her trust. He released her hands and, holding his torso completely still on his forearms, he lowered his mouth to hers. He placed tiny little kisses on each lip, barely more than a whisper. He could feel her warm breath on his throat, little gasps of terror.

His fault. He traced a path from her lips to her chin, across her throat. He nuzzled her neck, feeling her silky hair against his face, inhaling its light floral perfume. He ran his tongue around the edge of her ear and then softly probed the orifice. She shivered. She moved under him, he felt her arms encircle him. Felt her relax.

Sweat traced a cold path down the centre of his back as every muscle strained to hold his pounding need in check. He withdrew slowly, just a little, then slid forwards.

She lifted her hips, encouraging him now, welcoming him into her depths. Her courage humbled him. She was as brave as a warrior, and she was his.

'Ellie,' he groaned. 'Hold still, for God's sake.'

He heard her laugh low in her throat. 'I'm all right,' she whispered. She brought her legs around his waist. Unable to hold back, he thrust into her deeply, fiercely, and felt her rise to meet his every stroke.

She dug her fingers into his back. He welcomed the sting of pain and remembered to breathe.

Her heat engulfed him, making him forget all thoughts of restraint. He thrust faster, his body taking command. The storm built and swirled and raged and erupted in tearing, streaking light. Her back arched and she moaned sweetly and shuddered as she reached for heaven and found it. The edge of his abyss loomed close, hot and dark and welcoming. He withdrew from her body, spent his seed in the tangle of sheets and joined her on her downward spiral.

Panting, they lay together in heated bliss. He pulled her tight against his side, cradling her in the crook of his arm, stroking her until he was sure she slept.

Nom d'un nom. A virgin. If he had known, he would never have taken her. He shook his head in disbelief. Castlefield had not bedded her. Perhaps he scorned a mere servant, no matter that she had shown such love.

He couldn't help the feeling of triumph, even as he regretted her loss.

She'd given him, of all men, a treasure beyond price. He wanted to curl his body around her, shelter her from the world. The emotion tugged at a painful chord in the region of his heart. An emotion he couldn't afford.

He gazed down at her beautiful face, so young, so fragile in sleep. He brushed her silky hair away from her forehead and kissed each eyelid, with its sweep of fair lashes against fragile skin. Satisfied, he held her safe, then drifted off to sleep.

Shadows filled the room when Garrick opened his eyes. He stretched, feeling the wonderful pull of muscle from head to toe. None of the familiar feeling of panic of something urgent he needed to remember. Had he ever awoken feeling so utterly relaxed?

Ellie stirred. He rolled on his side, kissed her cheek, then her mouth, savoured the honeyed taste of his woman. 'Awake already, *chérie*?' he whispered. The wicked part of his body responded to the thought of her awake. Not a good idea, not when she'd be sore. And he was expected at the Court. He hung over the side of the bed and retrieved his watch, squinting at it in the fading light. Almost seven. 'I must hurry, if I want to be in time for dinner.'

Beside him, her body tensed.

He turned to face her, propped up on an elbow. 'What is it, sweet?'

Her gaze slid away. 'Nothing.'

In his experience, when a woman said nothing in that cool tone of voice it meant trouble. In the past he'd simply walked away, afraid to risk the heat of his anger. He didn't want to walk away from Ellie.

He tipped her chin with his hand and kissed her lips. They were as cold as ice and unresponsive. 'I'm expected. Surely you understand?'

Her lashes hid her eyes. 'Yes, my lord.'

'Call me Garrick. Ellie, I can't live here. What would your neighbours say? Besides, I have duties at Beauworth.' He'd promised his uncle and he would not go back on his word 'I will visit you every day.' He smiled. 'You won't be lonely, I promise.' He took her lips, kissed her long and hard, binding her to him, promising more. He felt the scorching heat spiralling around them, drawing them together, melting her against him.

For a moment, he surrendered to its power. More than anything, he wanted to stay, but he never went back on his word. He owed it to Beauworth and Le Clere to go home.

A week had passed. One of the most blissful Garrick had ever known. And he wanted Ellie to be happy, too. He'd thought of the perfect thing. So now with her at his side in the gig, he felt as nervous as a lad facing his first day at school. Ridiculous. And yet he hadn't felt this excited in years. Even the unpredictable weather had cooperated with a sunny summer day.

They turned on to the track winding to the barn where he'd been held captive. 'Where are we going?' The nervousness in her voice indicated she'd guessed their destination.

He kept his voice gruff. 'You'll see.'

Her body stiffened as if she expected some sort of trick. Perhaps he shouldn't tease, but he couldn't resist. She'd love his surprise. They turned through the gate. He tried to hold back his smile as her mouth dropped open at the sight of the two horses tied to the rail outside the barn.

'Oh,' she said. 'Mist.' She grabbed his arm. 'You remembered.'

'That you stabled him at Brown's farm? Yes.' He brought the horse to a halt and she leapt down without waiting for help. Skirts ankle high, she ran to the little white gelding, reaching out to him, petting his neck, murmuring soft words into his ear.

A huge warmth filled his chest, marred by a twinge of something small and mean. Jealousy for the damned horse? 'Struth. He must be losing his mind if he envied a bloody gelding.

Forcing a smile, he jumped down and strode to join her at the fence. 'Dan collected him this morning.'

'I never imagined you would do something like this.' Her laughter bubbled like champagne, even as her words cut through his joy and when she flung her arms around his neck and kissed his cheek, he forgave her careless dismissal and basked in her happiness. She could not have been more pleased than if he had brought her diamonds.

'Oh, I wish I had known, I would have worn my riding habit.'

'I can do better.' Garrick didn't try to hold back his smirk. He took her hand and led her into the barn. There, in a corner, was a suit of boy's clothes very much like those she had worn when they had fenced, and beside the pile, her sword leaning up against the wall.

She hugged him with abandon. 'I don't believe it.'

'Well, Miss Brown, first we ride, then we practise. I will teach you my sword trick, if you wish.'

Her face shone in the dim cool light. 'I do wish. Leave me, so I can change.'

Imperious and charmingly modest. A strange delightful mixture for a creature of passion and adventure.

Laughing, he tipped up her face with his knuckle. 'Do you need my help?'

'I'm used to doing for myself.'

Of course she was. Women of her ilk did not have maids to help them dress. Yet he would have liked to help her out of her clothes. Heat rushed to his groin. He could insist, of course. It was his right. But this was her day, and so he left and strode out into the sunshine where he paced in front of the barn, imagining her slipping out of her gown and into her other guise with increasingly lascivious thoughts.

When she emerged, her stride and the way she held herself reminded him what a great little actress she was, a woman who changed her persona with her clothes. Now, she was more boy than girl, swaggering in her form-hugging breeches with the sword belted at her waist and the cocked hat pulled down over her hair. The costume left nothing of her body to the imagination and the sight of luscious hips and thighs thickened his blood.

If he hadn't known how much she was looking forward to going for a ride, he might have pulled her down on to the grass where they'd kissed days before and teased her right out of her breeches. Instead, breathing hard, concentrating on the control he'd learned as a boy, he held his desire in check, merely nodding when she glanced from the horse to him.

In a flash, she mounted, a boy-like leap into the saddle, and urged the little white gelding into a gallop. Ah, but he would not let her get too far. He swung up on to Bess. The mare needed no urging to catch the fleeing pair. And when he came up on her, they rode side by side across the field. Not the sedate trot of an afternoon in Hyde Park, but a wild canter.

'A race,' she called out.

He grinned and dug in his heels. Bess easily outstripped the smaller gelding.

He looked back to gloat. Damn her. She'd cut off at right angles. Headed straight for the field's low stone wall. His heart rose in his throat. She'd break her neck if she fell at that speed. He wheeled Bess around and followed. He roared a warning. The gelding took the wall with a playful little kick of rear hooves, clearing the coping with inches to spare.

Even as his heart swelled in admiration, Garrick wanted to take his crop to her backside. He wanted to shake her. Make her promise never to risk her life in that fashion again. He had to catch her first.

Never had he seen a woman ride so hard, better than many men he knew. Admiration outstripped anger as he watched the perfect harmony between horse and rider. She rode like a madwoman, but she knew her horse and by the time they were heading back to the barn, he'd forgiven her madcap dash. He laughed out loud when she raised a brow in question from beneath her cocked hat.

As they walked the horses cool, a feeling of contentment washed through him. It was as if some great weight had gone from his shoulders, or some dark shadow had been erased from his soul. She made him feel…happy. A gift beyond price.

A happiness he didn't deserve, but would enjoy as long as it lasted.

'I'm starving,' he said.

'Me, too.'

'Lucky I thought to bring lunch.' He retrieved the hamper he'd left in the barn's cool interior and spread out a red-and-green plaid blanket on the grass overlooking the pond. She laid out the feast, small meat pasties in a feather-light crust, bread, cheese and fine red wine. Neither said much while they ate. It was good to see a woman eat with such gusto, unlike the ladies of his acquaintance in London, who picked at food as if it might be poison.

Crickets chirped a merry tune in the grass. A dove on the barn roof cooed softly. Appetite sated, Garrick stretched out, leaning on one elbow so he could watch her face. She sighed and, resting against his thigh, sipped her wine. 'Thank you for a most wonderful surprise,' she murmured.

The pleasure in her voice filled his heart with unaccustomed warmth. It burned like frozen fingers brought back to life. 'I'm glad it pleased you. Tell me, how on earth did you learn to ride and fight with a sword like a boy?'

She hesitated.

Would she lie? The warmth dwindled, but he tried to hold it fast. After all, he had his own dark secrets.

'I told you I was brought up with the Castlefield children,' she said. 'We spent a year or two in India. While travelling in some parts it was safer to dress the girls as boys. I took fencing and riding lessons with William…I mean, Lord Castlefield. I loved it. Sometimes I wished I'd been born a boy.'

William. Her familiarity with the man sent the heat of anger flooding to his brain even as he analysed her slight hesitations and carefully chosen words. No doubt about it. She was lying.

He kept his expression cool, detached. 'I envy you. I have never been outside England. The war with France made the Grand Tour impossible.' Not to mention his uncle's protectiveness.

She set down her half-full glass and stared at the rolling vista. 'It was the same for the oldest son, the heir. He hoped to go abroad once the war was over. He was killed in a carriage accident not long ago. Now William must return and take up the duties as heir. In a way, I'm glad.' Her voice caught. 'I hated thinking of him in danger.'

Garrick couldn't see her face, but he heard the note of deep longing in her voice. Clearly no matter what he did, she would prefer this man. Jealousy surged, twisted in his gut, knotted with a cold, hard lump of anger and bitterness. The thought of this other man wounded him in a way he hadn't expected, a way he'd never before experienced. He forced himself not to care. 'Is it your wish to go to him when he returns?' The hard edge in his voice told him he'd failed.

'Oh, no.' She sounded sincere, almost appalled.

More acting? And why would he care? His plans for the future didn't involve a woman. He eased away from her, rose to his feet and began packing away the remains of the picnic.

'One of your servants came to Castlefield, once,' she said, passing him her wineglass. 'He'd been in the same regiment as the old lord, and your father, I believe. A man named Piggot.'

His stomach lurched. The ground beneath his feet seemed to shift at the sound of a name he'd not heard in years. He stood stock-still. 'Piggot?'

'I can remember the Earl being quite upset after his visit, but he did not say why.' She rose to her feet and dusted off her breeches, her small hands patting the round curve of her derrière.

A tremor, so deep it did not disturb the surface of his flesh, quaked in his bones. Would Piggot have revealed the events surrounding his mother's death to Castlefield? Did the information that could destroy him lie in Castlefield's hands, awaiting imminent discovery? How Ellie would revile him if she learned the truth. And yet, in some dark corner of his soul lay a measure of relief at the thought of laying down a burden too heavy to bear.

Unseeing, he stared at the blanket in his hands.

'On guard.'

A sword point flickered in his face. He recoiled. 'What the deuce?'

She laughed, her eyes sparkling. She twirled her blade, then raised it in salute. 'You promised me a lesson.'

Sweat trickled off his brow and ran cold down his cheek. He let go a long breath and smiled. 'So I did.' He collected his weapon from the gig and took off his coat.

He bowed, then saluted. 'On guard.'

She took up her stance, lithe and alert. As their blades hissed together, he recalled her amazing skill. She'd been taught by a master. A worthy opponent, indeed, though she did not have the strength of wrist or the reach to best him. He demonstrated his technique of twisting a blade free of his opponent's hand. She grasped the theory quickly, but had trouble putting it into practice.

'It will work for you with a weaker opponent,' he said.

Clearly exhausted, the tip of her sword resting on the grass, she nodded and wiped her face on her shirtsleeve with a laugh. 'Enough, my lord. I can barely lift my arm.'

Her face was flushed, beads of sweat shone on her brow and her shirt was undone past what was decent. Delicious. Tantalising. His body quickened.

'Aye. It is time you changed, before my servant comes to retrieve the picnic, and he recognises you as the highwayman I kissed.' He led her into the barn.

Ellie tugged on his hand. 'Why did you kiss me that night? There was no legend, was there?'

He smiled at her frown. 'Because, like a fool I'd left my pistol in the coach.' And lucky it was he had. God, even now she might be dead.

'I was a fool to let you get so close. I'd not do so again.'

'There will not be a next time.' Cold fear struck his heart. He pressed her against him, the urge to keep her safe overwhelming. 'Will there?'

Against his arm, her spine stiffened. Her grey eyes cooled as she hid her thoughts. 'No. There is no reason for it any longer.'

He kissed her hard, trying to break through the barrier she'd put up. It worked. She melted against him and his blood grew thick and heavy with need.

'How do you do that?' His voice was low and husky with desire.

A laugh caught in her throat. 'I was going to ask you the same thing.'

He hoisted her into his arms, while she laughed and kicked. He put her down on the blanket amongst the straw, a lovely wild creature as comfortable in a barn as she was on a feather bed. An enigma. Perhaps that was the root of her attraction. She was unlike any other woman he'd known.

What was it about her that drove him to distraction? Perhaps not knowing how much of her was real and how much playacting held him enthralled. She'd been a virgin when she came to his bed, but there was nothing innocent about Lady Moonlight. Would he ever know the real woman behind the mask?

And if he did, would she disappoint? Was it better not to know?

She reached up and cupped his jaw in her small hand, dragging his face down to her lips with a saucy smile. Today, he had Lady Moonlight. God help him, he'd take whatever she felt free to give.

He wrestled with the buttons of her shirt while her lips were fastened to his, only breaking away to pull it over her head. When she did the same for him, he felt humbled. Honoured. He lay beside her, kissing her lips, her throat, the rise of her breast. Her nipples leapt to life under his tongue. Passion and adventure all rolled up in one unique woman.

While he nuzzled into her breasts to the sound of her delighted giggles, he unfastened her breeches, easing them over the curve of her hips. He caressed the soft skin of her buttocks and pressed her hard against his arousal.

She pushed him away. She laughed at his disappointment and, leaning forwards, nipped his shoulder with her teeth.

'Ouch!'

She slid slowly to her knees, her hands trailing down his chest and then his belly until they reached the waistband of his breeches. The white skin of her back melded into the roundness of her plump firm buttocks at its base. Groaning, he reached down and unpinned her silky golden hair so it flowed softly around her as she unbuttoned him and his shaft sprang free, rampant and ready. She kissed him, a quick shy brush of silky soft lips.

Mon Dieu, it felt good. A breath of pure pleasure hissed between his teeth. But he wanted more. He wanted to feel her soft curves against him. He lifted her to him and kissed her mouth. He plunged his tongue deep into her and felt her bold response.

'I need to be out of these clothes,' he whispered.

She cast him a shy smile of encouragement. He sat up and quickly stripped off his boots and breeches and turned to lay beside her. She gazed deeply into his eyes, seeking…what? Assurance. The passion in her smoky gaze drove blood from his brain to his groin.

He gathered her close, oblivious to everything except her warmth, her scent, the hint of vanilla. An honest, earthy scent. The sounds of desire from her throat while their mouths joined drove him wild with wanting. His fingers dipped into her moist, hot centre and he groaned. This was where he belonged. Somehow, he would make her forget her past.

He nudged his knee between her thighs and she, generous and yielding, let them fall open. He entered her and they became as one. He drove into her, thrusting again and again. Her gasps of excitement, the breath warm in his ear, her nails sharp points of wicked pain on his back and buttocks, drove him to new heights of desire.

The scent of her arousal filled his nostrils. Her cries, increasingly demanding, filled his ears.

So close. His own release threatened, demanded, tortured, tightened his groin until he thought he would explode. He clamped his jaw. Strained to bring her with him. Fought for control.

He shifted. Stroked her tight insides with his body, feeling the flutter and pull of her inner muscles goading him on. He reached between them, found the source of her pleasure, the swollen bud of her desire, and circled and rubbed, hard, fast.

'Oh God, Ellie, now.'

Her body clenched around his shaft, hot spasms against the sensitive head. He was going to die of pleasure. Not without her. Not alone.

Then she shattered. Crest after crest of heat and tight, clenching, muscles. In a panic, he withdrew, spilling his essence on her belly as he followed her into the surf. He collapsed on his side, grabbing his shirt to clean her skin. The scent of sweet-smelling straw and lovemaking in his nostrils, a harmony of breathing and slowing hearts, a paradise on earth. Blissful, sated, sweat cooling on exposed flesh, he gazed up into the ancient beams. If he stayed in England with her at his side, perhaps his inner demons could be vanquished.

With a smile, she nestled deeper in the crook of his arm, her straw-coloured hair trailing over her breasts like a silken veil. He ran a fingertip across her arm where it lay across her stomach, her hand resting on his hip. A beautiful, extraordinary woman.

His eyes drifted closed. When he came to and looked at her next she had turned on her back. His first thought was to kiss her awake and make love to her again. But tears were sliding from under her long, golden lashes and running down her face.

He reached out and captured a tear on his thumb and brought it to his lips. He tasted salt. What made her cry in her sleep? His stomach roiled as he forced his mind to recognise what his heart would not. She wasn't happy.

It was like a knife twisting in his chest, this sense of impending loss.

Yet perhaps it was as well. What if this thing inside him caused her harm? He'd never forgive himself.

Would he harm a woman he only wanted to protect?

The legends spoke of blind rage. He was almost sure he'd experienced it first-hand three times now, the sensation of control and memory slipping away. His gut churned.

Her eyes opened and she looked at him with a slight frown, as if she was trying to recall where she was, then her eyes cleared and she smiled.

'Why are you crying?' His voice sounded tight and hard.

'I didn't know I was.' Her laugh shook. She rubbed at her eyes with the back of her hand. 'A bad dream? I don't recall.'

A wave of guilt washed over him. He should have given her the money she needed and made her leave, instead of killing any dreams she must have of her noble patron.

He only wanted to give her happiness. In his selfishness, he had tried to win her heart, to make her want to stay, but if she cried for Castlefield after a day as perfect as this one, she'd never been his. Sadness rose up inside him, painful and dark.

He had spent years learning to control his deeper emotions, building a wall to keep out anything that might disturb his calm as a matter of survival. She had pierced that wall and he must make it whole again. He would tell her he was tired of her, send her away.

But not yet. Not today.

'Come, Dan will return soon. Let me help you dress.'

On the drive back to the village, Ellie rested her head on his shoulder, her body rocking against him with the horses' steady rhythm. Unconsciously he pulled her closer and she snuggled into him, nuzzling his neck. His heart felt tattered, torn to shreds, and he welcomed the pain.

They pulled up outside her front door. 'Goodnight, Ellie,' he whispered into her hair. He tipped her chin and brushed her lips with his thumb, aching for more.

'Goodnight, Garrick. Thank you for a wonderful day,' she murmured.

Tomorrow, he'd gather the strength of will to set her free. After all, she'd never been his to keep and a man with a stain on his soul didn't deserve happiness.

Chapter Six

Eleanor closed the door the moment the gig drove away. She busied herself preparing supper, trying not to think about the path she'd chosen and what it meant for her future.

He'd given her a beautiful day in idyllic surroundings and it hadn't been too hard to imagine herself spending the rest of her life with him. He was thoughtful, charming and fun. Most of all, when he made love to her, she forgot his reputation as a rake, forgot the duty she owed to her family, forgot she was ruined. It wouldn't matter how good he was to her, he could never marry her now.

Nor could anyone else.

And until their bargain was over, she must not let him steal her heart.

That foolish organ gave a funny little skip, a happy little hop in her chest. Too late, apparently.

She jabbed the fork into a slice of bread. What a fool. Each time she thought about bidding him goodbye, she cried. If she didn't take care she'd turn into a permanent watering pot. She'd always despised lachrymose females who complained about their lot in life. She'd made her bed and she'd lie on it, cheerfully, and think about the future when it arrived.

If she had a future. Drat it, there she went again.

She stared at the toast and jam she'd put on the plate, but there was no room in her stomach for food. Tea. She needed a nice cup of tea. In bed. And a book. She put the kettle on and changed into her nightdress and robe.

Her front door creaked open. Her spirits soared. Garrick had returned. She ran to greet him.

It wasn't Garrick outlined in the doorway, but a stranger. Large and threatening, with a wind-reddened face and heavy black brows above a red-veined, bulbous nose, he barged over the threshold. Oh, God. She must have forgotten to throw the bolt.

She backed away, her mouth dry and her heart beating loudly. While not tall, he was heavyset and could overpower her in an instant. Her stomach lurched as small black eyes ran down her body, eyebrows lifting. The worst thing about him was his grin, loose wet lips drawing back over broken yellow teeth beneath a greasy black moustache.

'Get out.' Her voice shook. She clasped her hands together, seeking strength. 'You have no right to be in here.'

'Now, now, my lady, don't get excited, I've come with a message from his lordship.'

'The Marquess of Beauworth?'

'The very same.'

Something jarred about his words. She gasped. He had called her my lady. Garrick knew? Her rapidly beating heart clogged her throat. She swallowed. 'Get out.'

He made no move.

She glanced around for a weapon. If only she had not left her sword at the barn.

The man closed the door with his heel, following step by step as she backed away. She daren't take her gaze from his face in case he attacked.

A weapon. She needed something heavy. She sidled into the bedroom, working her way to the brass candlestick on the night table. Breathing steadily, clutching fast to her courage, she backed around the bed. The table nudged her back. Her fingers fumbled behind her and found cool metal.

She held up her other hand in a warning. 'No closer.'

He reached into his pocket. He must have a pistol or a knife. She had to act.

She grasped the candlestick firmly, hefting it in her hand where he could see it. 'Stay back or I will put a dint in your face so large your mother will never recognise you.'

His hand emerged with a small brown bottle. He laughed, an evil, sneering sound. 'Them's fighting words, my lady.' The sound of the front door opening sent a chill down her spine.

'Where the hell are you?' a male voice called.

More of them. Bile rose in her throat.

'In here, Sarg.'

She might be able to deal with one, but two? Dear God, what did they want? Her chest tightened, making it hard to breathe. 'There is money in the chest under the bed,' she croaked.

'I'll keep that in mind,' bulbous nose said. 'Later.'

The chill down her back turned to ice. She launched the candlestick at his head.

He knocked it aside with his arm. 'Ouch,' he bellowed. 'You little bitch!'

He lunged at her. She ducked under his arm. He caught a handful of her hair. Pain shot through her scalp. Eyes blurring, she twisted in his grip. Lashed at his groin with her bare foot and hit his thigh. She stumbled. He yanked her back by her hair. More pain. Her eyes streamed. She flailed at his face with her nails.

Arms grabbed her from behind, around her throat and waist. A belt buckle jammed into her back. The second man. Panic chilled her to the bone.

'I told you to wait.' His voice in her ear was low and angry. 'Where's the bottle, Caleb?'

''Ere, Sarg.'

A grinning Caleb held the small brown bottle to her lips. She recognised the smell. Laudanum. She clamped her mouth shut. The man behind pinched her nostrils. Hard. Painfully hard, while Caleb pressed the bottle against her lips. The fingers around her throat tightened. Arms crushed her ribs. Her lungs burned. Her head swam. Air. She needed air.

One quick breath. Turning her face, she opened her mouth. A bitter-tasting liquid flooded in. She swallowed. Managed a breath.

'More,' Sarg said.

More liquid. She struggled blindly. Her movements became weaker. Dizzy, she felt her limbs loosen. The triumphant leer of the man Caleb faded.

The cottage had an air of desolation. An emptiness. Garrick sensed it the moment he entered and still he called out, 'Ellie?' Silence.

He placed her sword and scabbard gently on the pine table. He'd thought she might want to keep it. He wandered into the bedroom, just to be sure. The bed was stripped, the clothes' press empty. She'd taken everything.

A hollow, sick feeling hit the pit of his stomach. Knowing how unhappy she was, he'd planned to send her home, rehearsed what he would say over and over, all the while hoping she might want to stay.

It was better this way. She'd gone of her own accord. Less painful. Then why did his chest ache? A small scrap of white poked out from under the bed and he picked it up. A minute square of lawn edged in fine lace. He pressed it to his nose. It smelled clean, fresh with traces of vanilla. Ellie. It was the only thing left. No note. Nothing to show she had ever lived here. He stuffed the handkerchief into his coat pocket and went back to the kitchen.

Barely conscious of his actions, he pulled a bottle of brandy and a tumbler from the dresser and set them on the table. He fought his bitter disappointment. Why not say goodbye? Had she found him so lacking?

He pulled out the plain ladder-back chair, turned its back against the scrubbed table and sat astride. Chin resting on his sleeve, he glared at the honey-coloured table top, as if it could provide an answer. Had she somehow seen the evil in him? She didn't lack for courage, but it was enough to send anyone running off into the night.

Bloody hell. Why couldn't he accept she loved Castlefield instead of trying to place the blame elsewhere? An urgent need to drink one glass after another and dull the pain tightened his gut. He reached for the bottle, astonished at the way his hand shook as he splashed liquid oblivion into the glass and on to the table. The pungent aroma stung the back of his throat, brought tears to his eyes. Oh, yes. Fool yourself about this, too. He smiled wryly. Tomorrow reality would stare him in the face, the way it did every day. He ought to be glad she'd gone, glad she'd never look at him in horror.

He buried his head in the crook of his arm. Rage, despair, roiling emotions he couldn't name, made his skin feel too tight, as if he might burst like an over-filled water-skin. With a muffled roar, he rose and lobbed the glass into the fireplace. It shattered with the sound of hail on a tile roof. Then silence. Brandy fumes hung in the air like the stink of an inn on a Saturday night.

What the hell good had that done, except waste perfectly good brandy? He picked up the bottle to put it away. The front door slammed back against the wall. Ellie?

Garrick turned, his heart beating hopefully against his ribs. Without warning, a blond, red-coated soldier lurched across the room and grabbed at his throat. Choking, he tore at the man's fingers.

'Where is she, you goddamned thrice-misbegotten whoreson?' the man yelled.

Even as his vision blackened around the edges, Garrick knew this man. 'Hadley?' His enemy.

A red wash coated his vision, rage running like liquid fire through his veins. He embraced it. Used its strength. He brought his arms up and around. Broke the other man's hold, shoved him backwards and raised his fists, longing to beat the furious face to a pulp.

'Not so fast, my lord.' The muzzle of a rifle pressed coldly against the back of Garrick's neck.

With his back to the door, Garrick had not seen the man enter, but he recognised the deep rumbling voice. He released his breath in a long, shuddering sigh, gaining control, clearing the red mists from his sight, tamping down the killing rage. 'Well, if it isn't Ben.'

'No, my lord. Martin Brown, at your service. Put up your weapons.'

Martin Brown, the relative she'd spoken of, was also Ben the highwayman? *Merde.* How many more lies had she told him?

Garrick lowered his fists.

Martin Brown withdrew his rifle and held it ready across his chest.

Hadley fixed his hard grey gaze on Garrick and repeated his question. 'Where is she?'

What the hell was going on? What did this man have to do with Ellie? No. This must be about some other woman. He racked his brain for possible contenders, women he'd forgotten, while he kept his face a blank slate. 'What are you doing here?'

Anger boiled up again, at Ellie, at himself, at this man from his past. He curled his lip and glanced down at the man's twisted right leg. 'Come for another beating, Hadley?' He shouldn't have said that. Hell, he'd always denied being Hadley's night-time attacker.

The other man reddened. 'Castlefield now.'

Garrick reeled. The breath left his body as if he'd been struck in the kidneys. This was Castlefield? 'But—'

'Haven't you done enough, you bastard? Did you have to take your revenge out on my sister?'

For a long moment Garrick's mind stuck on the word revenge, the old issue between them, the fight over a woman and the accusations hanging over him at school. The reason for Castlefield's halting gait. The second occasion he'd lost control and couldn't remember.

Finally, the word 'sister' forced its way to the surface. The floor beneath his feet seemed to tilt. 'Ellie is your sister?'

'Lady Eleanor Hadley, to you. My twin.'

His twin sister? He could only stare in stunned silence. Finally he found a shred of voice. 'She left.' His mind scrambled to make sense of what his ears were hearing. 'She must have gone home.'

Martin Brown shook his head. 'The bailiffs are gone, but no sign of her ladyship.'

A sense of dread filled his stomach. 'Then she went to her sister.' He refused to think about where else she might have gone.

'Damn you, Beauworth!' Castlefield choked out. 'If I find that one hair of her head has been harmed, I shall hold you fully responsible.' He drew his sword.

'Put up, my lord,' Martin Brown said sternly, his ruddy face grim. This time his rifle was pointed at the Earl. 'This was all her own doing. I did my best to stop her and when I could not, I did my best to protect her.' He nodded at Garrick. 'He became involved when we held up his coach and he followed us. She said she would set him free and go to Scotland.' He flushed. 'I had a feeling there was more to it. That was why I waited for your ship in Portsmouth. But if she's gone, she's gone to your aunt, or to her friend in Scotland. We should look for her there.'

Oh God, Ellie. What were you doing? He stared at her enraged brother. No wonder she'd longed for him to come home. The bastard had left her to face everything alone. Well, now he'd know the truth, because he wasn't fit to take care of her.

Garrick crossed his arms across his chest and stared down his nose at the other man. 'You were right to worry, Martin. She became my mistress to retrieve the mortgage and pay his debts.' He curled his lip as the other man squirmed. 'Not once did she tell me the truth.'

Horror etched on his features, Castlefield limped to the sofa and collapsed. He covered his face with his hands. 'Eleanor,' he moaned. 'Why?'

A wave of remorse washed away Garrick's anger. 'I'm sorry you had to find out this way, but you have only yourself to blame.'

Martin Brown assisted his young master to rise. 'Come, my lord, we have to find her and bring her home.'

Castlefield glared at Garrick. 'You despicable cur, taking advantage of a woman. My sister is worth two of you.'

What had he done? She'd been trying to save her brother, and Garrick had taken full advantage of the circumstances. Dear God. He'd ruined a noble-woman, taken her virtue. Were there no depths to which he would not sink? If only she'd told him who she was. Let him help her. *Nom d'un nom.* She'd lied rather than give him the chance to help because she didn't trust him.

He had to make it right. Offer her his name. It was all he could do. What he wanted to do. He felt a surge of hope. 'I will marry her, of course.' His voice sounded thick and hoarse.

In the doorway, Castlefield swung back around, granite eyes blazing, his pale skin flushed. 'Do you think I'd let her marry a cur like you?'

Cringing inside, Garrick somehow managed to keep his voice calm. 'It will be up to Ellie to decide.'

'Will it?' Castlefield's voice dropped to a whisper. 'When I tell her what you did to me, you know how she will answer. Eleanor will do my bidding in this. Say one thing to a soul about my sister and I swear I will kill you. Come near my family again and you will die.'

The bitterness in his voice rent Garrick's sympathy to shreds. 'Next time you find yourself in debt, don't leave your sister to rescue you.'

'Damn you to hell, Beauworth!' Castlefield

shouted, following Martin Brown out of the door and slamming it shut.

Hell looked inviting. Garrick sank on to the sofa. What a bloody mess. How could he not have seen what she was? Hell! He'd known she had secrets, but how could he have guessed she was a noblewoman? Liar. The signs had all been there—her conversation, her bearing, even her modesty and innocence. The selfish bastard in him hadn't wanted to see. He'd wanted the rogue, the woman in the mask, the woman he could not hurt.

He scrubbed his palm over his chin. She had no choice but to take his name. Castlefield would come to his senses, once he got over his anger. His heart lifted. In a way, it wasn't so bad.

'She's waking.' Shuffling footsteps crossed the room.

Eleanor turned her head towards the coarse female voice. Light sliced pain through her temples and she tried to swallow what felt like sand in her throat. The room spun like a child's top. Oh God, she was going to be sick. A basin appeared before her as if by magic. She vomited. Again and again.

Exhausted, she lay back, eyes shut. What was wrong with her? She'd never felt so ill in her life. Then she remembered. They'd dosed her with laudanum. After a few moments, she opened her eyes again and peered through a watery blur at four bare stone walls, a grimy window and flagstone floor. Where was she?

She struggled to rise. A dumpy old crone in black shoved her back against the pillow.

'Here, lovey,' the woman said. 'Drink. It'll 'ave you right as rain, it will.'

Feeling a glass against her lips, she gulped at the liquid. Bitter. Disgusting. Oh, no, more laudanum. 'Why are you doing this to me?'

'Rest, missie.'

'How long will she sleep?' A man's voice, low and harsh from across the room. Eleanor tried to raise her head to see. Too heavy. Too tired.

'A few hours.'

'Good. Keep the door locked. Caleb will keep watch.'

Caleb. A rush of fear engulfed her as she remembered the man's ugly face, the last person she'd seen before darkness sucked her down.

The next time she opened her eyes, she was alone. She felt better, stronger. The musty-smelling room remained steady. A chamber with crumbling plaster, and empty except for the cot on which she lay. A spyhole pierced the blackened wood door. Had they watched her sleep? She shivered. A blanket, rough to the touch, covered her nightgown and robe. Her skin crawled at the thought of those men with their hands on her in such flimsy attire.

Nausea rose in her throat. If she was sick, they would hear her. She swallowed.

'Is she awake?' Caleb's voice. Outside the door. A voice of nightmares. A voice she'd heard in vague dreams of being carried and shoved into a vehicle. Shuddering, she closed her eyes and lay still. She wasn't ready to face them. Not yet. Not until she felt stronger.

'Nah,' the woman replied, obviously peering through the hole in the door.

'Sarg will be back soon.'

'Aye. I'll make tea and wake her. He'll want her ready.'

Ready for what? There were noises, crockery rattling and footsteps. Eleanor imagined the woman moving around in the other room. The scraping of a chair being pushed back and heavier footfalls made her tense. Careful not to move, Eleanor opened her eyes a fraction.

'She's awake,' Caleb said. 'I know it.'

'Get away from there, you big lummox. You leave her to me, just like Sarg said. Get yourself back on guard or he'll have your guts for garters.'

'I've got a score to settle with the bitch for my arm,' Caleb growled. He clumped away and a door closed with a bang.

Barely clothed and a prisoner at their mercy. Her body trembled. Her heart raced. She couldn't breathe. They were going to kill her. She was going to die here in this horrid little hovel.

Ellie, calm down. Father's voice stilled her panic. Remember what he used to say? The reason many soldiers died was because they froze in fear and stopped thinking. Pull yourself together and you will be all right.

She hauled in a deep breath. Then another. Her heart-beat slowed. Her breathing evened out. She forced herself to listen to the sounds from the other room and was sitting up when the key turned in the lock and the woman entered with a tray.

'Where am I?' Eleanor said, looking down her nose at her female jailor. 'Who are you? What do you want with me?'

The woman set the tray on end of the bed and pulled her grey woollen shawl tight around her hunched shoulders. She looked like any woman you might see on the street in a village—black gown, grey hair scraped back, wisps escaping around her lined suntanned face. 'You'll get your answers soon enough, my lady. Now, drink your tea and eat something. You'll feel better.'

More drugs? Eleanor eyed the tray askance. Yet her stomach felt uncomfortably hollow. How long since she had eaten? 'What is the time?'

'Getting on for noon. You slept all day yesterday.'

She'd lost a whole day? Garrick would be worried. But how would he find her? 'You can't keep me here. The Marquess of Beauworth expects to find me at home.'

'Does he now?' The woman's smile was grim, but she didn't seem perturbed. 'Eat. Or go hungry.' She marched out and locked the door behind her.

Eleanor glanced at the tray. She needed strength for whatever they had in store for her, but not more laudanum. She carefully smelled the bread and the tea. Nothing obvious. Nor did she taste anything odd. She ate and drank her fill.

Feeling stronger, she strolled around her prison. The floor was cold and gritty under her bare feet, the air smelled of mould. Daylight struggled though a small window hung with dusty cobwebs high above her head. To see out, she would need to pull the cot beneath it and battle the spiders. She eyed the corners of the room. No doubt the horrid beasts lurked there, too. She shuddered and swallowed the urge to beg.

She peered through the peephole in the door into a kitchen much like the one in her own cottage, but not nearly as clean. From this angle, she had a view of an outer door and one end of the kitchen table.

The outside door swung open and a dark-haired burly man stepped in with an air of command.

'Is she awake?' this new man asked.

'Yes, Sarg.'

The man who'd grabbed her from behind. Her heart picked up speed. She retreated to sit on the cot. The door of her prison opened, admitting the newcomer. Eleanor clutched the collar of her robe tight.

'My lady, I hope you are feeling better?' Polite, well spoken, but not a gentleman. And he'd also addressed her as my lady. How did he know? Who was he? Her chest felt terribly tight as her heart drummed a warning. She gave him her haughtiest of stares. 'You have no right to keep me here against my will. I demand you release me, immediately.'

Sarg laughed softly. 'Very hoity-toity, my lady, and you a lightskirt and all.'

Eleanor gasped. Her face heated. 'How dare you? I am under the Marquess of Beauworth's protection.'

''Tis the Marquess bade us keep you here. Do as you're told and no harm will come to you.'

Her stomach dropped in a sickening rush. Garrick knew who she was? She couldn't believe it. Wouldn't. 'You lie, you cur.'

'Do I?' His voice hardened. 'Your brother has Beauworth's property. And you are going to make sure it is returned.'

An odd sort of numbness enveloped her mind. It was as if she didn't want to feel the pain of the truth. For if this man knew her identity, then Garrick must know, too. How? Had she said something unwittingly? And why had he said nothing? Her stomach churned. She'd trusted him. Trusted his word that William was safe. Apparently Garrick, having enjoyed her favours, was striking out at her brother. But why? What on earth could he want? 'Lord Castlefield has nothing belonging to the Marquess.'

Caleb entered the room, grunting under the weight of a table and a wooden stool. 'Where do you want them, Sarg?'

Sarg pointed to the far side of the room under the window. 'There. Bring paper and quills.'

The man cast her a leering glance, then shambled out, only to return with writing implements. He set them on the table, all the while casting sly looks in her direction, seeming to peer right through her clothing. Revolting beast. If only she had a pistol or even her sword, she'd teach him a lesson in manners.

Sarg raised a brow. 'We brought your clothes, my lady. I will have Millie bring them to you, once you have written the letter to your brother.'

'My brother is abroad, fighting for his country.'

'Was abroad. His ship docked in Portsmouth three days since.'

She stifled a gasp with her hand. 'How do you know?'

'We've been watching.'

Someone had planned this very carefully. The realisation rolled up from her stomach, dark and sour and thick, like the winter fogs that slid up from a river. What could Garrick possibly want? 'I'm not writing anything to William.'

'Perhaps Caleb can change your mind.' The threat was delivered without a change of expression in the grim face staring down at her. Her heart missed a beat as Caleb grinned over Sarg's shoulder. She closed her eyes briefly. She couldn't suffer that man to touch her. 'Very well. I will write your letter.'

Caleb stomped out of the room.

At Sarg's gesture, she seated herself at the desk. The sheet of paper was blank. She glanced up in question.

'Write this,' Sarg said.

If you care to see me alive again, dearest William, please obey the bearers of this note. Only then will I remain, as I am now, unharmed. She signed, *Your sister, Lady Eleanor Hadley.*

She jumped when Sarg placed a calloused hand on her neck. She desperately wanted to jerk away. Instead, she held perfectly still. 'Don't touch me, you fiend.'

'Will your brother recognise this little trinket?' His finger looped under the ribbon around her neck.

'Yes.'

The man undid the clasp. Eleanor could not repress her shudder as his fingers touched her nape. The moment he drew the chain from her neck, she got up and moved away. He picked up the letter and left without a word. Caleb followed him out.

Drained, Eleanor sank on to the bed, her hands covering her face. This was all so dreadful. It seemed the Marquess had fooled her completely, taken her in. What could William have that was so important to him? The note told her nothing.

What a fool she was, to be sure. Every step she took exploded in her face like a faulty pistol. Never again. She had learned her lesson. In future she would never interfere in things that were not her business. If she had a future.

Millie shuffled in. 'My lady, here are your clothes. Would you like help?'

The woman seemed genuinely regretful, far more kindly than the men. 'No, thank you. I am used to looking after myself.' Eleanor eyed the modest grey gown with longing. 'I would, however, appreciate something to cover the hole in the door.'

'Ye can use my apron.' The woman undid the tapes

and dropped it on the end of the bed. 'Just while ye dress.' She left.

After covering the peephole, and half-afraid that Caleb might decide to check on her progress, Eleanor dressed quickly. She tidied her hair, though without pins she could only leave it in a long braid down her back. Properly clothed, she felt a whole lot less exposed.

On the other side of the door, the woman moved around, humming softly to the sound of chopping and stirring. The revolting smell of boiling meat filled the air. Of Caleb and the man they called Sarg, she heard nothing.

The window offered her only hope of escape. Past the spiders. She shuddered. She had to try now, while they couldn't see in. She climbed up on the desk, pulled her sleeve down over her hand and swiped at nasty clinging webs. One floated against her face. Ugh. She brushed at it wildly. The table wobbled. She grabbed at the ledge. *Don't think about hairy bodies and long legs.* Gritting her teeth, her mouth dry, a lump in her throat, and her shaky breath loud in her ears, she peered outside.

Nothing but trees. No view. No landmarks. If she managed an escape, which way to go? It didn't matter. Anywhere would be better than here.

She pushed up on the sash. It refused to budge. She banged upwards with the heel of her hands. The rough wooden frame dug into her palms and the window shot up with a bang. A cobweb tickled her nose. She squeaked, yanked the window closed and jumped down. She tipped over the stool and smashed her plate on to the floor just as Millie and Caleb ran in.

'Oh, ho,' said Caleb, looking from the stool and the plate to her. 'There's that temper again. I'll tie you to the bed if you're going to start them sort of tricks.'

He loomed over her. Eleanor shrank away. 'I'm sorry. I won't do it again.'

'Aye. Well, you threw it down, you pick it up. Nay, Millie, do not help her. She better learn some manners right quick, or I will give her a lesson she won't forget.' His hand went to the belt at his waist.

Eleanor knelt swiftly and picked up the shards of pottery and crusts of bread. They watched her silently. She scooped them on to the tray and righted the stool.

Caleb pulled down the cloth that covered the peephole and ushered Millie out, leaving the door open. 'Break another platter, my lady, and you'll eat off the floor.'

Not until she was sure no one was watching her did Eleanor glance up at the window. Would they notice the lack of dust and cobwebs? She wiped her hands on her skirts with a grimace. After dark, she'd have to brave the spiders again. No choice. She must reach William before he paid her ransom. Then she'd decide what to do about Beauworth.

She recalled the words he'd spoken at the barn. *No abductor ever lets his victim live.* Had his charm been nothing but a ruse? Was he paying her back for what she had done as Lady Moonlight? Or did William really have something he wanted and she had let herself be fooled? Which meant somehow, he'd known who she was all along. Something squeezed in her chest. The horrid sensation of a heart in denial. But her heart was probably wrong.

'We need more wood for the fire.' Millie's announcement in the room beyond broke through her agitated thoughts.

'That's your job, woman. I'm guarding the prisoner,' Caleb said.

Millie cursed.

Through the open door, Eleanor watched Millie pick up a basket and head outside. Caleb remained sitting at the table, his half-closed eyes fixed on her. Her heart picked up speed. Now she knew how a mouse felt when faced by a cat. Finally, unable to stand the tension, she got up and closed the door. It swung back before she could step away.

'Leave it, wench,' Caleb said.

'Hoping I'll try to escape?'

He stepped threateningly over the threshold.

Damn. Why could she not keep her mouth shut?

Hand on the doorjamb, he raked her body with a hot greedy expression. She wanted to back away, to get as far from him as possible. Giving ground would be a fatal admission of weakness. She watched him warily.

Caleb smiled. His mottled skin flushed dark as he reached out to touch her. Calloused skin brushed her cheek. Sour breath filled her nostrils.

'Hands off, you oaf.'

He rocked back on his heels, clearly taken aback. He grabbed at the doorpost, unsteady on his feet. Drunk. 'Come on, pretty lady. Old Caleb only wants a little bit of what the Marquess 'ad.' He frowned. ''Twould be better if you gave it to me nice like, than if I 'as to take it.'

Every nerve in her body warned of danger. Flee or fight. Cunning was better. Eleanor smiled. 'Well…' She took a half-step forward.

His lips rolled back over his rotting teeth. She grasped the edge of the door and swung it with every ounce of strength. The corner hit the middle of his forehead with the crack of a hammer. His nose burst and blood spurted. He stood there staring, unblinking, unmoving, blood dripping off the ends of his moustache. She'd not hit him hard enough. She backed away. Now he'd come after her and she had nowhere to run.

His eyes glazed. He fell slowly backwards and crashed to the floor like a felled tree.

Oh, God, she was going to be sick. She had never in her life caused such damage to another human being. No time for regret. This would seal her fate if she didn't leave. She needed a weapon. A gun, or a knife. She dropped to her knees beside the unconscious man and feverishly searched his pockets. She found a pistol in one pocket and a dagger in the other. She ran for the door. Lifted the latch. Footsteps clattered on the flagstones outside.

Blast. She dodged back, hugging the wall behind the door. Her heart in her mouth, she cocked the pistol.

Chapter Seven

Something hammered against Garrick's skull.

'My lord!'

It wasn't in his head. There was someone at his door. 'Go 'way.' He could barely get the words through the fur lining of his mouth.

'Please, my lord. It's Dan.'

Garrick groaned and sat up. He was still wearing his shirt. The curtained room was dark and enough of the haze cleared from his head to wonder what time it was.

'My lord.' Nidd entered through the door to his dressing room. 'That lad says he needs to talk to you right bad.'

'Damn it all,' Garrick muttered. Couldn't a fellow get drunk in peace? If Uncle Duncan hadn't gone off to Portsmouth on business, he would have broached the old man yesterday, instead of a bottle of brandy. Now he had to face today with a bloody headache. 'All right, send him in. Nidd, can you find some of those miracle powders of yours?'

'Aye, master, right gladly.'

A few seconds after Nidd had left, Dan stood in front

of Garrick, his hat clutched in his hand, his face troubled. Bloody hell. Clearly the lad had been up to mischief. Garrick glared at him. 'What is it?'

'It's M-Miss Brown,' the boy stuttered.

Garrick narrowed his eyes. 'What about her?'

'I was having a drop of blue ruin on the quiet, like, late last night and I…' Dan gazed at his shuffling feet. Garrick had forbidden him to indulge the taste for gin he'd developed in childhood. 'I fell asleep in the loft. I woke up this morn when Mr Matthews rode in. His lordship came out to meet him.'

Good. Uncle Duncan was back. He must have returned after Garrick went to bed. He realised Dan was staring at him. 'Catch you, did they?'

'No, my lord. They were right under me. I couldn't help but hear what they said. I think Miss Brown is in some sort of trouble.'

Garrick straightened, the mists in his brain receding. 'You must be mistaken. Miss Brown left Boxted two days ago.'

The boy winced, but continued doggedly. 'Mr Matthews said something about a letter, but she was still sleeping. I didn't know what they meant. Then his lordship said it was kind of you, my lord, to hand them a weapon. It didn't make no sense.'

'Any sense.'

'Yes, my lord. Then Mr Matthews says for a lady she was a hellion and he looked forward to taming her. Then his lordship said no, that Mr Matthews was to leave the Marquess's ladybird alone. That's when I knew they meant Miss Brown, my lord, for I knows she's—'

Garrick scowled. Dan flushed to the roots of his hair. 'I didn't mean no disrespect, my lord.'

The boy had a screw loose. Unless Le Clere had some misguided notion of saving Garrick from himself. Hardly likely. Perhaps the boy had misheard. 'Did they say where Miss Brown was?' His voice creaked like an old door.

Dan curled into his shoulders, a picture of defiance underpinned with fear. 'I followed.'

'Followed who?'

'Mr Matthews, my lord. I couldn't hear no more, they walked away, but I got down from the loft and when I saw him ride away I followed. He went over by Standerstead, to a cottage.'

Utter nonsense. 'Did you see Miss Brown?'

'No, my lord, there was this big ugly cove standing outside. Looked to me like he was carrying a brace of pops as if he was guarding somethin'. Like them soldiers at Horse Guards.'

Garrick narrowed his eyes, cursing the fog in his brain. Dan had no reason to lie. It didn't make sense, but he had to be sure. 'What time was this?'

'Not long ago, an hour mebbe.'

'Can you find the place again?'

'Yes, my lord.'

'Good lad.' Garrick squeezed into his coat. 'Ask Nidd to hurry up with that powder, then meet me at the stables. Have Johnson saddle Bess.'

The boy touched his forelock and dashed off, looking exceedingly pleased with himself.

Garrick retrieved his duelling pistols from the case in his dressing room and shoved them into his waist-band. He was struggling into his boots when Nidd arrived with the promised potion.

'Oh, my lord, look at you putting fingerprints all over them new Hessians.'

'Never mind that, Nidd. I'm off on some urgent business.' He tossed off the cloudy liquid and made a face at its bitter taste. 'Have you seen my uncle?'

'I understand he's busy in his study, my lord.'

'Good. No need to disturb him.'

Garrick reached the stables without seeing anyone at all, and found Dan standing in the yard holding a skittish Bess and the reins of the bag of bones he'd ridden before. Garrick shook his head. 'I'm sorry, Dan. Stable your horse and return to your duties. I will get there faster alone. Give me the directions.'

Dan's face dropped, but he complied.

For a city lad he had given very precise directions and Garrick had no trouble finding his way to the one approach leading to the cottage, a narrow cart track winding through the woods. The smell of smoke gave away its location. Garrick tied Bess to a blackthorn bush and surveyed the thatched half-timbered hovel. A woodcutter's cottage. No sign of any guard. He crossed the clearing and strode up the flagstone path. No sound emanated from within. The door was ajar. He pushed it open.

A tub o' lard lay on his back on the stone floor, his face a bleeding pulp. What in hell's name had happened here?

Garrick crossed the room swiftly and knelt beside the injured man. He felt for a pulse. He swung around at a rustle behind him and stared from the barrel of a pistol to the rigid, white face of a very determined young woman.

He got to his feet and held out his hands, wariness and relief coursing through him. 'Ellie, you are here. Are you all right?' He hesitated and then bowed with a regretful smile. 'I mean, Lady Eleanor.'

'If I didn't know better, I might think you were pleased to see me.'

What the hell was she talking about? He stepped forwards. She waved her pistol. 'Stay back.'

'My lady, you seem to be in some danger. I think we should leave.'

Eleanor frowned. 'We? I think not. Where did you arrange to meet William?'

'Your brother? I made no such arrangement.'

She glared. 'Don't think to fool me again. Just tell me the meeting place.'

He recoiled, shocked by her obvious distrust. He kept his voice gentle. 'We have to leave before anyone comes, then we will talk.'

'*We* are not doing anything. Don't think me a fool. Your man here told me everything.' She levelled her pistol at his head. She backed towards the door. 'Don't make the mistake of thinking I don't know how to use this weapon, will you, Garrick? Make one move and you're a dead man.'

Clearly he was dealing with Lady Moonlight. 'As you wish. Go on your own. But go now.'

A shadow fell across the flagstones outside. He moved to get a better view. Her pistol followed him. Damnation. Matthews. With a gun in his hand and a smile on his face.

'Stay where you are, my lord,' she warned in a low voice.

Matthews's gun was levelled at her back. If he warned her, she would look. And she might die.

Garrick dived to the floor, rolling, yanking free a pistol. She kept her weapon trained on him. Garrick fired. Her shot came a second later. The burning, ripping pain of her bullet tore into his bicep. He reeled from the numbing force. Thank God she hadn't shot to kill.

She jerked around at a sound behind her. Face twisting in pain, Matthews shook his hand, blood trickling from his fingers, his pistol at his feet.

Garrick launched himself upright, staggered forwards, reversed his pistol and struck the steward behind the ear. He measured his length with a dull thud beside the first man.

'Go,' Garrick said. 'Get out of here. Take my horse. She's ten yards off to the right of the path. For God's sake, hurry.'

Eleanor pressed the back of her hand against her mouth. 'I shot you.'

'Never mind that.' Garrick bent to pick up Matthews's pistol. He forced it into her hand, relieving her of her discharged weapon. 'Run.' He pushed her ahead, urging her out the door and down the path. With one hand in the small of her back, he guided her to his horse.

A raucous shout came from behind. A woman running from the back of the cottage. They were done if she was armed. He kept going. His shoulder blades tensed, anticipating yet another bullet. More noise, ahead of them this time, a rider thundering down on them.

Garrick drew his second pistol. 'Keep going,' he shouted. 'I'll catch you up.' His left arm useless, he dropped to one knee and steadied his forearm on his thigh, ready to shoot the rider as he came in sight. He would only get one shot.

'My lord.' The rider turned his horse at the last moment. The blond curls were unmistakable. Dan? By thunder, the lad needed a good hiding if this was the way he followed orders. Garrick released his finger. 'You young idiot. I told you to stay at Beauworth.'

The boy stuck out his bottom lip.

'Never mind. Come on.' Garrick turned to follow Eleanor and almost tripped over her, crouching behind him with her weapon cocked and ready to fire. He cursed. Would no one obey anything he said?

She stared at him, a puzzled frown on her face. 'You don't really know anything about this, do you?'

If only that was completely true. 'We don't have time for talk. Move.' Grasping her arm, he guided her to Bess cropping at the grass. Dan leapt down, untied the reins and boosted Eleanor into the saddle. He helped Garrick to get up behind her, before remounting.

'Where to, my lord?' Dan asked, his eyes bright with excitement.

Good question.

'Brown's farm,' Ellie said. 'My horse is there.'

So, Lady Eleanor was taking charge. But since his head was spinning, it was just as well.

The Brown kitchen was like any other farmhouse kitchen in England: tiled floor, polished copper pots and hearth with a kettle steaming on a hook over a large brick fireplace. Or it would be, Garrick thought, had a Marquess not been sitting at the kitchen table with his shirt off while an apple-cheeked farmer's wife wielded a bowl of water and a bloody cloth.

The back door opened to admit a burly man of middle age with a craggy face. 'What's all this I hear from the lad in the stable about Beauworth needing help?' The man was a younger version of Martin Brown and, Garrick recalled, one of Beauworth's tenant farmers.

'His lordship had a bit of an accident. A fall from his horse,' Mrs Brown said.

'The lad said it were a bullet. Those highwaymen we've been hearing of, I'd wager.'

'Oh, my,' Mrs Brown said, her blue eyes widening.

Damn. They should have remembered Dan needed to know the story they had concocted for the farmer's wife.

Hands clasped at her waist, Ellie moved back to the table, whether seeking or offering protection Garrick couldn't tell, because her gaze was fixed on the farmer.

'The lad is mistaken,' she said firmly. 'Please, Mr Brown, do not concern yourself. We came only to fetch my horse. We will leave right away.'

Protection, then. It made Garrick want to smile, to pull her close and kiss her, but perhaps she'd change her mind about wanting to protect him, when she learned his secret.

John Brown scratched behind his ear and stared at Garrick's arm for a second or two. 'I'll send to Beauworth for the carriage.'

'No need,' Garrick said. 'It's nothing. I'll be back on my horse in no time at all.' He winked at Mrs Brown. 'Isn't that right?'

She batted her eyelashes. 'Yes, my lord.'

Brown touched his forelock. 'As you say, my lord. But we need to catch them villains. Terrorising decent folk they are. Mr Le Clere should be sent for. As magistrate, he'll know what to do.'

The irony of it struck Garrick hard. 'I'll bring it to my uncle's attention the moment I get home.'

'Aye. Well, you'll find me mucking out in the barn, if you needs me. That good-for-nothing cousin of mine has disappeared again.' He stomped out.

Mrs Brown continued her dabbing. 'It's just a graze, my lord,' she said. 'The men gets worse cuts at haying time.'

'I told you,' Garrick said to Ellie. She smiled absently. Damn it, they needed to talk about what had happened and then make some sort of plan to get her to safety.

'I'll just fetch a bit of liniment and we'll bandage you up,' Mrs Brown said. She bustled off into what must be the scullery.

'What do we do now?' Ellie asked.

'Now we have to get you back to your brother. He came looking for you at the cottage.'

If anything her face grew paler. 'You've met William?'

'Yes.'

'At the cottage?'

'Martin brought him.'

She winced. 'He knows, then. About us.' Her look of devastation pained him worse than the wound on his arm.

'Ellie, we'll be married right away. Everything will be all right.' He hoped.

Her lips tightened. She got up, taking the bowl of water to the sink under the window. He had the strangest feeling of loss, as if it wasn't mere feet, but miles she'd put between them.

She turned to face him, her back against the sink, her expression hidden by the light from the window behind her. 'What is going on, Garrick? Caleb, the man you found on the floor, said you arranged my abduction. Why?'

Garrick shot to his feet. 'Ellie, no. You can't possibly believe—'

Mrs Brown bustled back into the kitchen with a jar of something yellow and a roll of white bandage. The kindly woman must have sensed something amiss, because she hesitated, looking from one to the other. 'If you would sit down, your lordship, I'll have you better in a trice.'

'Thank you. You are a wonderful nurse.' He smiled at her.

She bridled like a young girl. 'Go on with you, my lord.' She waved her pot. 'Hold still now.' She removed the paper cover.

Garrick almost choked on the dreadful smell. 'By Gad, that stinks.'

The woman smeared a dollop on his arm and proceeded to wrap the bandage around it. 'We use this on the horses. Heals 'em up lovely, according to my John.'

She cut the end of the bandage with scissors and tied it off in a knot.

'Thank you.' Garrick reached for his shirt and pulled it on. He thrust his arms into his waistcoat and coat and knotted his cravat at his throat. 'Mrs Brown, I wonder if there is somewhere Lady Eleanor and I could converse for a moment or two?'

'Oh, yes, my lord. What was I thinking? Me keeping you here in the kitchen, with my parlour much more the thing. This way.'

She led the way to the front of the house, to a room full of highly polished chairs, their seats stuffed with horsehair and covered in plush. It reminded Garrick of a visit to his grandmother's house when he'd been a lad. 'Will this do, my lord?' Mrs Brown bobbed, all formality and humble apology now he looked more like himself.

'What a beautiful room,' Ellie said. 'Thank you.'

Mrs Brown beamed.

'Yes indeed,' Garrick said. 'A well-appointed chamber, and the view is very good.'

Mrs Brown smiled. 'I'll bring you that tea.' She left, closing the door.

'Good people,' Garrick said.

She nodded. 'They've been good to Martin, while he's been living and working here.' There were shadows in her eyes.

Garrick crossed to her side. 'Ellie, I had nothing to do with your imprisonment or the ransom. An over-heard conversation between my uncle and Matthews led me to you.'

'Matthews?'

'The man I shot at the cottage.'

'Oh. They called him Sarg. He said—'

Anger clawed up his spine. 'I don't care what he said. I had nothing to do with it.'

She recoiled.

God, now she was afraid of him. He fought for calm. 'I would never do anything to hurt you, Ellie. I swear it.'

He held her gaze for a very long moment, saw acceptance slowly dawn on her face with a deep sense of relief.

'I didn't want to believe it,' she said softly. 'They made it sound true.' A sob caught in her throat. 'I should have known better than to think so ill of you. I'm sorry.'

He caught her to his chest and patted her shoulder. 'Please, *chérie*, don't cry. None of this is your fault.' He tipped her chin with his hand and his heart clenched at her tremulous smile. He brushed a wayward tear with his thumb and something welled in his throat. Tenderness. It didn't mix well with rage. It felt strange, confusing. He wanted both to comfort her and kill the men who had caused her harm. 'That's better.'

'Why did they blame you?' she asked.

He took her hand, kissed her small fingers briefly and gazed into her face. 'I think you should sit down.'

Gripping her hand as if it could anchor him to rational thought, he led her to the sofa. She sank on to the seat, clearly worried. He braced for the coming storm.

She gazed at up him, her eyes fearful. 'They said they wanted something from William.'

He wished he couldn't guess what they wanted. He wished her chance remark did not lead him into hell and he could deny all knowledge. He took a deep breath. 'Le Clere is behind your abduction. Without my knowledge, I promise. I believe it has something to do with Piggot's visit to your father.'

Silent, eyes wary, she stared at him. His palms felt suddenly damp. 'There was an accident. Years ago. My mother fell down the staircase at the Court. Piggot accused me. He said I pushed her deliberately. Then he fled.'

'Did you?' she asked.

He glanced down at their interlaced fingers. Dammit. He was avoiding her gaze and yet he didn't want to see her revulsion. 'I don't know.'

She pulled her hand away. 'How can you not know?'

'I can't remember.' He got up and went to the window. Looked out at the very fine view of English countryside, rolling hills, neat fields and woodland and saw only black-and-white tiles, black hair and white limbs sprawled...

'I remember nothing.' He glanced over his shoulder. She was watching him, her face serious, her eyes huge, her sweet lips pressed firmly together. 'Except her body on the floor at the bottom of the stairs, and Piggot, a footman, accusing me.' *He did it on purpose.* 'He disappeared. The other day you mentioned he visited your father. I can only assume he told him the tale. But unless you heard something, or your brother did, I can't understand my uncle's actions. Did you hear Piggot's story, Ellie?'

'No.' Her voice was a whisper, full of shock and horror. 'Did you…?'

He hadn't wanted to tell her like this, with so much at stake, and so much doubt in his heart. His voice grew thick and rough. 'I loved my mother. Adored her. I can't believe I would have hurt her, not deliberately. And yet…' He swallowed. 'The Le Clere blood carries a taint. Blind rage with the strength of several men. The blood of Norse berserkers shows up every generation or two. Good for battle. Not good around people. That's why Beauworths are always soldiers, not politicians.' He hated it. 'Uncle Duncan, my father's cousin, believes what happened to Mother was an accident.' He'd spoken the way adults pander to naughty children, leaving Garrick in doubt. 'I knew nothing of this disease until long after my mother died. Le Clere devoted his life to our family. He loves Beauworth. Far more than I. I think he is trying to protect me.'

'So you did not have anything to do with my abduction.'

What could he do to make her believe? 'I swear it. On my honour.'

'Then why would they say you did?'

'If they did it in my name, I suppose I am as guilty as they are.' He turned back to the view. 'There is only one way to end this nightmare. I have to go to the authorities and admit the truth.'

A light touch fell on his shoulder. He'd not heard her approach. Half-afraid of what he would see in her face, he turned and saw pity and the shimmer of tears. His heart cracked open and pain flooded in. The pain of guilt he'd held back for so many years.

'You really can't remember?' she murmured.

He shook his head.

'It must have been an accident,' she said.

Ellie. Sweet gentle Ellie. Even now she would give him the benefit of the doubt.

He forced a laugh, heard the bitterness. 'I don't need to remember. There was a witness.' He brushed the thought aside. 'The most important thing is to get you home safe. Then I will deal with my uncle.'

'But—'

A scratch at the door and Mrs Brown, her hands full of tray, entered. 'Here we are, at last. And look who came to see how you are, my lord. My John though it best to send word to the Court after all.'

Garrick's heart dropped to the floor as Le Clere stepped into the room behind Mrs Brown.

Ellie could not restrain her gasp.

'Why don't you all have a nice cup of tea before you set out?' the farmer's wife said with a beaming smile, placing the tray on the table in front of the sofa. 'There are some scones here and preserves and a nice dollop of cream.'

Ellie wanted to scream. While the sweet, well-meaning Mrs Brown chattered about cakes and set out plates and cups in front of her, she wanted to charge past the portly noble looking over the woman's shoulder with the sorrowful expression of a bloodhound.

Garrick stood pale and stiff, his hands clenched at his side. Why didn't he object, consign his uncle, or cousin, to the devil, if they weren't in league? This was a nightmare. At any moment she'd wake up in Castle-field and discover it had all been a horrible dream.

But it wasn't.

'That will be all, Mrs Brown,' Le Clere said, moving aside. Then Ellie saw the reason for Garrick's posture. Le Clere held a pistol. This really was too much. How many more men were going to hold her at pistol point today?

She started for the door, intending to follow Mrs Brown out.

'Don't move, Ellie,' Garrick said.

She darted a glance at him. It was two against one. If they rushed Le Clere, surely they could overpower him? His face a mask, Garrick shook his head, refusing her aid. Was he in this with his uncle, after all? Her stomach fell away, a sickening sensation.

'Well, well, isn't this pleasant,' Le Clere said in genial tones the moment Mrs Brown closed the door. 'And here I thought Matthews had lost the pair of you.'

'What the deuce do you think you are doing?' Garrick said tightly. 'This is Lady Eleanor Hadley.'

Eleanor let go of her breath. He knew his uncle better than she. Perhaps he thought he would listen to reason.

Le Clere raised a heavy black brow. 'I know.' He bowed. 'By now your brother should be in possession of your letter, and be following his instructions. The exchange will continue just as planned.'

'No,' Garrick said. 'I will not allow it.'

'You won't allow it?' Le Clere's face hardened. He no longer looked like a bloodhound, more like a bull-dog. 'After everything I have done for this family? Either Lady Eleanor co-operates or she dies, as will every member of her family.'

Horrified, she stared first at Le Clere, then at Garrick, who paled.

'Uncle Duncan, what the hell have you done?' Garrick started forwards. 'This must cease now.'

Le Clere tightened his grip on his pistol and moved closer to Eleanor.

Garrick stopped short. 'Why are you doing this?' Garrick asked, his eyes intent. 'What does Castlefield have that is so important?'

'Sit down, Garrick,' Le Clere said mildly. 'We might as well have this conversation in a civilised manner. Perhaps, Lady Eleanor, you would be good enough to pour the tea?'

Back to kind elderly gentlemen. It was uncanny. A shiver ran down her spine. Garrick sat. She followed suit. With a sense of unreality, she poured each of them a cup of tea. Le Clere's pistol didn't waver as he took a sip from his cup.

Garrick refused tea. Eleanor poured a cup for herself. Perhaps if she threw it in his face…

'To answer your question, Garrick,' his uncle said, 'we need the letter Piggot left with this young lady's father and everything can go on as before.'

'Piggot left a letter?' Garrick squeezed his eyes shut as if the words caused him pain. 'How can you know?'

'He sent me word of a letter to be opened at his death,' Le Clere said. 'Do drink your tea, Lady Eleanor. And don't think about throwing it in my face. I can assure you a bullet travels faster than hot liquid.'

Eleanor put down her cup. 'It would be a waste of good tea.'

Garrick whipped his head around and gave her a hard, warning stare. Well, it had been a feeble idea, but she hoped he'd think of something better, and soon, or she'd be forced to give it a try. Perhaps the teapot would make a better missile.

Le Clere smiled. 'Very wise, Lady Eleanor.' He returned his attention to Garrick. 'Piggot warned what would happen if anything happened to him or his family. What I didn't know was the letter's location. I should have guessed he'd go to one of your father's army friends. When the man I hired finally tracked him down, Piggot was dying. It seems he wanted it all off his conscience and told his nurse the whole story. A few guineas later, and I knew exactly where to look.'

Garrick looked as if the walls of the farmhouse were folding in on him. 'You never told me any of this.' He looked genuinely shocked and horrified.

'Why did this all come to a head now?' Eleanor asked.

'The impending arrival of your brother made action imperative. He is bound to find the letter sooner or later. When he does, he will see it as his duty to bring it to the authorities. I could not allow that.' He sounded as if it was the most natural occurrence in the world.

Garrick leaned forwards, his face dark. 'Did you kill Piggot? Is there more blood on my hands I don't know about?' He was white beneath his tan, looking ill.

'Don't be foolish, my boy.' Le Clere almost chortled. 'What would that advantage? All the while he remained alive your secret was safe. Now the letter is to be opened. Fortunately your older brother died before he had time to go through your father's papers, Lady Eleanor. We needed more time to look.'

The words were like hot pebbles dropped on ice, the import fracturing the surface of her mind, the cracks spreading out, until the surface weakened and the stones fell through, sinking to the bottom with a threatening hiss. She gripped the fabric of the sofa, needing to feel something solid in her world. 'You killed Michael?'

'Let us say the timing was fortuitous,' Le Clere said.

'No!' The word seemed to be ripped from Garrick's chest. 'No,' he whispered. His fists clenched. The knuckles white.

'Control yourself, Garrick,' Le Clere said. 'Anyway, by foreclosing on the mortgage and forcing you out, I hoped to find it before the next brother returned to England. William, isn't it? Brave young man. Mentioned in dispatches more than once.'

A wave of fear rushed over her. William. She closed her eyes, as strength drained from her limbs like water running through her fingers. She wanted to collapse. To scream. But William's life was also in danger. She had to find a way to warn him.

She glanced at Garrick. He seemed frozen, his shoulders rigid, but his dark eyes blazed fury.

Unlike Le Clere, who looked calm, a relaxed, well-dressed gentleman taking afternoon tea, if it weren't for the evil hanging about him like a cloak. She repressed a shiver. She would not let him see how afraid he made her feel.

He leaned back in his chair, his face smug. 'I paid one of the bailiffs to search the house. He found nothing. Not even a safe.'

The room behind the panelling. Built in Tudor times as a priest hole. It would take a clever thief to find it.

'Ah,' Le Clere said, his gaze narrowed on her face, 'I see you know where it is.'

'Ellie,' Garrick said. 'Tell him nothing.'

Perhaps he'd let her guide him to it. Once at Castlefield, she'd be in familiar territory. It might give her an advantage. 'I've never seen this document, but my father did have a safe.'

Le Clere nodded. 'I would have found it given time,

but I made a mistake.' He looked at Garrick. 'I took advantage of Garrick's weakness for a certain young lady. I thought it would keep him at Beauworth.' He looked sorrowfully at the Marquess. 'We can solve all this right now, Garrick. Marry Lady Eleanor, get an heir and leave me as guardian. I'd be more than happy for you to go off and get yourself killed.'

The kind way he spoke the words made Eleanor's stomach heave. 'You are disgusting.'

'Despicable,' Garrick said. 'And the game is up.'

'Is it?' Le Clere rose to his feet. 'By now, Matthews should be outside with the carriage. All we have to do is meet your brother at the assigned place and everything will be all right.'

'I think not,' Ellie said with dawning fear. 'I know what he did.' She pointed at Garrick. He winced. A wry smile curved his lips and it wrenched at her heart that he did not deny it. How could she feel such a pang of sympathy when so much evil had been done in his name?

Le Clere pursed his lips, his head cocked on one side. 'You think anyone will pay any attention to the words of a jilted lover? Just do as you are told and you can return home safe and sound.'

He lied. Something in his face told her he would not leave any of them alive. Including William and Sissy. A cold wind seemed to brush across her shoulders and penetrate her bones. Fear. Deep and terrifying. She fought its numbing weight. 'You planned it all. The ship I invested in. The debt.'

Le Clere had the gall to laugh. 'Dear lady, your man of business works for me.'

'Jarvis?'

'The same.' The more this man said, the more she felt like a fly spinning around in one of those horrible sticky webs, and no matter how she struggled she would never get free.

Garrick must have sensed something similar because he leaned forwards, glaring at his uncle. 'I'll expose you. I'll go to the authorities the moment your back is turned.' He looked ready to spring at his uncle, his shoulders tense, his face a mask of fury.

Eleanor braced herself, ready to follow his lead.

'And Lady Eleanor will die,' Le Clere said softly. 'Now, or later. And it will be your fault.'

A hiss of breath left Garrick's lips. He sagged back against the cushions. 'Damn you.'

Mrs Brown stuck her head in the door. 'The carriage is here, my lord.'

Le Clere reached across the table and grabbed Eleanor by the arm. The pistol jammed against her ribs. 'I know you won't mind helping an old man out to his carriage, Lady Eleanor.'

If she resisted and Le Clere killed her, she would have no chance to warn William. She inhaled a shaky breath and rose to her feet.

Le Clere drew her close. 'Garrick, do go ahead. One misstep and Lady Eleanor will find a nasty hole in her stomach.'

Fury rolled off Garrick in dark waves. Lines bracketed his white-edged lips. The sinews in his neck stood out against his collar, his hands opening and closing as if he was ready to strangle his uncle. His eyes bored into Le Clere's for a long minute, as if he debated what to do, then his shoulders slumped and he walked ahead of them into the hallway.

Le Clere put an arm about her shoulders, let her feel the press of the weapon into her side, then urged her forwards. The front door stood open. In the farmyard beside the carriage, Matthews, a livid bruise on his temple and a bandage around the knuckles of his right hand, looked as if he would very much like to shoot someone.

Two horses were tied to the rear of the carriage and Caleb, his face a bloody ruin, glared at them from the box. She certainly didn't have any friends she could turn to for help among this lot. Not even Garrick, it seemed.

Of the helpful John Brown, there was no sign. Besides, what could a farmer do against his landlord? A movement in the barn, a flash of yellow. A slight figure peering out. Dan, no doubt. The poor lad could be of no help, either. No one could. The realisation sent a cold shiver down her spine.

Garrick climbed into the coach. Matthews followed him in. Then Le Clere shoved Ellie inside and climbed up behind. He pointed his pistol at her head. 'Tie their wrists at their backs, Matthews. We don't want any more problems.'

Blood pounding in his ears, vision hazed, Garrick stared at Le Clere. His father's cousin. A man he'd known all his life. His flesh and blood. Why had he never seen this side of Le Clere?

He had. Years ago. A faint memory of loud voices, his mother weeping. And later, when Garrick refused to admit pushing his mother down the stairs, the man had lost his temper and taken a cane to Garrick's back. Le Clere had changed after that, Garrick realised. Become his friend. His mentor. His kindly conscience, always reminding him what he'd done without coming out and saying it in words. In the close confines of the carriage, Le Clere's lust for power pervaded the air, rank and toxic.

The thought that Le Clere had done it on his behalf horrified him. Worse yet, Garrick wanted to kill him for what he'd done to Ellie.

The rope around his wrists bit into his flesh as he strained against them. He glared at the pair of them, Matthews and Le Clere, and smelled their blood in his nostrils. He wanted that blood on his hands. He pulled on the ropes binding him. But Matthews knew his work. The rage inside Garrick grew until he could see little more than their faces through a red mist.

Beside him, Eleanor sat rigid, watchful and coolly remote, when she should have been having a fit of the vapours after all she'd heard. Courage shone in her eyes, but how she must hate him now she knew what lay beneath his skin.

Control. He needed control or he'd be lost. He took slow, deep breaths. 'Where are we going?'

'You'll see,' Le Clere said.

He would. And when he did, he'd be ready to act. Surely he could outwit a man who had clearly lost his reason?

Chapter Eight

The carriage pulled to a halt. Garrick peered out. They were only a few yards into the lane beyond the farm. Matthews leaned over and tested first his ropes and then Ellie's. 'They won't be getting free in a hurry.'

'Good,' Le Clere said, and leaned forwards to open the door. Garrick's heart picked up speed.

His uncle laughed. 'Don't worry, Garrick. I'll be a few feet behind you all the way.' He stepped out, followed by Matthews. The two men mounted their horses, no doubt with a view of discussing their plans in private. The carriage set off once more.

Ellie stared out of the window, her shoulders stiff, her face white and her expression forlorn.

The rage in his gut unfurled like a dragon full of fire, heat rushed up from his belly. He took a deep breath. It wouldn't help. When she didn't say anything, he fished around for a way to break the silence. 'I'm sorry you got dragged into this.'

'I don't suppose you have a knife?'

He didn't like the way her gaze raked the interior of the coach. 'Please, Ellie, whatever you do, no heroics. Trust me to get you out of this and follow my lead.'

Nor did he like the way her determined chin came up in challenge. 'Do you have a plan?'

'I'll take advantage of whatever opportunity is offered.'

She curled her lip. 'An excellent plan.' She turned her head to gaze out of the window.

'Sarcasm won't help.' He huffed out a breath. 'Ellie, believe me, I won't let my uncle harm you.'

'He killed my brother. For you.' Her voice was husky. She turned her head slowly. The glitter of tears she'd tried to hide with harsh words cut a swathe through his heart. She'd been so brave up to now and to see her spirit leach away weighed heavy on his soul. Nor could he think of a word to say in his defence.

He couldn't afford to let himself feel her pain, because if he allowed the emotions through, the anger he held at bay would take over and he'd be nothing but a raging unthinking beast.

He stared out of the window. They were approaching the crossroads beyond the village. The place where the first Lady Moonlight had ended her life on the gibbet. With a wry twist of sick humour, he hoped it wasn't an omen.

The carriage halted behind a stone wall at the edge of the common where the villagers grazed a few sheep and a scrawny cow. Garrick watched Caleb take off at a run, a musket over his shoulder, heading for a ridge to the east where scattered boulders and gorse provided plenty of cover.

Matthews opened the door, blocking his view. 'Out you get. Ladies first, if you please.' He bowed.

Garrick thought about head-butting the man on his

way down the step, but saw Le Clere watching from a short distance off and could only watch in helpless fury as Matthews's hand clenched around Ellie's elbow. At the steward's nod, Garrick leapt down and glanced across the open tract of land to where Caleb had disappeared. The man had ducked out of sight.

A perfect place for an ambush.

Trust him? An admitted murderer? Ellie wanted to. He'd been naught but a child. Could such an act be the sign of some horrible disease, as Garrick seemed to believe, or simply an accident? It seemed incredible to believe he'd killed his mother on purpose. But both he and Le Clere seemed convinced of his guilt. And then he'd asked her to trust him.

Up to now, everything she'd done had turned out for the worst. Like a fool, she'd trusted Jarvis to guide her in the matters of business, and look where that had led. With William's life in the balance, the only person she dare trust was herself, and even there she didn't have a lot of faith.

Michael. A pain carved through her chest. Don't think about what had happened. Not now. Concentrate on what you need to do.

Her mind whirling in circles of indecision, she picked her way through the long grass to the wooden stile at Matthews's direction. Garrick followed.

'Wait here,' Matthews said. 'And don't try nothing funny. I'll be watching.' He marched back to Le Clere, who had remained with the carriage, scanning the surrounding countryside with a spyglass. Watching for William?

Should she run? Not with Matthews's shotgun pointed her way. If she wanted to escape, she'd need a distraction. She looked at Garrick. He seemed oblivious to the man and his weapon, gazing off into the distance with a faint smile on his face, as if he didn't have a care in the world.

He must have felt her gaze because he turned his head and raised a brow. 'I wish to hell you'd let your brother get himself out of his own financial difficulties. You might never have got involved in this at all.'

Was he bent on annoying her? 'If wishes were horses… And besides, they were not his financial problems. They were mine. I forged his signature.'

He groaned. 'I might have guessed.'

'Your Mr Jarvis said it was an opportunity of a lifetime.'

'He is not my Mr Jarvis. He works for the estate.'

'Your estate, my lord.'

'As trustee, Le Clere makes all the decisions until my twenty-fifth birthday.'

Well, that explained some of it. 'Not a wise choice for trustee.'

'He was like a brother to my father. I don't understand it.'

'He's protecting you.'

He sighed. 'I know. But he's far beyond the pale with this.'

'You could say that.'

'Squabbling is not going to help us.'

Her turn to raise a brow. 'What do you suggest?'

'We work together.'

She glanced up to find his eyes searching her face. Eyes full of bleakness, as if he guessed her doubts.

'All right,' she said.

Matthews was eyeing them suspiciously. 'What are you two lovebirds talking about?'

'None of your business, you cur,' Garrick said, glowering at the man from beneath lowered eyebrows.

'I could make it my business, your lordship,' Matthews said, clearly undeterred.

'Matthews!' Le Clere's voice held a warning.

Matthews closed his mouth like a fish on a hook, but the expression on his face threatened a future discussion, with fists.

Instead of blustering and squaring up like a contender at fisticuffs at a fair, Garrick should be focusing on their problem. She poked his ribs with an elbow.

Garrick watched his uncle direct Matthews to a position further along the wall. But where the hell was Caleb? And how many more men did Le Clere have up there? He scanned the rough terrain, with its clumps of gorse and shadowed folds.

A glint. A quick flash beside a rock he'd almost missed. And another, to the right. There were at least two of them. Garrick gauged the distance and the angle in relation to Matthews's position at the wall. Oh, yes, Le Clere had it all worked out very nicely. Whoever crossed the common would be caught by intersecting lines of fire.

They were running out of time and he couldn't find one weakness in Le Clere's strategy.

Garrick turned, casually leaning his elbows on the rough stone wall, reviewing the open ground. Not a scrap of cover, not even a clump of grass left by the hungry sheep.

A lone horseman walked his horse on to the far side of the common.

Le Clere strode over to Ellie. 'Your brother is right on time.'

The look of hope and joy on Ellie's face pierced Garrick's heart. What must it be like to have a family who cared the way she cared for her brother? What he had thought was caring, a bluff distant kindness, had turned to dross. His mother had loved him, he remembered dimly, but it hadn't served her well.

He had to reunite Ellie with her family.

The man on the other side of the common raised a hand to shield his eyes. Clever. With the sun in his eyes, he'd have trouble spotting the sharpshooters.

He must have seen the party gathered at the wall because he urged his horse into a walk. When he was in the centre of the open space, he stopped. Good.

'Where is my sister?' he yelled.

Le Clere thrust Eleanor through the gap in the wall, a pistol held to her temple. 'Come and get her.'

'William,' she yelled. 'Go back. It's a trap.'

Bloody hell. She'd caught them all by surprise.

Le Clere cursed and pulled her back behind the wall.

Castlefield remained where he was, tension in the set of his shoulders. The horse shifted uneasily.

'I ought to wring your neck,' Le Clere said.

Garrick felt like doing a bit of wringing himself. Or maybe not. Perhaps she'd given him the opening he needed. 'Leave her be. He won't come any closer. Not now. Withdraw and find another way to get the letter.'

Le Clere swore. 'No.' He put his glass to his eye. 'I've a good mind to… Bugger.'

Garrick straightened. 'What is it?'

'He didn't come alone. There are soldiers with him.'

Beside him, Ellie squinted across the field. She was starting to look hopeful. Garrick mentally groaned. What foolhardy idea would she take next into her head?

Le Clere pulled a knife from his belt and cut

Garrick's ropes. 'See for yourself.' He handed Garrick the glass.

Surprised, but not about to object, Garrick looked. There were two officers at the edge of the common behind Castlefield. Infantry. 'Men from his regiment by the look of it. Two of them.'

'A couple too many,' Le Clere growled.

'Beauworth,' Castlefield yelled, 'I want my sister.'

'Wait here,' Le Clere said to Garrick. 'One move in the wrong direction and the girl dies.'

There was cunning in his uncle's eyes. A sort of clever madness. Keeping that gaze locked with his, Garrick nodded.

Le Clere trotted off to join Matthews.

Her eyes full of shadows, her shoulders drooping, Ellie shivered. To see her so beaten down was more than he could bear. 'He won't harm you all the time your brother has the letter. I pray to God he hasn't opened it.'

'Or your neck is on the line.' The red flag of anger flew in her cheeks. The spirit he liked to see.

'Something like that.' If Castlefield had followed orders, then perhaps Le Clere could be convinced to let them go. It wouldn't be easy to convince him. Ellie knew too much. But without any solid proof...

Le Clere headed back in their direction and Garrick turned to face him.

Pistol steady on Eleanor, Le Clere handed him the knife. 'Set her free.'

What now? Garrick cut the ropes.

Le Clere retreated a step. 'Walk her to her brother, collect the document and return to me. No tricks or she dies. You can't escape, my men have every inch of the common covered. Are you clear?'

The scene played out in his mind. 'Absolutely.'

'And consider this, Garrick. By walking her out there, you are my accomplice. If anything goes wrong, you hang.'

Since if the contents of the letter were made known he'd hang anyway, it seemed a strange thing to say. 'Good point, Uncle. Thank you.'

Ellie stared at him, shock on her face. Well, he'd wanted to fool Le Clere and in accepting his defeat so meekly, he'd fooled her, too. The thought left a bitter taste in his mouth.

He helped her over the stile. 'Walk. Nice and steady.'

She tugged at her arm. 'Why are you helping him?'

He thrust her ahead of him. 'Keep walking.'

Only a few more feet and they'd be level with her brother. Castlefield's horse sidled. The man sawed at the reins, his face red.

Garrick raised his voice. 'Throw the letter on the ground. Be very careful, there are armed men behind us. One false move and I won't answer for what happens.'

Castlefield nodded. He pulled a packet from his saddlebag, a sealed document, and tossed it on the ground. The word Beauworth in black ink mocked Garrick from the ground. He kept going, pushing Ellie ahead. Eleanor gave him a startled look over her shoulder.

'Aim for the corner of the field. They cannot shoot you without hitting me.'

'Hey.' Castlefield cursed and brought his horse around.

'Hurry,' Garrick said.

Castlefield rode up alongside. 'What the devil are you playing at, Beauworth? Go back where you belong.'

'Ride ahead if you want to live.'

'Garrick!' Le Clere's bellow. Garrick did not turn.

Castlefield pulled his pistol. 'Get away from my sister. Or I'll kill you.'

'Don't be a fool,' Garrick said. 'I am the only thing between your sister and a bullet. Look out for yourself.'

'William, listen to him,' Ellie said.

Thank God she understood. Bright, bright woman, his Ellie. A ray of light in his dark, dark world.

A shot rang out; Castlefield's chestnut took off at a gallop.

'William,' she cried.

Garrick grabbed her arm. Stopped her from giving chase. Time was running out. Once Le Clere's men realised what he was doing, they'd shift position, if they hadn't already.

'Run,' he said. It was their only chance.

Her face pale, she lifted her skirts and took off at a steady clip. He breathed a sigh of relief and followed. A minute more and they'd gain the wall's protection.

'Hold your fire,' Le Clere shouted. The panic in his voice gave Garrick a moment of glee.

Another shot. Not Le Clere's men this time. A rifle. It came from ahead. Martin Brown, perhaps, trying to pick him off. Better he aim at Le Clere's men. Garrick glanced back. He couldn't see any sign of Caleb or Matthews or the other man he'd spotted. Perhaps they hadn't yet worked out what was happening.

More shots rang out. From all directions. A stinging sensation in his side. A tearing pain. His legs buckled. He stumbled on. The pain in his side sharpened. Keep moving. Keep between Ellie and them. The wall rose up like a grey mossy cliff. Hampered by her skirts, Ellie got stuck halfway over. Any moment another shot would find them. He pushed her over the top. Somehow he got a knee on the coping and fell to the ground on the other side. He lay gulping air and clutching his side.

He looked around for Ellie, found her bent double and panting. 'Are you all right?' he asked.

Gasping, she nodded. 'Did you see what happened to William?'

William. Always worried about her brother. He wanted to hit something. He reined in his anger. It was only right she should care for her brother. It was what real families did. 'His horse cleared the wall further down. I don't think he was hit.' He pushed to his feet.

Eleanor grabbed his arm, her face full of worry. 'Le Clere was right. You will be implicated in this. Go now, while you can. Save yourself. Take a ship to America.'

His heart soared. She cared about him, too. If it wasn't impossible, he would have sworn his vision blurred. He cupped her cheeks in his hands, capturing her storm-clouded gaze. 'Come with me.' He held his breath, hope a pale flame in a dark future. His heart drummed against his ribs.

She swallowed, her eyes glistened. Tears. Damn it. He'd made her cry. He'd no right to ask after what Le Clere had done in his name.

Before she could answer, Castlefield galloped up, pistol in hand. 'Stand back, Eleanor. I've got him in my sights. You're safe now.'

Glowering with righteous anger, the man who looked so like Ellie pointed his cocked pistol at Garrick's head. Strange he hadn't seen the similarity before. But Castlefield had been a chubby schoolboy the first time they met. Garrick curled his lip and held his hands clear of his sides. 'She's all yours, my friend. I'm done with her.'

Tears on her cheeks, Ellie put a hand to mouth. 'You should have gone when you had the chance,' she whispered.

Should he? Had he wanted to go without her? What would be the point?

Castlefield flung himself off his horse. 'I'll kill you for that.' Better a bullet than the noose.

Ellie stepped between them. 'William, he saved my life.'

'More likely he saw it as a way to save his own skin, the coward.'

Castlefield yanked off his cravat, swung Garrick around by the shoulder and pulled his arms behind him. Using the strip of fabric, he tied Garrick's wrists together. Garrick flinched as his ribs protested against the rough treatment.

Castlefield grunted approval. 'That will hold you until they put the chains on.'

Eleanor gasped. 'William, no!'

The heartbreak in her voice was like balm to Garrick's soul. He flashed her a grin. He didn't want her to think he was surprised by this turn of events.

Castlefield pushed him toward the two officers and a couple of farm labourers with a cart. 'My friends can't wait for the honour of escorting you and your pack of villains to prison.'

Eleanor's heart seemed to have been cut in two, her chest hurt so much. Garrick had looked so hopeful. If William hadn't arrived at that moment, what would she have said? Her breath stilled. She had the strangest feeling she would have said yes.

She stared after Garrick's tall, straight figure, so proud in his defeat. The pain intensified. Her eyes misted. She felt as if she might fly apart. She wrapped her arms around her stomach.

If only she didn't love the way he smiled at her as if

there was no one else in the world but the two of them, the way he teased and made her laugh, the way he held her, and the sensations he brought to life in her body.

Oh Lord. After all she knew of him, how could she feel this way?

A drop of something dark glistened on the ground at her feet. With a horrible premonition, she bent and touched it with a fingertip. Blood, sticky and red.

Garrick's wound must have opened. He needed a doctor. She hurried after the two men.

By the time she'd crossed the open ground, Garrick lay on the straw in a cart, a prisoner in his tumbrel, looking as calm as if he were out for a Sunday drive. Ellie trembled to see his lips looking bloodless and the skin on his cheeks ashen.

William, talking to Martin, didn't see her until she tugged on his arm. 'He's wounded. He needs a doctor.'

'Not now, Eleanor. There are more of these criminals to be rounded up.' He turned back to Martin. 'Follow them as best you can.'

'Yes, my lord.' Martin strode off as Caleb's unconscious body was thrown on to the cart beside Garrick.

She grabbed William's arm. 'Beauworth had nothing to do with my abduction.'

'The courts will decide innocence or guilt,' William said, and began walking away as if she was of no more importance than a bothersome insect.

'Damn you, William.' She ran after him. 'Give me your knife.' She snatched it from his belt. 'I can at least bandage the wound before he bleeds to death.'

William hunched a shoulder. 'Be careful. He's chained, but he's a dangerous man.'

'Not when he's half-dead,' she muttered. 'Where are you going?'

He stared across the common, his eyes narrowed. 'There's something I need to take care of. Wait here for me. I'll be back in a moment.' He marched toward the Beauworth carriage, his limp more pronounced than usual. Too much time on horseback, no doubt. He wouldn't welcome her suggesting he rest and arguing would keep her from Garrick.

She ran back and scrambled up on the cart. Once there, she slashed a strip from the bottom of her petticoat.

One eyebrow raised, his gaze on her ankle, Garrick smiled. 'Very nice.'

'Let me see where you are hurt.'

He lifted his hand from his side, revealing a sticky dark patch. 'A scratch,' he said.

A new wound. Oh, heavens. So much blood. 'I need to bind it.'

He frowned, his gaze flickering to Caleb. 'This is no place for a lady.'

'I'm Lady Moonlight, remember.'

He grinned at that.

She pulled his shirt free of his pantaloons and found a jagged tear below his ribs, blood oozing in a steady flow. She swallowed the urge to gag. 'I hope this is the last time today you are going to walk in front of a bullet.'

He chuckled, then winced with a hiss of breath through his teeth. 'Me, too.'

Panting, fearful, she pressed the wad against the gash. 'Hold this.' His fingers covered hers for a brief second, his skin chill. 'Thank you.' She glanced up to find gold flecks danced in his eyes and his lips curved in a smile, a smile she might never see again.

Her eyes blurred. Blinking, she pulled her hand

away, bound the second strip around his torso. Would it be enough?

He lifted a hand, touched her cheek. The ugly chain attached to the manacle encircling his wrist rattled. 'Now go.' He looked over at his companion. 'I don't want you here. Do you understand?'

The words hurt. But of course he didn't want her here. She'd rejected him.

He pushed forwards, as if he planned to get up. 'Leave now, Ellie.'

The labourer guarding the cart hefted his pitchfork. 'Miss?' he said. 'You shouldn't be up there.'

She didn't want to leave him like this, but if she didn't go, more bad things would happen. 'I'm leaving. Garrick, please, take care of yourself.'

He slumped back against the side of the cart and closed his eyes, pain etching deep lines around his mouth.

By the time she reached the ground, she was shaking so hard her legs wouldn't hold her. She leaned against the cart's wheel. A hand pulled on her shoulder. She jumped and whirled around.

'For God's sake, Len,' William said. He pulled a handkerchief from his pocket and wiped her face. 'You cannot be crying over that blackguard.'

She hadn't known she was crying. 'He needs a doctor. Please, William. You can't be so cruel.'

His lips flattened in a thin line, William stared into her face. 'You don't understand, Len. You don't know what he did, to us. To me.'

'It was his uncle.'

'No. It wasn't. There are things you don't know.' He let go of a long breath. 'We will discuss it later.'

'He needs a doctor.' She was beginning to wonder if

she had any other words. Never again, she swore
silently. Never would she be anything but a model sister,
if he would just get Garrick a doctor.

'All right. I'll see to it. But then enough until we get
home.'

'Thank you.'

A young lieutenant approached leading a couple of
horses. 'Lucky thing we accompanied you from
Portsmouth, wouldn't you say, Wills?'

'Very lucky,' William said. He gestured to the cart.
'Can you escort that rubbish to Haverstock for me while
we mop up here? Have a doctor sent to attend Beauworth the moment he is behind bars.'

The lieutenant snapped a salute. 'Certainly, sir.'

A few moments later the labourer was driving the
wagon down the road, with the lieutenant in attendance.

Eleanor watched it go. There was nothing more she
could do.

The steady sound of dripping water never ceased in
this accursed place. Shivering, Garrick pulled the
blanket tighter around his shoulders and leaned back
against the wall. The damp of his cell pervaded every
bone in his body. His teeth chattered uncontrollably if
he let them. He clamped his jaw tight.

Out of respect for his rank, they'd put him in a private
cell. As if it made any difference. Still, he'd glimpsed the
condition of some of the other poor wretches who inhab-
ited this filthy place and had no cause for complaint.

The hole in his side had been cleaned and his arm was
on the mend thanks to Ellie insisting on a doctor. He'd
cut a good strong figure on the gibbet, the doctor had
said. Nothing like a little gallows humour to cheer a
man up.

If they'd also caught Le Clere, he wouldn't feel quite so bitter. But what the man had done, he'd done in Garrick's name and the piper would be paid.

A sharp twist of regret squeezed his chest. He would have liked to marry Ellie.

Ellie. So dear and so brave. Right up to the last, she'd tried to save his worthless hide. He didn't blame her one bit for not wanting to fly with him. She deserved so much more. Though the thought of her with another man sent hot blood rushing to his head. Ah, well, soon he wouldn't have a head.

God, this place was really getting to him.

He did like thinking of her safe with her family, safe from Le Clere. It was the only thing making this stinking pit bearable. Not that he'd be here much longer. He swallowed. They'd take him to London for trial. A jury of his peers in the House of Lords. A chill ran down his spine.

He'd brought shame to the proud name of Beauworth. Harry, bluff, cheerful Cousin Harry would have to carry the burden. Good thing the man was well liked by his fellows. He'd make an excellent Marquess.

The noise of boots in the hallway echoed through the cells. Was this it? His heart picked up speed. He'd been expecting them all day, but deep in his heart he had hoped something would save him. If Piggot hadn't left the letter, he could have died honourably, serving his country in battle. No doubt his old enemy, Hadley, or Castlefield as he was now, would make sure he met a just end. Justice. The gods must be laughing their heads off at the irony of it all.

The footsteps drew closer. If only Eleanor had trusted him with the truth. His fist clenched. He slammed it into the wall, welcomed the jarring pain. He would never have ruined her. It was his one regret.

That and what he had done to his mother.

He smoothed his lank hair, and scratched at three days' worth of stubble. He must look like everyone's idea of a desperate killer.

The cell door opened. Letting the blanket fall, he pushed to his feet and held out his arms for his manacles. Thank God, they did not also chain him to the wall of his cell.

The warder ignored his outstretched hands. 'This way if you please, my lord.'

Stiff, joints aching, Garrick took a deep breath and straightened his spine. He followed the warder out of his cell and up the worn stone steps. This was it. A journey to London, a public humiliation and death.

At the head of the stairs the warder ushered him into a room. An office. For the first time in three days, Garrick felt some of the bone-chilling cold leave his body.

A man of medium height, middle-aged, grey at the temples, and his blue eyes twinkling, sat in one of two chairs in front of the desk. He rose at Garrick's entrance.

'My lord? Andrew Calder, at your service. I am your barrister.'

'I don't need a lawyer.' A guilty plea needed no argument.

'As to that, my lord, you are probably correct. However, Lord Dearborne asked me to meet you before your appearance.'

Dearborne was a local magistrate. He wasn't to be tried in the House? 'The trial is today?'

'No, my lord. You will be released today.'

Legs weak, Garrick dropped onto the other chair. 'I don't understand.'

'My lord, I have been asked by Lord Dearborne to

offer apologies for your wrongful arrest. You have been cleared of any involvement in the crime against Lady Eleanor Hadley. Caleb Trubbs has confessed the whole. His evidence proves you were a dupe in Le Clere's plans. Lady Eleanor herself confirmed his testimony.'

The room seemed to shift around him. At any moment he would awaken in his cold cell, lying on the filthy pallet, and discover he was hallucinating. It wouldn't be the first time. Usually it was Ellie who occupied his dreams.

The dapper little man continued to look at him with a kindly smile. Garrick began to believe. Slowly he felt his shoulders relax. Until he remembered. A bitter taste filled his mouth. 'There is another matter, Mr Calder. The death of the Marchioness of Beauworth, my mother.' He swallowed the dry lump in his throat as if the words would choke him.

Calder frowned. 'I know nothing of this matter.'

His hands gripped the chair arms, clinging to the only solid thing in the room. 'There was a letter. From an eye witness.'

Calder shook his head. 'There is no letter, my lord.'

'It was there.' Castlefield had dropped it at his feet. He'd seen it and so had Ellie.

'I have no reports of a letter, my lord.' Calder was beginning to sound just a little impatient, no doubt wondering why the prisoner wasn't leaping for joy. Garrick shook his head, trying to sort his jumbled thoughts into some sort of order. The letter had been there. Addressed to him. Lying among the sheep droppings on emerald grass. Something about it had puzzled him. And now it had disappeared.

This was his chance to confess. *Why admit to something you don't remember?* Ellie's words. He'd be confessing to something he didn't believe in his heart. Had never believed. The realisation dawned slowly. Before he said anything, he had to know for sure.

'Shall we go, my lord?' Calder said, rising to his feet. 'A carriage is waiting outside.' He coughed discreetly behind his hand. 'You might wish to, er…freshen up.'

Garrick looked down at himself, filthy, ragged and stinking. 'Yes. I would like that.' He stood up.

'Good. Lord Dearborne would be glad if you could call on him two days from now. At that time, you will be required to give a statement and the proper paperwork will be drawn up.'

'And Duncan Le Clere and Matthews?'

'The search continues.'

'I want to help.'

The lawyer grimaced. 'Leave it to the authorities, my lord. By all accounts Le Clere is a dangerous man.'

Only a Le Clere could deal with Duncan. But right now Garrick had something more important on his mind. A wife. His heart swelled. He would make things right for Ellie.

'Beauworth for Lady Eleanor.' He handed his card to the Castlefield butler. At least his voice sounded calm, despite his inner turbulence.

The butler ushered him into a saloon painted pale blue with white trim. Large windows overlooked an expanse of formal gardens. The house was a sprawling Tudor mansion, but this room occupied one of the newer wings. 'If you would wait here, I will see if her ladyship is at home.'

Why hadn't she replied to his letter of a week since? Unable to sit, he wandered the room. A room full of family treasures, Meissen china, paintings, statues. The clutter of generations of Earls and their families. Nothing like Beauworth, where few reminders remained of his parents. Le Clere had put them all away, even the portraits, supposedly out of respect for Garrick's feelings, but now he wondered if the old man hadn't tried to make him forget the happy part of his childhood.

He studied the portrait of a woman above the mantel. Eyes grey and clear like Eleanor's looked back at him from beneath a powdered wig. Eleanor's mother, no doubt. She seemed to smile down at him.

He swept her a bow. 'Lady Castlefield, you have a most beautiful daughter.'

'Garrick.'

He spun around.

She looked lovely, almost ethereal, in her white muslin gown. Tiny curls framed a face that seemed thinner and paler than he remembered. He could see no sign of Lady Moonlight in this very proper young lady, with her hands clasped at her waist in a dignified manner. This was Lady Eleanor.

In two strides he reached her, kissed each cool hand. 'Ellie.' He cupped her lovely face in his palms, brushed his mouth across her lips, losing himself in her taste as she parted to his questing tongue.

God, he'd missed her. He dropped his hands to her shoulders, enfolded her in his embrace. She arched into him. Kissing him with avid desperation, clutching at his shoulders. He cupped her buttocks, pulled her against his length, felt the stirring of his blood and sighed. His woman. He pulled back, smiling into her lovely face.

She bit her lip.

'What is it, sweet?' he asked, tipping her chin to look into her eyes.

They were shadowed, wary. His stomach plunged in a sickening rush. 'What is wrong?'

She pulled away, paced to the other side of the room before facing him. 'Why are you here?'

The ground felt unsteady beneath his feet. 'Didn't you receive my letter?'

Her eyes widened. 'Did you write, indeed?' She shook her head. 'I suppose William…' She made a small helpless gesture.

Suspicion writhed in his gut. 'I wrote to your brother for permission to pay my addresses to you. Didn't he tell you?'

'William is angry, disappointed in me.' She averted her face. 'I am fortunate he didn't turn me out.'

Turn her out? The heat of terrible rage flowed like lava in his veins. The accursed Le Clere temper gripped him in vice-like claws. His clenched fists shook with the effort to hold them at his sides and not strike out blindly.

He drew in a deep breath, forced his hands to unclench. 'Believe me, had I known who you were, I would never have offered you a *carte blanche*. I'm here to make it right as honour demands.'

'Honour?' She stiffened, drawing back. He felt as if he'd missed something important. He crossed the room to her side, took her hand in both of his, held tight so she could not pull away. He dropped to one knee and gazed into her face. 'Lady Eleanor Hadley, please do me the honour of becoming my wife. I will protect and cherish you all the days of my life. I swear, I will never cause you harm. Please, Ellie. Give me a chance.' He was begging and he didn't care.

Her eyes glittered with moisture. She pulled her hand free. 'You don't understand.'

He rose to his feet, paced away from her, then looked back, where she stood stiff and pale. She had never fully given herself to him and never freely. She'd only come to him because she'd needed money for her brother, but he'd been sure there was more between them than lust.

She swallowed. 'What about what you did?' The agony in her voice ripped through his heart. In her eyes, he saw fear.

Pain speared his heart. She knew him better than anyone. Did she sense the evil lurking in his blood? The thought filled him with a grief so deep, he didn't know how he remained standing. He forced himself to answer. 'You said it yourself. Why admit to something I don't recall?'

'What about what you did to William?' Her voice was a strangled whisper of pain. 'Do you deny that, too?'

A knot balled in his gut. He felt as if he'd entered a maze to discover all of the exits blocked and a monster breathing at his heels. 'Yes, I deny it. My friends vouched I never left the dorm.'

'Your friends.' Her lip curled. 'How very convenient. He bested you in a fight and everyone heard you swear your revenge. What kind of monster beats a boy in his bed? He wanted a cavalry regiment. Because of you he can't sit on a horse for more than an hour or two.'

She spun away. Left him standing mute, accused, trembling with rage and something deeper. Fear. Fear he was losing her.

She covered her face with her hands. 'Back then, he told us it was an accident. After all, men don't tell tales. If I had known, I never would have come to you. Never.'

'I didn't do it.'

She raised her gaze, the grey of her eyes fractured, as if something inside her had broken. 'Or do you simply not remember?'

The bitterness raked him like a cat-o'-nine tails. He hesitated. Oh God. His friends had said he never left his bed. But if he was honest, he really wasn't sure. Because he feared it might be true. He shrugged to hide the pain of her words stabbing his heart. 'I was asleep.'

'My older brother died for Beauworth's cause and once again William's dreams were shattered. He's angry, Garrick. He swears if I have any more to do with you, I will never see him or Sissy again. I can't let that happen.'

An iron band seemed to tighten around his chest. 'You care more for your sister than you do for me.' A painful truth entered his mind. 'You believe I did those things.'

Tears ran silently down her face. 'I don't know any more. I want to believe you. But…how?' She flung her arms wide. 'And besides, it doesn't matter what I believe. I promised Sissy I wouldn't leave her.'

Her tears ran and he couldn't think straight. Her family came first. She'd given up everything for the sake of her family. He'd ruined her and all she could think about was her sister. 'What about you? About your reputation?'

She stared at him, silent, sad, an island, a lonely rock, the tears drying on her face. 'No one else knows about us, unless you tell them,' she whispered.

She was ashamed of her time with him. And how could he blame her for keeping her word to a child? He felt as if someone had pitched him headlong into a bottomless well. He couldn't see a glimmer of light, or any way to climb out of the depths.

A bitter laugh rose in his throat. All those days in his cell, thinking about her, about her kisses, about the warmth in her eyes for him, were the dreams of a fool. He'd been nothing but a means to save her family. If she cared at all, she'd trust in his innocence.

You don't trust yourself, a small voice whispered in his head.

The sorrow in her face slid like arrows, wicked and barbed, between his ribs, tearing into his flesh, into his battered soul, releasing a monster of anger, a writhing twisting being with fangs bared and ready to strike.

'If you ever change your mind, Lady Eleanor,' he said softly, his lips drawing back in a caricature of a smile, 'you will need to tell me so on your knees. After all, you owe me the rest of my three months.'

Her soft gasp didn't ease his pain, nor did the glisten of moisture in her eyes. If anything, it made him feel like a wolf wounding a fawn and it was far too easy. None of this was her fault. He swung away, opened the door, pausing with his hand on the knob. God, he was a bastard. 'I apologise. I did not mean that. I truly wish you and your family well.'

How he left the room on his feet, he wasn't sure, because he seemed to be walking through chest-high water, wet and cold and sluggish. He felt older than England's green hills as he crossed the hallway.

A child ran down the stairs. She halted at the sight of him. 'Oh, it's Len's wicked Marquess.' She beamed and started towards him.

'Lady Sissy,' he said harshly, 'I bid you good day.'

He stormed out of the door to his carriage and Johnson set the horses in motion. As the carriage drew away, the truth seeped like bitter bile into his mind. She was right not to trust him.

Desolation, cold and empty, filled every corner of his being. She'd left him with nothing. Not even hope.

It was no more than he deserved.

Chapter Nine

London—May 1815

'Such a lovely girl, your sister,' Mrs Bixby said, touching Eleanor's arm. 'And so unaffected.'

Did the old bat mean Sissy enjoyed herself too much? William always said she did. Eleanor forced a smile. 'Thank you.' Cecelia certainly sparkled like a ruby among pale pearls. Her deep-rose gown showed her dark hair and eyes to splendid advantage as she laughed up at her partner in a cotillion. Did she stand out too much, as William said? Perhaps she should have worn white after all.

'She's a handful,' Aunt Marjory said on the other side of Mrs Bixby. 'Never know what harum-scarum thing she'll take next into her head.'

'Really, Aunt Marjory. It is simply high spirits,' Eleanor said. 'Nothing more.'

'She's a credit to you,' Mrs Bixby said.

Unlike herself, had Mrs Bixby known it, Sissy did indeed bring credit to the Hadley name. She was popular with her peers, also making their first Season, and the young gentlemen flocked around her without any sign of loose behaviour.

'Who is she dancing with now?' Aunt Marjory asked. The poor dear just couldn't keep up.

'Lord Danforth. Unexceptionable family,' Mrs Bixby said. 'He'd make a good catch, if he came up to scratch.'

'It is far too early to be thinking of marriage,' Eleanor said. Unless of course Sissy fell in love, which would be wonderful.

'Speaking of coming up to scratch,' Aunt Marjory said, 'I haven't seen Mr Westbridge this evening.'

'He is most likely in the card room,' Eleanor replied. 'He knows I will not dance.'

Mr Westbridge, a serious man in his middle years, asked Eleanor to marry him at least once a week. He refused to believe she would never change her mind. Wouldn't believe she was happy keeping house for William and Sissy.

Idly glancing around the room for another suitable partner for her sister, Eleanor's heart stumbled. Head and shoulders above the man at his side, hair the colour of chocolate and his olive skin startling among the pale English faces around him, stood Beauworth. After four years she recognised him in an instant. He looked broader, more assured and certainly sterner of eye. Older, of course. All that she saw in a second. Her heart steadied, but her breathing remained irregular. What changes would he see in her, if he knew her at all? She looked away, determined not to notice.

As if compelled by some unseen hand, her head turned to once more bring him into view. Time had taken its toll. Deep lines bracketed a far more sardonic mouth than she remembered. Lean and axe hard, his face offered no quarter as he gazed with dark and cool remoteness at the world. As dark as a Moor, he must have spent years beneath a harsh sun. The legends of his female conquests, his dissipation, his hedonistic lifestyle, whispered of in salacious detail in the salons of the *ton,* hung over him like a dark cloud. The ladies of the *ton* loved hearing of his exploits. At first, she'd felt pain, a sharp jealousy. As the years passed, it had reduced to a dull ache she could ignore most of the time. To be jealous of a man she'd sent away seemed impossibly selfish. The females in the room, young and old, eyed him with barely concealed fascination, while some of the men looked strained. He was, after all, a close friend of the Prince Regent and commanded their respect, if not their friendship.

In the brightly lit room, dressed in sombre black, he had the look of a living breathing shadow.

She shivered.

Perhaps she felt chilled by the cold half-smile with which the Marquess listened to his fair-haired male companion. His gaze swept the room apparently without interest, moving swiftly and unerringly towards her corner.

Heart beating wildly, Eleanor lowered her gaze. Even if he did recognise her, he would surely not approach, not after what lay between them. Would he? Was that hope in her heart?

Dimly, she realised the set was ending. She started to rise, to go to her sister. Perhaps if she pleaded a headache, Sissy would leave. If not, perhaps she could leave her in Aunt Marjory's care.

'Lady Eleanor, a pleasure to meet you again.'

The deep voice with its trace of a French accent thrummed a chord low in her belly, a long-forgotten thrill. Trembling inside, she raised her head and gazed into brown eyes flecked with gold. Cold eyes. The charming smile she remembered curved his lips, his teeth flashing white. Yet he made her think of a predator, a panther, dark and sleek and hungry. He held out his hand.

Her throat dried. Heat rose in her face. Her heart pounded so hard she couldn't breathe. If she reacted like this to a simple greeting, people would talk. They would make guesses, gossip. She must not make a breath of scandal. She rested her fingertips on his pristine white gloves for no more than a second. 'Lord Beauworth.'

She turned in her seat to the ladies beside her. 'Aunt Marjory, Mrs Bixby, allow me to introduce the Marquess of Beauworth.'

'A pleasure.' Aunt Marjory gave him a speculative glance, assessing his worth and his lineage.

'My lord,' Mrs Bixby said, her eyes alive with curiosity and surprise.

'Ladies, a pleasure. May I have this dance, Lady Eleanor?' The words were no more than a polite murmur, but the slight quirk at the corner of his mouth issued a challenge.

Stunned to speechlessness, she could only stare. To feel his arms around her again would be wonderful, awful.

She never danced.

Mrs Bixby was nodding as if it was the most natural thing in the world. How would it look if she accepted? If she refused, would people think there was a reason and talk? Mrs Bixby loved to talk.

She inclined her head. 'Thank you, my lord.'

He brought her to her feet. Two layers of cotton separated their skin, yet she felt his touch as if their hands were naked. Did he notice the way her fingers trembled in his? Hopefully not.

The orchestra struck up a waltz. Of all things. Had he known? She glanced up at his face, thinking to cry off, but he gave her no chance, sweeping her into the steps of the dance, masterfully, gracefully, powerfully in command. He swung her around the floor in soft glides and elegant twirls. How strong his hand felt beneath hers. He guided her steps with the lightest of pressure, yet his hand was all she could feel. The room disappeared into a swirl of pastel and shimmering candles. She saw nothing but shoulders hugged by a black coat, a froth of white cravat above a pale cream waistcoat embellished with tiny forget-me-nots. The scent of his cologne filled her nostrils. The warmth of his body reached out to caress her skin, though he held her no closer than was proper.

Sissy, who had not yet received permission to waltz, stuck out her tongue as they passed.

'Your sister is as charming as ever,' the Marquess remarked. He sounded almost wistful, which must be her imagination.

'Her first Season,' she said. 'Lady Cecelia is a huge success.'

'I can see why. Are you also enjoying the Season?'

She glanced up, seeking assurance that this wasn't some sort of barb. He looked merely interested. He raised a brow.

'Seeing Sissy so happy, why would I not enjoy it?'

'Why not indeed? You look lovely.'

'Fustian,' she said. 'I look exactly what I am. A woman past her first blush of youth and firmly on the shelf.'

'Then perhaps I should rephrase my words. You look lovely to me.'

Her insides fluttered. An instant flare of arousal, her body crying out for completion. She swallowed her gasp of shock. The pink in her cheeks must have turned carmine, because her face was scalding. 'Why are you here? Why are you doing this?'

His hard mouth twitched at the corner, as if he guessed she spoke of her body's reaction, not his request to dance.

'I need to ask you something,' he said.

A twinge of disappointment pierced her heart. Had she expected he would seek her out for herself? If not expected, then hoped, perhaps? Against all reason. 'Then ask it and be done.'

A woman gliding by in emerald and gold turned her head to look at them. She must have heard the sharpness in Eleanor's tone.

Chagrined, Eleanor pinned a smile to her lips. He whirled her around the end of the floor, tucking her against his side, his strong arm at her waist in an almost lover-like embrace, then he turned her under his arm.

'Not here,' he murmured into her ear, his warm breath sending a shiver down her spine.

Breathless, she glanced up. 'I beg your pardon.'

'We can't talk here. Drive with me tomorrow afternoon.'

Not a request, a command. She stiffened. William would be furious if he knew she had danced with him. What would he say to her driving out? And yet she was tempted. Her heart was galloping like an out-of-control colt, all fits and starts and wobbly. 'And if I say no?'

The warm light in his gaze fled. 'Then I must seek my answer elsewhere.'

An undercurrent of something dark coloured his voice. Not a threat exactly, but then she saw he was looking at Sissy.

The dance drew to a close and he escorted her back to her chair. Mrs Bixby had departed, no doubt eager to regale her cronies with Beauworth's foray into the realms of respectable women. The news would cause a bit of a stir and some beating of matchmaking breasts, and Eleanor couldn't help feeling the tiniest bit triumphant.

'I'll call for you at four,' he said.

Blast. She'd hesitated too long. And besides, he knew very well she wasn't going to let him anywhere near her sister. 'I will be ready.'

With a bow to her aunt, he departed.

'Ready for what, dear?' Aunt Marjory asked.

Watching him make his way through the crowded room without effort, almost as if those before him cleared a path for a dangerous creature, she answered absently, 'He wants to take me driving tomorrow.'

'Oh, my dear. Such a handsome man. What will you wear?'

The Marquess disappeared from the room. Had he come tonight for the purpose of seeking her out? She felt breathless at the idea. And then horrified. Nonsense. He'd probably headed for the card room like most of the other gentlemen not on the marriage mart.

She turned to her aunt. 'I'm sorry, I missed what you said?'

'I think you should wear the celestial-blue morning gown you had made at the beginning of the Season.' Her aunt nodded as if the matter was settled.

It was a ridiculous gown. Not the sort of thing a woman past her prime should wear. The reason she had never taken it out of the press since it arrived. 'I'll think about it.' When she could think, when her heart settled into its normal comfortable rhythm and her gaze stopped searching the crowd for a tall dark figure. 'Aunt Marjory, where is Sissy?'

Her aunt pointed her fan. 'Dancing with Felton. The poor boy is quite besotted.'

Lord Felton was an honourable young gentleman who would not take advantage of Sissy's high spirits. Eleanor breathed a sigh of relief. The slightest hint of a scandal would bring William back to town in an instant. He'd been so distraught by what had happened four years ago he'd turned into a mother hen where his sisters were concerned, no matter how often she promised she'd sown all her wild oats.

Pulling his greatcoat close against the cool breeze, Garrick set out on foot from his house in St James's. At this late hour, there were few people on the street. A dank mist stinking of muddy river obscured all but the closest objects. He hunched deeper into his coat. If he hadn't promised Dan, he'd have preferred to down a bottle of brandy in his chamber and drown the memory of a pair of cool dove-grey eyes.

When he arrived, Dan grinned from ear to ear at the door of his small bachelor rooms off Piccadilly. 'I'd almost given you up, Major.' There was little of the old cockney left in Dan's speech.

'You'll get used to calling me Garrick one of these days, Dan.'

'No, my lord, it wouldn't be right.' Dan never made any pretence of being other than a man up from the gutter, no matter how high he rose or how highly his regiment sang his praises. It was all a source of wonder to the modest Lieutenant Dan Smith. 'Come in. Take your ease.'

Undernourished and small as a child, he now topped

five foot eight inches. His shoulders were broad and his expression open beneath his cropped blond hair. With his handsome face and bright blue eyes, he was as sought after by the ladies as Garrick himself. Too bad Dan was far too shy to take advantage of their lures.

Garrick settled into one of two armchairs by the fire and Dan poured a glass of whisky for him and a gin for himself.

'Did you see her?' Dan asked.

'I did.'

Dan looked ridiculously hopeful. 'And…'

'And…nothing. We met. We spoke. We danced and I left. I felt nothing, nor did she.'

'You danced?'

'Yes.' He did his best to sound bored, despite the jolt low in his gut.

'How did Lady Eleanor look?'

Garrick thought hard. She had looked…beautiful, womanly. Paler than he remembered, almost drab in the muted grey of her gown. She seemed restrained, as if she held her emotions in check, the lively spirit he'd admired replaced by severe English spinsterhood. And yet something had sparked between them when they had danced. Or had he imagined it, because he'd hoped to feel something? He closed his eyes briefly at the pang of something sharp in a place where he didn't have feelings at all. 'She looked well enough. A little older, I suppose.' He sipped at the fiery liquid. 'I had forgotten how stuffy these London parties are. What news do you hear?'

Always sympathetic to his moods, Dan let the subject go and grimaced. 'We expect to receive orders to leave at any moment. London will awake one morning and we will be gone.'

'I agree. The Duke will move swiftly once Cabinet makes up its mind. But their shilly-shallying will cost our men dearly.' The War Cabinet had bungled too many times to do any better now. Only Wellington's instincts had saved their bacon time and again in Spain.

'What about you?' Dan asked.

Only Dan would ask. No one else knew of his work for the Allies. Many suspected his loyalty even though they were careful not to show it, not when Prinny had admitted him to his closest circle. But the scavengers were circling. If one more person sighted him in France, things were going to get very difficult. But he trusted Dan with his life as he trusted no one else. 'I'm to go at the end of the week.'

Dan whistled through his teeth. 'That soon. You will take care.'

The only person who cared enough to worry. 'I will.'

'And after? When Bonaparte is back under lock and key?'

He never thought about after. He had never expected to live this long. He wouldn't come back to England. There was nothing for him here. 'Find another war? Hire myself out as a mercenary.'

Dan looked far from happy. 'And the other matter?'

'I asked her to drive out with me tomorrow.'

'And she agreed?' Hopeful had returned.

'She did.' He'd thought she would refuse. He shouldn't have threatened her, but she'd left him little choice.

'Will you tell her Le Clere has been seen in England?'

'I don't see the point. Not when we aren't sure. I plan to snare him before he gets anywhere near the Castle-field tribe. No more of this, Dan.' He smiled and reached across the space between them. He clinked his erstwhile tiger's glass. 'Here's to you and yours and may you come home safe.'

'And you and yours, my lord.'

Garrick swallowed the rest of his drink in one gulp. There was no one he called his. Not any longer.

He pushed the thought away and held out his glass for a refill. Better to take whatever pleasure life offered when it came along. Like a few hours of her company on the morrow, though he expected it would hold little in the way of delight for either of them.

In the end she did wear the blue gown. After all, one did not drive out with a gentlemen of Beauworth's standing looking like someone's governess, as Sissy had pronounced earlier with all the assurance of youth.

When Eleanor walked down the stairs a few minutes before the appointed time, she felt satisfied with her appearance. Her pulse beat a little too fast, her stomach was tied in a tight little knot that made breathing more difficult than usual, but the gown masked all of that. To the world, she looked cool and calm.

Sissy dashed out of the drawing room as she set foot on the last step. 'You look ravishing,' she said. 'I told you that gown was perfect. It makes your eyes look bluer.'

'Sissy, don't be a hoyden.'

'Hah.' Sissy's dark eyes sparkled. She brushed a tumble of chestnut curls back off her shoulder. 'Don't be such a stick in the mud.'

The case clock struck four. Someone rapped the knocker on the front door.

'Quick,' Sissy said. 'Into the drawing room. You don't want to look too eager.'

'Sissy.' Eleanor couldn't help laughing. Her sister

had certainly adopted all the niceties of a débutante in her first Season with alacrity and enthusiasm.

Eleanor allowed herself to be chivvied into the drawing room, while the butler hurried to open the front door.

'Very nice, dear,' Aunt Marjory said, glancing up from her embroidery.

'Thank you, Aunt.' What the old lady would say if she knew just how annoyed William would be was a whole other matter. By the time he learned of it, there would be nothing to discuss. Today she would answer Beauworth's questions and tell him not to bother her or her family again. If he had any sense of honour, he would abide by her wishes. And that would be that.

Her heart squeezed a little at the thought, but she ignored it, firmly.

She perched on a chair by the window.

'Not there, Eleanor,' Sissy said. 'The light obscures your face.' She frowned. 'And why are you wearing that horrid cap under that perfectly lovely chip straw as if you are an old maid?'

She was an old maid. 'Too late to do anything about it now,' she said calmly, although her heart thundered as the door opened and Beauworth entered.

If he could not see her features, she could see his very well indeed. Still handsome, but harsh, like granite carved by the wind, the furrows around his mouth and creases at the corners of his eyes deeply etched. Only a shadow of the young man she had known remained in his smile and the angle of his jaw, the wave of brown hair on his forehead.

He took Aunt Marjory's hand in his and murmured a suitable greeting. Then he moved on to Sissy.

She peeped up at him. 'I don't suppose you remember me?'

'The last time I saw you, you had soot on your nose,' he replied with a flash of his charming smile. Eleanor's stomach tumbled in a long slow roll. Would she never be able to see that smile without melting?

Sissy laughed. 'You are still Eleanor's wicked Marquess.'

'Sissy,' Eleanor said as Beauworth turned to her with a raised brow and one of those devastating smiles. She was going to be mush if this continued.

'What did you say, dear?' Aunt Marjory asked.

'Nothing,' Sissy said, with a blithe smile and a wink.

'Are you ready to leave, Lady Eleanor? Much as I delight in the company of your family, my horses do not like to be kept waiting.'

He took her hand and brought her to his feet. As he did so, his gaze searched her face. Seeking what? She lifted her chin and regarded him coolly. 'Indeed. I am quite ready, my lord.'

Sissy ran to the window. 'Oh, my,' she said. 'A high-perch phaeton. And matched chestnuts.'

'Come away from the window, dear,' Aunt Marjory said. 'Do take care with my niece, my lord. The thought of her up on those high things gives my heart palpitations.'

'Fear not, Miss Hadley,' the Marquess said. 'I will take care of Lady Eleanor's person as if it were my own.'

His velvet tones were like a caress on her skin. An insidious yearning filled her body. She managed a tight smile. 'I have no fear, my lord.'

'You never did.'

He was wrong, of course. She'd feared greatly for him all these years. But she could never show it.

He guided her out of the house and down the steps into the street.

Sissy was right, his equipage was high and dangerous. The horses, held by a groom, tossing their heads in the traces, were fresh, high-strung and beautifully matched. A team she'd love to drive, or she would have in her misspent youth.

While she didn't need his help, she allowed him to assist her up the steps. She sat on the seat and settled her skirts. The ground looked astonishingly far away and the slightest movement caused the coach body to sway on its swan-necked springs.

The Marquess went around the other side and climbed up beside her. He took the whip from its holder, catching the points deftly in his fingers and gathered up the ribbons in his other hand.

He glanced at her with a quizzical expression. 'Nervous, Lady Eleanor?'

'Certainly not,' she said. The fact that her heart seemed to be performing an endless drum roll against her ribs and had been since she awoke this morning had nothing to do with him. It was lack of sleep.

'Good. Then we will dispense with the services of the groom.' He raised his voice. 'Jeffers, spring 'em. You can walk home.'

Before Eleanor could protest against the breach of propriety, the liveried groom touched his hat, released the off-side leader's bridle and stepped back. The Marquess moved his equipage into the street and soon they were bowling down the quiet road at a clip.

'It is an open carriage, Ellie,' he said with the ghost of a laugh. 'I want our conversation to be private.'

Ruffled, she glared at him. 'We have nothing to say to each other of a private nature. And you should have asked me first.'

'Asking doesn't get me anywhere.'

Now what did he mean by that pithy little comment? Surely he wasn't referring to his disastrous proposal of marriage? And surely he wasn't going to ask her again? Her throat dried. A patter of hope ran through her heart.

'What did you want to ask me?' There, she sounded cool and collected.

He turned on to Piccadilly and headed toward Hyde Park. She admired his skill as he negotiated around a hackney coach stopped to pick up a fare and neatly avoided a brewer's dray coming the opposite way. He made it look easy, but the horses required all of his attention, so she sat quietly, content to enjoy being driven by a master, content to look at the hard-angled profile, the curl of his hair on his temple, the confident set of his shoulders. Her reckless gaze lingered on the firm line of his sensual mouth, the angle of his chin. He was still beautiful and very dangerous. She would not let him catch her unaware again and she'd already spoken to Sissy about keeping her distance.

They entered Hyde Park and started along Rotten Row. Because of the early hour, only a few carriages paraded their occupants.

'Now,' he said, 'I can concentrate on you, instead of these beasts.'

The thought of him concentrating on her made her breathless with longing. But it was not what he meant, surely it was not. She tried to ignore the trickle of hope sliding around in her stomach. She stared at the horses tossing their heads at every pedestrian they passed. 'What they really need is a good long run.'

'Should I have whisked you away to Brighton? I have the key to the Pavilion.'

The words were said with a teasing note, but she sensed an undertone of challenge, or perhaps a shadow of hope. She fought the very real urge to say yes, to kick over the traces she'd forced herself into these past years, the curb of propriety and duty.

'It was simply a comment.'

'Naturally,' he said.

'Well, here I am, all attention. What was so important that you must speak to me alone?' The words sounded sharper than she had intended, sharp enough to ensure her heart was not hanging on her sleeve like a flag.

The teasing light in his face disappeared and her foolish heart regretted the loss. 'You've changed, Ellie.'

'I'm older and wiser.'

'And none too happy, if I'm not mistaken.'

'My happiness is not your concern.' How could she ever be happy, hearing about his conquests, knowing other women were enjoying favours that could have been hers? And like a fool, she drank up every mention of his name because it brought him closer, when it was quite obvious he never thought of her at all. Until he wanted something.

'It could have been,' he said.

But she'd chosen. And she lived with the choice no matter how painful. 'Your question.'

'Quite honestly, I'm not sure how to ask.'

'Ask.' The torture of having him close, of hiding the warmth running beneath her skin, was a bit like trying to hide a fever. A fever with no cure.

'After you…after it was all over, Beauworth held no interest for me. I joined the army. Rumours circulated that I'd ruined a noblewoman.' The words were spoken calmly enough, but bitterness rang in his voice.

'I never spoke of what happened to anyone,' she said.

'Except your brother.'

She recoiled. 'Are you saying William blackened your name?'

'Yes.'

The flat statement knocked her off kilter. The carriage remained steady, but she felt as if she was being buffeted on all sides by a strong cold wind.

'There is something I want you to tell your brother.'

She could just see herself talking to William about Garrick. 'I—'

'Tell him it wasn't me who crippled him.'

The cold wind turned into an icy gale. She put a hand to her throat, felt the hard beating of her heart. 'What?'

'Your brother caught me exiting a window of the porter's lodging. He knew whose chamber it was and went off to report my despicable behaviour. I think he had some sort of boyish crush on the girl. Believe me, she wasn't the angel he thought.'

'Is that what happened? He never told me the full story.'

'He doesn't know the full story.'

He guided his team past a young gentleman in a phaeton who had stopped to greet some ladies on foot.

'Your brother hit me from behind. Stunned me. I called him a sneak and a tell-tale in front of his friends and threatened him with a sound thrashing.' He winced. 'I lost my temper. Later that night someone went to his room and beat him with a club as he slept.'

'He says it was you.'

His mouth tightened. 'I wasn't the only one punished. The porter was removed from his position, but someone forgot to retrieve his keys. Or perhaps he had an extra one. He'd lost far more than I. A month of waiting on the teachers' table doesn't warrant beating a man to within an inch of his life.' His voice was grim. 'Losing your livelihood might.'

Oh, God. And she'd believed William. She felt as if her heart might break. She stared at his profile. He looked unmoved. Completely unaffected. How could he be so cool, so icily calm, when he'd been so unjustly accused? Perhaps he no longer cared. 'And you have proof of this?'

He glanced at her with a cynical curve to his mouth. 'Still doubting me?'

'No. I was thinking of William. It will not be easy to change his mind after all these years.'

He nodded slowly. 'I found the daughter a year ago. Her father is dead and she's fallen pretty low, but she remembered me. She was happy to tell me the truth. She'd do so on the Bible and can point to the men who helped him. Ellie, more important than William, do you believe me?'

An odd bubble of joy filled her heart. The relief of knowing she'd been right about him all along seemed to take a heavy weight from her shoulders. 'Yes. I do. I wish I had known when—'

'So do I. Setting the record straight about your brother, however, wasn't my primary reason for wishing to have a private conversation.'

'Then what?'

'Cast your mind back to the day of the ransom. To Piggot's letter, if you will?'

They passed a barouche with an elderly woman and a pretty young lady. Garrick bowed an acknowledgement as they shot by.

She remembered too much about those days. But the letter? She frowned. 'William dropped it at your feet.'

'I left it there. Didn't want to give them a shot at you.'

He'd been brave that day, saving her life and William's. 'It was addressed to you. That is all I remember.'

His grip tightened on the reins as the horses started forwards. It was a few moments before he had them in hand again. 'Why?' he said.

'I beg your pardon?'

'Why was it addressed to me, the accused? And what happened to it?' While his expression remained calm, if a little grim, anger tinged his voice.

'I have no idea. I'm sorry.'

'I want that letter.'

What did this have to do with her? 'Le Clere must have picked it up during the mêlée.'

'Impossible. No. Someone else picked it up.'

'Who?'

He looked as her sideways. 'Who do you think?'

'If William had retrieved the letter, all he had to do was hand it over to the authorities and send you back to prison.' Her stomach dipped.

'Precisely. I want that letter, Ellie.'

The blood in her veins seemed to have been exchanged for melted snow. She took a breath. 'You think I have it.'

He didn't have to answer.

She did not have his stupid letter, but from the look on her face he wasn't going to believe a word she said. 'Why would you want it after all this time?'

His gloved hand tightened on the reins. 'Because it was addressed to me.'

'I don't have it.'

He sighed. An impatient male huff of breath. 'All right. Let me tell you what happened. You climbed aboard that cart and bandaged me up. For which I thank you. Then you walked back across that field and picked up the letter. Did you read it?'

She pressed her lips together.

'Answer me, Ellie. Did you read it?'

The man of ice from minutes before evaporated in the heat of his anger. And beneath the rage, she heard the cry of a small boy, afraid and hurt and very lonely. It made her feel sad. Hot prickles burned behind her eyes. Her heart felt wrenched into a thousand pieces. 'I do not have your letter. Even if I did, why dredge up history?'

He inhaled a long, slow breath and let it go. 'For the sake of my sanity. If you won't help me willingly, I will find the truth without your help.'

She reached out, put her hands on his forearm, felt the quiver of sinew and muscle as he steered the horses in a tight circle. 'Please, leave well alone. If anyone had the letter, they would have used it by now. Perhaps the wind blew it away.'

He shook her hand off, flicked his whip above his leader's head and set the team into a gallop.

'Slow down,' she said as they turned on to the Mall. He didn't seem to hear. Too busy driving to an inch, setting his team at impossibly narrow spaces with mere inches to spare, his face set like granite. He was angry, but he really had the wrong end of the stick.

It wasn't very many minutes before he set her down at her door. He didn't bother to escort her inside. He helped her climb down, then whipped up his horses and left her standing on the curb.

She nibbled at the tip of her glove, remembering those long-ago days. They'd all changed so much. Her, Garrick, William. Only Sissy remained the same.

She shivered.

Chapter Ten

Eleanor thought she might expire from lack of air. The Smithwicks's ballroom was far too small for the number of guests invited. She couldn't see the dance floor for the crowds as she squeezed her way back to her aunt from the withdrawing room.

She sat down. 'Where is Cecelia?'

'She was here a moment ago. Beauworth asked her to dance.'

Her heart jolted. 'Beauworth?'

'Mmm. Asked very prettily, too. Made her laugh.'

Why would Beauworth ask Sissy to dance? She didn't like the unpleasant little twinge in her stomach. She craned her neck to see around the group of friends clustered in front of her. 'I don't see her.'

I will find the truth without your help. That was what he had said. He had better not involve her sister in his plans. A chill breeze came out of nowhere, lifting the hairs on the back of her neck, a feeling of impending doom. 'I'll go and look for her.'

'She'll be back when the music stops,' Aunt Marjory

said. 'I've never heard it said Beauworth had a taste for misses in their first Season.'

He'd had a taste for one young miss. Years ago.

'I will be less than a moment,' she said. The air reeked of attar of roses, bay rum and hot bodies. Eleanor plied her fan, hoping to stir up enough air to give some respite from the heat as she strolled around the dance floor, twice. No sign of them. Nor were they anywhere else in the room. She was sure of it. She'd know if Garrick was present.

She headed for the doors, squeezing between tight knots of people trying to make themselves heard over the din.

Finally, she made it into the hallway. It was like going from Bedlam into a sanctuary. She took a breath. Where would they have gone? She would certainly have a word with Cecelia about disappearing without a chaperon. And Garrick would also get a piece of her mind.

Halfway along the corridor, she met a blond fresh-faced lieutenant in a dark green uniform coming the other way. He hesitated as she approached.

'Lady Eleanor?'

Eleanor frowned. He looked familiar, but she could not place him.

He smiled and bowed, his vivid blue eyes twinkling. 'Dan Smith, my lady.'

'Dan? Oh, my goodness, I would never have recognised you. A lieutenant, too. Congratulations.' He had been a bright young lad four years ago and the war had obviously given him a golden opportunity for advancement.

'My lord, the Marquess, put in a good word.' Dan spoke with pride and affection.

His words brought Eleanor back to her quest. 'Have you seen the Marquess and Lady Cecilia?'

'I believe they went into the drawing room. They have cards set out there. May I escort you?'

She smiled her agreement and took his arm. They walked along the brightly lit corridor, their footfalls making no sound on the thick Aubusson rug. Her heart knocked a protest at the thought of facing Garrick. She'd hoped to avoid him entirely.

The card room proved to be vacant except for a couple of elderly men playing whist. Dan looked around nonplussed. Disappointed, she turned to leave. The curtains rippled in the draught of an open window. She glanced at Dan. His expression tightened.

Before Eleanor could say anything, the young man strode to the curtain and drew it back, revealing an open French door. He stepped through. Eleanor followed on to the torch-lit balcony.

Sitting on a stone seat with her skirts above her calf, Sissy's stockinged foot rested on the bent knee of the gentleman kneeling before her. The Marquess, for that was who it was filling her pink satin slipper with champagne, glanced up with a wicked grin.

Eleanor's ribs squeezed tight. She could not hold back her gasp. 'Cecilia! What are you doing?'

Her face alight with laughter, the child looked up. 'Len? Isn't he the most ridiculous man alive?' She giggled. 'I think I'm going to lose my wager.'

She sounded foxed. They were on the brink of disaster. Scandal loomed a mere whisper away. Eleanor's lips felt tight, her jaw felt tight, her skin felt tight—if she took a breath, she might fly apart. She kept her voice low. 'And what did you wager, may I ask?'

'A kiss.'

Dan stiffened.

Even a commoner found this kind of behaviour appalling. She snatched the slipper from the Marquess and emptied its contents over the railing. 'Sissy, put this on, at once.'

As he rose to his feet, Garrick's mouth curled in a cynical smile. 'Good evening, Lady Eleanor.'

She ground her teeth, rather than throw the slipper at his head.

'Lady Cecilia,' Garrick said softly, 'I'm afraid your sister doesn't believe in the principle that one's word is one's bond, do you, my lady?'

A low blow, indeed, directed at her reneging on their bargain and far more painful than a slap to the face. Eleanor knew she must have gone red from the prickling heat in her cheeks and throat. Pretending not to hear, she pushed Cecilia's foot into her damp footwear and pulled her upright. 'Come back to the ballroom before anyone notices.'

'My lady,' Lieutenant Smith said, his voice low, full of concern. 'Might I suggest that if I escort Lady Cecilia and my lord takes your arm, it will look as though the four of us took a stroll?'

Eleanor glanced at him with gratitude 'You are very kind, Lieutenant Smith.'

'An outflanking manoeuvre, Dan?' The Marquess's voice from the shadows sounded dangerous. Then he gave a short laugh. 'I surrender. This time.'

Dan offered his hand to Cecilia and she looked up at him.

'Cecilia, this is Lieutenant Dan Smith,' Eleanor said.

'Lady Cecilia,' Lieutenant Smith murmured, his ears pink.

'Lieutenant, a pleasure.' Cecelia's smile was a little lopsided, but very sweet.

A slightly bemused expression on his face, the young man placed her outstretched hand on the green sleeve of his uniform.

Eleanor closed her eyes briefly. Heaven help them all. Cecilia was positively dangerous.

She ignored Garrick's glower and took his arm. 'How dare you?' she muttered.

He glanced down at her. 'I dare anything to get what I want, Lady Eleanor. As do you.'

A rush of heat flared in her face. 'You have no idea how much I regret what I did.'

His breathing changed, a slight hitch, and she had the sense she'd touched a nerve, yet when she glanced up, his expression was one of utter boredom.

'Promise me you will stay away from Sissy,' she said.

'Would you believe my promise?' he asked with a cynical smile.

She had no time to answer. They'd already entered the ballroom, where any chance word might be overheard. Whether he promised or not, she would make sure Sissy didn't come within ten feet of the Marquess of Beauworth in future.

A few heads turned in their direction as they traversed the room, but no buzz of conversation or sly whispers. Eleanor breathed a sigh of relief. Lieutenant Smith saw Sissy to her seat and bowed very properly. Eleanor took the chair on the other side of her aunt. 'Thank you, both,' she said, intending it for a dismissal.

'Do you not dance, Lieutenant?' Sissy asked.

Lieutenant Smith turned as red as a poppy. The Marquess, rot him, grinned wolfishly at his protégé's obvious discomfort. Eleanor wanted to bash him over the head with her reticule. She pretended not to notice.

'I do, my lady,' Lieutenant Smith said. 'I would be honoured if you would grant me a cotillion later this evening.'

The little minx grinned. 'I have one free after supper.'

Serious and courteous, the young soldier bowed. 'I will return then. Thank you.' He took the Marquess by the arm and led him away.

A considering expression on her face, Cecelia watched the angelic soldier and the dark rake depart, an odd combination to be sure. And the poor young lieutenant was no more suitable for Sissy than the Marquess of Beauworth.

Eleanor sighed. 'Really, Cecilia, what has got into you, going off alone with a well-known rake? You could be facing ruin right now. Not to mention it is shockingly rag-mannered to ask a man to dance.'

'You are a jealous old maid.'

It was unforgivably rude and hurtful, but Eleanor swallowed her pride. It was Garrick's fault Sissy had drunk too much champagne and there was no point in getting into an argument with her in a crowded ballroom. And besides, after playing mother to Sissy for so many years, she felt like an old spinster.

Her summer of madness with Garrick was the last time she'd felt truly young. It had been a wild and won-derful adventure and had led to nothing but pain. Not to mention the financial disaster she'd caused. No more adventures for her. She'd settled down. She was happy. Very happy. She sniffed into her handkerchief, blinked, then turned and entered a conversation between her aunt and the elderly widow beside her, just as she ought.

* * *

'What are you about letting her make a fool of herself with a man who comes straight from the stews?' William paced the floor in front of the table where she sat waiting to pour him a cup of tea.

It had been too much to hope that he would not hear the gossip and the guilt written on her face wasn't helping. She loved her twin dearly, but since inheriting the title he'd become one of the world's most intolerant men.

'William, dear, Lieutenant Smith is a brave and honourable young man. Everyone likes him, despite his lack of birth. He is but one man among many in Cecilia's court and I promise you she does not favour any one of them. You should be proud of her success.'

'I am proud of her,' he said. 'But, Eleanor, the man hangs on Beauworth's lips.' And that was the real reason for his anger. Dare she speak to him about Garrick? Her heart picked up speed.

'About Beauworth…'

His brow lowered.

She gulped a breath. 'I met him the other day.'

'I told him I would kill him if he came near you.'

'William, he has proof he was not the person who injured you.'

'Are you really so gullible? Stay away from that man. I don't want him near this house.'

She was unable to control the pain in her expression.

He sat down beside her. 'I'm sorry, Len. But if anything were to happen to Cecilia, I would never forgive myself.'

As he had never forgiven himself for what had happened to her. The reason she forgave him his ill humours.

He grimaced. 'Beauworth was seen in France, you know, but no one will come right out and accuse him to his face, even though he is half-French.' His lip curled. 'He curries favour with the Prince.'

'Rumour, William. Not fact.' She kept her face calm and her voice steady. 'William, there are other rumours about Beauworth, involving me. You didn't tell anyone, did you?'

'What do you think I am?'

He sounded defensive and he hadn't answered the question. Her heart sank. What had he done?

She handed him a white bone-china cup with a smile. 'You know, I always wondered what was in that letter Le Clere asked you to bring that day. Did you read it?'

He shifted in his seat, the cup rattling in the saucer. 'Of course not. Do you think I would have risked your life?'

Her heart softened at his obvious indignation and yet the way he sat sipping his tea, all stiff and uncomfortable, not meeting her gaze, stirred up a feeling that something wasn't right. 'And you didn't pick it up afterwards?'

'Eleanor, you are changing the subject. Make sure that young puppy Smith keeps within bounds and Beauworth does not enter this house and I'll say no more.'

It was he who had changed the subject, and he'd given in far too easily on the issue of Captain Smith. He was hiding something. Something to do with the letter? Surely not. What would it benefit him to keep Garrick's guilt a secret? Dash it all, now she would have to look for the letter. If only for her own peace of mind. She would send word to Martin. Ask him to look for it. As steward, he had access to all of William's papers. He wouldn't like it, but somehow she'd convince him to help her one last time.

She realised William was watching her, expecting some reaction to his generous surrender. She smiled. 'Thank you. Besides, I think the question will soon be moot. Lieutenant Smith expects to be called back to his regiment any day now. He thinks we will go to war again.'

His brow furrowed. 'No doubt about it.'

'Thank heavens you are out of it.'

'Damn it, Eleanor. I wish I could go. See the end of the little Corsican once and for all.' His expression betrayed an unusually boyish eagerness. A look she hadn't seen for years. Her stomach dipped.

'William, no! Think of me. Of Sissy. How would we go on if something happened to you? Your duty is here.'

He huffed out a breath. 'To be in at the end would be tremendous. If Michael hadn't died, I would have been there.'

'I wish he was still with us, too, but not if it meant you going to war again.'

He smiled at that, but still, frustration showed in the set of his shoulders and his pursed lips. He'd given up his military ambitions for the sake of the title, for his family, a sacrifice she knew he regretted deeply.

He set down his cup. 'I must be off. I am meeting with the fellows from my old regiment at Whites'.'

He rose awkwardly to his feet and kissed her cheek. 'Promise you will keep a close eye on Sissy?'

'Yes, William, I promise.' She walked with him to his carriage and waved him farewell. She sighed. He had his purpose, he would not shirk his duty, and she had hers, though what she would do when Sissy married, she couldn't imagine.

A footman approached her as she turned to re-enter the house. She didn't recognise the livery. 'Do you live here, miss?'

Lord, did he take her for a servant? She knew her gown was plain, but really. 'I do,' she said.

'Got a letter for one of the ladies of the house. Lady Sissy.' He thrust it in her face and ran off. Affronted, she watched him go.

She glanced down at the note, turned it over to see from whence it came. It was fastened with a red seal she recognised. Beauworth.

Her stomach sank. Why was Beauworth writing to Sissy? What mischief was he up to now? *I will find the truth without your help.* Was he trying to involve Sissy in his quest?

Feeling guilty, she took the letter and made her way to her chamber. Seated at her dressing table, she turned the paper over and over. It was addressed to Cecilia. She should not open it. But William trusted her to keep Sissy safe. If it was harmless, she would explain her motives. Sissy would be angry, but she would have to understand Eleanor meant it for the best.

Hand shaking, she cracked the seal. Bold words slashed across the page.

Meet me tonight after Midnight
At the corner of the Square. We will finish
Our wager, on my Honour.
Do not Fail me.
B.

That was all. No words of love, just a command. He must be very sure of himself. A surge of anger made her hot, followed swiftly by a cold feeling around her heart. Did he plan to seduce Sissy into helping him? To ruin her sister for his own selfish purposes?

She stared at the letter. It was lucky that the footman

had handed it to her instead of the butler, or she might never have discovered the plot. A careless mistake for a man like Garrick. She gazed down the street after the footman. A very careless mistake.

From inside his coach, Garrick watched the cloaked and hooded female figure pick her way along the footpath. The watch called midnight. Right on time. A streetlight on the corner revealed little but her height as she paused to glance around. He didn't have to see her face to recognise Ellie. He breathed a sigh of relief. After his escapade on the balcony had failed to flush her from cover, this was all he could think of to force her hand.

Lord knew what he'd have done if Lady Sissy had shown up instead. Given her a lecture and sent her home.

Still, he'd wondered whether Ellie retained any of the courage he'd loved in her, the reckless wench. A carriage rumbled past, cutting her off from view and he waited with baited breath for her to reappear. He bared his teeth as she stepped into the road.

Walking right into his trap.

He flung the carriage door open and leapt down to kiss her hand. Under the hood of her cloak she wore a hat with a veil.

'*Chérie,*' he whispered huskily, leaning close to her ear. Vanilla. Memories stirred. Seductive. Full of languor and heated flesh. They always did when he smelled that particular scent. Her small gloved fingers trembled in his hand. Nervous, then, afraid of what he might do when he discovered her ruse. And rightly so. If he was her brother, he'd lock her up. God. He'd love to lock her up in a room with him. But it wouldn't happen. Not when she learned of his treachery.

Without a word, she stepped into the carriage, settling into the corner.

He'd thought of every last detail, planned his strategy to an inch. The only wild card had been her. He leaned inside. 'I will drive, *chérie*. It is more discreet that way.' He didn't dare give her a chance to demand they turn back. He closed the door and climbed on to the box.

Startled, Eleanor made a lunge for the door. The carriage lurched into motion. Dash it. Why hadn't she noticed the lack of a driver? Too terrified by her own bravado to notice anything but his large form waiting in the dark. She hadn't expected him to leave her in the carriage alone with no chance for conversation.

She peered out of the window. Where on earth was he going? To his house? No, they had left St James's and were now heading out of town.

She stared at the trapdoor above her head. Should she knock to get his attention? Or wait until they arrived at their destination? Where was he taking her? Wherever it was, they'd be alone together. Despite her effort to remain calm, her heart picked up speed.

What if she was wrong about him? What if he lost the temper he feared? Things could go very ill.

After what felt like hours, but could not have been more than one, the carriage halted outside a small but elegant house, somewhere near Chelsea, she thought. She shrank into the shadows when he opened the door.

'Where are we?' She no longer felt quite so brave.

'Still veiled, sweet?' Garrick held out his hand. 'How very discreet. A good friend loaned me his love nest for the evening. I promise we shall not be disturbed.'

The announcement sparked her anger. Eleanor had heard hints of such places from the ladies of her acquaintance. Houses tucked away on the outskirts of town, where married men took their pleasure once they had fulfilled their duty as husbands. To think he would consider bringing her sister to a place like this. If that had been his plan.

She dredged up the words she'd practised at home, but before she could open her mouth he reached in, grasped her hand and tugged. 'Don't be shy, little one.'

Missing her footing on the step, she tumbled into his arms. Strong arms she remembered so well. His hand encircled her waist and he let her slide down his length before he set her on her feet. She shivered at the hot sensation of remembered bliss. How long since he had held her thus? A lifetime. The yearning she had buried deep returned with sharp vengeance.

He laughed at her gasp, his white teeth gleaming wickedly in the torchlight over the door. She was barely able to stand on legs as soft as warm butter; her heart beat a wild rhythm. Surely he heard it?

As if sensing her weakness, he swept her off her feet, picking her up as though she weighed no more than a child. If only he knew how she had longed to feel his arms around her again.

For one blissful, heavenly moment, she leaned her head against his shoulder, revelling in the oft-thought-of warm strength while he rang the bell. Oh Lord, someone would see them. She struggled and he set her down with a warm chuckle. 'Patience, woman.'

The door opened and, holding her elbow fast, he ushered her straight past a footman in dark green livery, into a small salon off the marbled and mirrored entrance hall.

From beneath her veil, she took stock of her surroundings. The dark green walls absorbed much of the light from the single candelabra. A brown velvet sofa guarded an intricately carved, white marble hearth. Beside it, a small round rosewood table held a bottle of champagne and two glasses. A thick white rug covered the floor in front of the fire. She could imagine him stretched out on that rug, caressing one of his women. Except the face of the wicked woman in her mind was hers. If her heart had raced before, now it galloped. Her skin warmed from head to toe.

Across the room, a door led to an adjoining chamber.

He stood behind her, his hands at the hollow of her waist as he nuzzled her nape.

Delicious shivers raced down her spine. The years rolled away and she ached to lean against him, to let him carry her away into bliss. 'My lord,' she said firmly.

His lips stilled. He drew back.

She turned and threw back her hood and the veil. 'You and I need to talk.'

He smiled. All white teeth and little humour. A wolf inspecting his prey. His gaze travelled from her head to her feet in a slow appraising look that made her feel hot and cold by turn.

'Well, well, here you are, just as I expected.'

'Of course you did. You had your footman hand me the note. You didn't think I'd see it and not open it, did you?'

He looked a little stunned, but she had to hand it to him, he recovered quickly. 'Aah, *chérie,* I knew you'd do anything to protect your sister. Even this.' He bent his head and pressed his lips against her mouth, hard, demanding, ravishing. His tongue traced the seam of her lips and rivers of fire raced along her veins to burst into flame at her core. Her heartbeat drummed. She stood stiffly, resisting him with every fibre of her being.

He lifted his head. 'You resist me now, but you won't. You never could.'

'Any more than you could resist me?' she said, only too aware of the breathiness of her voice. 'Garrick, I don't have your letter. I swear it on my honour.'

His face fell. He spun away, anger and disappointment writ large on his face along with belief.

'I think William does,' she said to his stiff back. 'He went back across the field, while I was in the cart. He must have protected you all these years, for my sake.'

He turned back. 'William?' He lifted his hands from his sides, his shoulders rising. 'It makes no sense. I'd swear he'd do anything to pay me back. Unless…' His expression turned to horror. 'Oh God. It could not be that.'

He strode for the window and stared into the dark.

'What? Tell me. You are scaring me.'

He turned his head and met her eyes, his gaze clear, but his expression shuttered as if he was afraid she might see too much. 'What if that letter exonerates me?'

'I don't understand.'

'Why would he keep it hidden, if it proves my guilt? Think, Ellie. He hates me.'

William wouldn't. He couldn't.

Garrick must have seen the denial in her face because his mouth twisted in a wry smile and his eyes held pain. 'You always believe the worst of me and the best of him. Get me that letter and you will never hear from me again.'

He offered it like a bribe. Was that what he thought she wanted? 'What if it proves your guilt? What then?'

Agony blazed in his eyes. 'It is not your business,' he said harshly. 'I want that letter before I leave for France.'

She froze. 'France?'

'Where else would I go? The beloved emperor returns.' Bitterness charged his voice, gave it a hard edge.

'Are you telling me you are a traitor?'

'I'm telling you nothing.'

Fear constricted her throat. 'And once you have the letter, I will never see or hear from you again.'

He swallowed. 'I swear it.'

Her heart ached as if it had been pounded by a hammer. He truly believed she didn't care. And if he went to France, he would be lost to her forever. Even the little flicker of hope she carried deep in her heart would go out. 'Garrick—'

'Don't say another word.' He grabbed her cloak, tossed it to her, turning away as if he couldn't bear to look at her. 'Just find the letter.'

She clutched the soft fabric in her arms, struggling to comprehend his anger. 'You hate me.'

He turned slowly. Two strides took him to her side. He gripped her shoulders. 'How could I hate you? You saved my life, remember?'

A mistake, Garrick thought. Touching her, feeling her skin beneath his fingers. Seeing the flare of longing in her eyes, knowing the depths of her passion. It made letting her go all the more difficult. He'd been wrong to think he could seduce her all over again and feel nothing.

She reached up with her other hand, smoothing his hair back from his forehead—a gentle, intimate caress.

'I've missed you,' she said. 'Did you ever think of me?'

He bit back the words in his heart: *I never stop thinking of you, wanting you, looking for you.* He dared not admit it. She'd find a way to use it against him. And still he wanted her, body and soul. As if without her he was incomplete, insubstantial, a wraith, walking through life on the outside looking in.

Struggling for control, he breathed deep and stepped back. 'Ready to go?'

'Must we?'

Anger at her naïvety sparked a brush fire in his veins. 'What did you want to do? Reminisce about old times? There is only one reason a man brings a woman to a place like this. If you don't go now, I can't promise nothing will happen.'

'Oh. I see.'

Damnation, she looked hopeful and it was all the encouragement his raging desire needed.

He caught her wrist and pulled her close. He fastened his mouth to hers, ravaging, demanding. And she kissed him back, arching against him, her mouth fervent, insistent. Four long years of loneliness rolled away as if they'd never been. Her kisses, the feel of her against him, was as familiar to him as his own face in the mirror. Perhaps more so, for his face had changed as she had not.

In a wonder that felt almost reverent, he lifted his head to look into her face and found her eyes heavy-lidded with desire and with an expression of such abandon, it sent him beyond the edge of reason. Groaning with passion so intense his body shook, he swept her up into his arms.

'*Chérie,*' he whispered as he entered the bedroom lit only by a fire. He set her down gently on her feet next to the bed covered in snowy white linens.

She reached up to twine her arms around his neck, her fingers running through the waves of hair that fell over his collar.

He pulled her hairpins free, letting her hair fall in a golden river around her face and over her shoulders. He grasped a handful of it and held it to his face. He inhaled deeply. The unique scent of her. '*Ma mie, je t'adore.* It is the colour of spun gold and soft like silk.' It was part of his memory.

Then his hands were behind her, expertly unfastening her gown, as he carefully placed tiny, fluttering kisses on her face. She whimpered, a sound so small, but so filled with longing, it stole his breath and any shred of reason he had left. Her hands shaped the curve of his shoulders, then grazed his chest, caressing, stroking, as if they remembered.

A moment later, she was pulling urgently at the buttons of his coat. He stopped unbuttoning her gown to allow her to push his jacket over his shoulders and shrugged it off. He tugged at his cravat till it, too, followed his coat to the floor. Feverish, on fire, he undid the top few buttons of his shirt and pulled it over his head. He heard the intake of her breath and drew in a hissing breath of his own as she pressed her lips to his chest.

He placed his hand beneath her chin, desperate to feel her mouth on his lips and as he crushed her close, her back arched, her hips hard against his thigh. His heart drummed so hard he thought his ribs would crack.

She wanted him. Always in this, he had her trust.

'Turn around, *mignonette*,' he whispered into her mouth. 'I need you out of this gown.'

Eleanor did not want to let him go, to lose his heat, the feel of his skin under her fingers in case she lost her nerve. It was dreadfully wrong, but this would be their last time together. He seemed to sense her need for his touch, for even as he pulled at the tapes he kept one arm around her waist, pressing her buttocks against his thighs, his erection evident. An illicit thrill clenched between her legs. Rough and fast, he pulled her dress down over her arms and her hips to the floor. The brush of cool air sent shivers down her spine, and her knees trembled. The stays went next, tossed aside, and she turned to face him, smiling, clad only in a fine white-lawn chemise, silk stockings and slippers.

In the warm flicker of firelight, he loomed over her, tall, dark eyes licked with golden flame. Her gaze drifted down his lean body, fixed on a white indentation on his shoulder. Her gaze travelled over his chest, the dark curling patch of hair around his flat male nipples, a line running down his ridged hard belly. His muscles were taut as he held himself tense, a danger-ous wild animal ready to spring, ready to devour and she longed to be tasted. Another scar zig-zagged across his side, ragged and badly puckered, a blasphemy in such masculine beauty. Her gaze flew to his face as she re-membered. She touched it gently, for this was her fault.

He grasped her fingers and brought them to his lips, never taking his gaze from her face.

He smiled then, warm, open and wicked. The smile she loved. This was no ravening beast to be feared. This was her own wicked Marquess, his full mouth soft, his eyes gilded with longing. She slid her arms around his shoulders and he picked her up and deposited her upon the bed.

She was just as Garrick remembered, just as he had seen her every day in his mind. He always denied any thoughts of her at all. Now she was his for the taking and he exulted.

Nothing else mattered.

Not France, not England, and not his quest for truth.

He leaned over her, gently stroking her breasts, down the soft plane of her belly, measuring her slender waist, his hands remembering the silken feel of her skin on his palms, the sweet rounded curve of breast, the valley between ribs and flare of hip. Slender, yet luscious.

She reached for him, pulling him towards her. She'd always been a bold, sensual wanton beneath the prim-and-proper miss. His body tightened, urging him on. He smiled down at her.

She frowned as if uncertain and touched his lips. Would she change her mind? Dear God, he prayed not, yet he waited. She grasped his shoulders, pulled herself up to kiss his mouth.

He closed his eyes in brief thanks. 'Give me a moment, *chérie*.' He sat on the edge of the bed and dragged off his boots, hurrying, half-afraid she'd change her mind, stripping out of his pantaloons.

He turned to find her watching. His member pulsed at the touch of her gaze. His groin felt heavy and full. Placing one hand on each side of her head, he covered her body with his. Skin of satin, soft yielding flesh, welcoming warmth. His woman.

His breath left him in a long sigh and he plundered her mouth with his tongue, savoured the sweetness, triumphed in the way her tongue tangled with his, giving him pleasure, the way her body cradled him, her eyes glazed with desire. Then, with only the gentlest of pressure, he slid his knee between her thighs.

She opened to him, sweetly, honestly.

Desire writ strong in smoky eyes, she smiled and his

heart cracked asunder at the sweet curve of her lips. This she wanted. His body. His pleasuring. Her hands wandered his arms, his shoulders, his torso, encouraging, urging. And this he would give.

He thrust into her, hard, deep. Tight and hot and wet, her body welcomed him home. Her moan of pleasure drove his own pleasure to heights he'd forgotten all these long years.

He groaned, and captured her mouth.

The feel of his body within her and the touch of his mouth on hers made Eleanor feel alive for the first time in years. Time returned to when she'd been happiest, if only she'd recognised it.

He was wrong about why she had come to him tonight, though she hardly dared admit it to herself. Taking Sissy's place had been the fulfilment of a purely selfish need to spend one more night in his arms, taking joy for herself one last time.

Each movement of his body sent glorious sensations rippling beneath her skin. His tongue teased her lips, filled her mouth and she succumbed to the heat and the fire. Conscious thought became impossible as, hot and moist, his mouth licked and nibbled at her jaw, her throat and finally the rise of her breasts.

And she panted for more, as he lingered in the valley between her breasts, nuzzling and kissing the sensitised skin. With a whimper, she grasped his hair, brought his mouth to peaks tingling with anticipation.

He licked one, then the other. Circling his tongue around each hardened nub, nibbling, promising bliss, until she thought she might go mad. At last, his mouth, hot as fire, closed around her nipple. He suckled.

Sweet agony. Back arched, her hips rose off the bed.

He slid deeper inside her, tormenting her, as she sought her release.

And he held her there, between bliss and torture, driving her higher, tightening the connection between them, yet never letting her reach the precipice, where bliss awaited in silken black depths.

'Garrick,' she moaned, 'please.'

Supported by arms knotted with muscle and sinew, he lifted his head, eyes molten and heavy as he gazed into her face. She clenched her inner muscles around his flesh as he'd taught her so many years ago. A growl of hunger rumbled up from his chest, and then his hips drove him into her, hard and fast, almost furious, his lips drawn back in a feral snarl.

Yes. Hard and fast, and very good. She clung to his shoulders, feeling his heat, his skin slippery, rising up to meet each forward thrust.

He tilted his pelvis, the base of his shaft grinding against the sweet place between her legs.

Every nerve tightened, until she thought she must break. Agony twisted his features as he stared into his own abyss. 'Now, Ellie.' The plea in his rough voice tipped her over the edge. She shattered.

A tide of heat rushed outwards, turning her limbs to molten lead. She lay gasping for breath and he slipped out of her body and, shuddering, spilled his seed into the sheets, then stretched beside her and pulled her into the crook of his arm.

Even as she lay, blissful, warm, panting for breath, a faint tinge of bitterness twisted her heart. Even in the heat of passion he'd been in control, where she'd been completely abandoned, thoroughly wanton.

She turned her head to look at him and he brushed her lips with his mouth, a brief caress, as soft as a but-

terfly wing. 'Rest, sweetheart,' he murmured, pillow-
ing her head on his shoulder.

Was it minutes or hours later when she opened her
eyes? Held fast in the circle of his arm, her cheek on
his warm chest, his breath tickling the lock of hair on
her forehead, she watched fire weave patterns on his
skin, gleam on the arc of his cheekbone, shadow the
hollows of cheek and throat.

The scent of his musky cologne filled her nostrils.
Tenderness seeped into her heart, the trickle building
into a stream, then a river, perhaps even an ocean, it felt
so vast. She raised her head and kissed his jaw, the
stubble rough against her lips. He was lovely in sleep,
relaxed, his deep, even breaths stretching the muscles
of his chest, which might have been carved from marble
if it weren't for the dark sworls of hair.

She drank in his well-remembered features. The
hard planes of his lean cheeks, the firm, sensual lips.
The face she saw each night in her dreams was softer,
more boyish. This hard new face had character, determination, and perhaps even shades of cruelty.

The thought shimmered through her body, frightening and exciting. Impulsively, she pressed her lips
against his. If only she could tell him what she'd locked
in her heart. Too late. Unless she went down on her
knees.

He tensed, his eyelids snapping open, his gaze at
once alert. His vision focused and he huffed out a
breath. 'It's you.'

'Yes. Me.' Her heart twisted. Had he hoped for
someone else? No matter. Tonight he was hers alone.
And because she could, she kissed him again. And his
hand came up to catch her nape, to angle her head and

he deepened the kiss. He rolled on his back, bringing her with him, drawing her up on to his body.

His strong muscled body. His burgeoning erection. A thrill shot though her core as she felt him harden. Perhaps she could show him how well she remembered, with her hands, her lips, her body.

She traced the seam of his mouth and when his lips parted, she swept his mouth, teasing his tongue with hers, tasting. He grunted, a low guttural sound of approval, and sucked. Ripples of pleasure rushed outward from low in her belly.

God help her, the man knew her too well.

Thoroughly aroused, she rocked her hips in small circles against his groin.

'I want to be inside you,' he said, raising his shoulders, reaching down, using his hand to press the head of his erection against her mons. 'Now. Lift up.'

'Not yet,' she said, her voice huskier than she had ever heard it.

'Heaven forefend, woman, do you want to kill me?' He dropped his head back on the pillow.

Smiling, she claimed his lips in a swift kiss. 'Only a little.' She kissed his forehead, his nose, the hollows of his cheeks, the hard line of his jaw. He squirmed and hissed in a breath when she explored the depths of his ear with her tongue, salty and bitter, and very sensual.

His hands gripped her buttocks, large and firm, squeezing gently. He ground his hips against hers with a groan.

'Let me inside you.'

'Hush, let me play a while.'

Shifting to her side, she pressed her lips to his throat, wandered lower, across his shoulders, to his chest, the springy curls rough, the flesh beneath hot and salty and musky. She ran her palms over his flat male nipples and they puckered and hardened. Next she traced the plane of his belly; muscles beneath tanned skin rippled like waves on an ocean, as they tensed beneath her mouth. Too shy, too young, to do more than peek at him before, now the strength and the beauty of his body left her in awe.

'God. Ellie. Don't stop.'

She glanced up at his face. His eyes were closed, his jaw clenched, his expression one of agony.

She took pity on him and her hand found the hard, hot length of his erection. Watching his face, she wrapped her fingers around him, then squeezed.

His eyes opened wide. 'Harder.'

'Won't it hurt?'

'God, no.'

Taking him at his word, she squeezed and he moaned and took her hand in his, showing her how to stroke, from tip to base and back without releasing the pressure.

The tip darkened, while the shaft hardened and pulsed against her palm. 'Oh, my.'

A small drop of moisture glistened in the tiny slit at the tip. She licked it away. Salty, warm, musky.

His hips shot off the bed. He grabbed her around the waist, lifting her over him. 'Enough.' It sounded more like a growl than a word.

A shudder of pleasure held her enthralled and instinctively she straddled his hips, somewhat like mounting a horse astride, except her naked female flesh pressed against his hard penis and the heartbeat beneath his skin matched her own little pulses. The rough hair on his leg grazed her inner thighs. Quite wicked and absolutely tantalising.

Lifting her with one hand under her bottom, he

guided himself inside her body. Rigid and hot, he stretched her. She slid down the delicious intrusion. Hands about her hips, fingers digging into the swell of her buttocks, he helped her set a tantalising rhythm. Definitely like riding a horse, but far more enjoyable as the friction brought new and delightful sensations. If it were not for the tension in his face and the corded muscle and sinew in his large powerful body, she might have thought him submissive to her command of their lovemaking. Hers to do with as she willed.

Would that it were true. The wicked thought thrilled her to the core.

Wanting his touch, she brought his hand to her breasts. He curled his fingertips into her flesh, weighing, massaging, shaping to fit his palms. He caressed her nipples with his thumbs, strumming them, bringing them to life in aching little bursts of pleasure. At each downward stroke of her hips, his pelvis rose to meet her, pressing himself deeper into her heat, but leaving her to set the pace.

He lifted his head and suckled, hard. The thrill shot all the way to her centre. Little quivers, deep earth-quakes of passion drove her to find completion. Her body hummed with tension. 'Garrick.'

'Let go, darling.'

He touched where they joined, at the sensitive spot above where he entered her body, pressing and circling with his thumb. A sensation like nothing else, pleasure and sweet, sweet pain, unbearable.

'Oh, yes,' she said. The tension inside her vibrated, the breaking point just out of reach.

'Harder?'

'Faster.'

By increasing the tempo, he brought her to new

heights. The world narrowed to one arching stretch of pleasure.

She flew apart. Burst in glorious quivers of delicious pleasure. He groaned and withdrew, spilling his seed into the sheets while her own shudders went on and on.

He rolled on his side and kissed her forehead, the corner of her mouth, her throat, a delicate brush of his lips against her breast.

'You were glorious,' he said. 'Thank you.'

She lay in his arms with her skin cooling and tears a blink away. Loss of what might have been as real as the death of a loved one.

'Your hunger was great,' he said into her hair.

Before, he had always been the driving force in their lovemaking.

'Yes,' she whispered. 'It…has been a long time. But not for you, I think.' She couldn't help the little knife of jealousy.

'You have an itch. You scratch it.'

An itch. Well, she should have expected no more. 'William always said you were an unprincipled wretch.'

'William.' He rolled away, flung the sheet back and stood up, his bare flanks lean and muscled. She repressed an urge to lean out and caress the lovely firm rounded flesh.

'I did offer marriage,' he said. 'You chose otherwise.' He shrugged, a lift of broad shoulders. 'You would have had my name, my title. What more did you want?'

A declaration of love? Would it have made any difference? She'd made so many wrong decisions that summer, caused untold harm. Now was not the time to open old wounds. And yet he deserved an answer. She swallowed. 'I could not abandon my sister.'

His back stiffened, then he picked his shirt up from the floor and pulled it over his head. 'Admit it. You were afraid.' He continued to dress, his focus entirely on his articles of clothing, as if her answer made no difference.

She slipped out of her side of the bed. She drew on her chemise and tied the bow at the neck. 'Afraid?'

He turned to look over his shoulder. 'Of me. Of what I might do.'

'It wasn't like that.' She struggled with the laces of her stays at her back. 'I made a promise.'

'And so you made your choice. And here you are once more, the sacrificial lamb.' He strolled to the mirror over the mantel and in swift, sure movements tied his cravat. 'What about you, Ellie? When will you choose you?' He laughed, a short mirthless crack. 'Please. Don't answer. I don't want to know. Just get the letter and you can forget me, and go back to your safe little life.'

He had changed. She really didn't know him any longer. But he was right about her life. It was little. And it was all she had left. 'Take me home.'

Garrick glanced at the clock. A flash of concern crossed his face. 'Yes, you should leave now. My friend will be home soon.'

He hurried her into the sitting room, picking up her cloak, shoving her bonnet and veil into her hand, clearly wishing her gone. She'd lost him. So quickly. She could see it in his distant expression. Her heart sank.

What had she expected? That he would renew his offer of marriage after a brief encounter? He was using her to get what he wanted, the way she had used him. Mayhap, it served her right.

He opened the door and she followed him out of the chamber.

In the hallway, a footman was in the process of opening the front door.

Garrick cursed under his breath as a rather bosky young gentleman and a scantily dressed woman stepped over the threshold. He handed his cane to the waiting lackey.

Ellie gasped and pulled up her hood.

'Morning, Beauworth,' he said, grinning beneath his fair moustache. 'Finished gambling a bit early. Pleasant night, I assume?' His glance shifted to Ellie and he bowed unsteadily. 'Lady Eleanor.'

Her stomach dropped away in a rush. Once more, impetuosity had led her to ruin and this time she'd well and truly stepped over the brink.

She lifted her chin. 'Lord Goring.'

Chapter Eleven

What had she done? Alone in the carriage, Eleanor wanted to bang her head against a wall or throw herself beneath the rumbling wheels. Years she'd spent making sure not a breath of scandal besmirched her name. And now this.

Impetuosity.

It had got her into trouble in her youth and here she was again, acting without thinking. Only this time her reputation would never recover. A little hot rush of something naughty sang in her veins. Since she was ruined, why not go the whole hog and finish out her bargain with Garrick? The mere idea of it made her feel hot and breathless.

Oh, yes, and ruin Sissy's chances of making a good marriage. She couldn't do it. She'd have to retire to the country in disgrace. She struck the cushioned seat with her fist. Idiot.

After swearing she'd never do anything rash again, here she was, a fallen woman. And it was all her own doing.

When the carriage pulled up to her front door, Garrick helped her down and escorted her up the steps without a word. She scrabbled in her reticule for the key.

'What the devil!' William's voice from behind her.

Heart tripping, Eleanor whirled around. Garrick's hand gripped her elbow, whether for support or to stop her from fleeing she couldn't be sure.

William bounded out of a hackney carriage wearing a scarlet uniform. Open-mouthed, shocked, confused, Eleanor watched him toss a handful of coins at the driver and limp across the footpath to stand at the bottom of the steps.

He glared up at Garrick. 'You bastard.' His voice sounded choked.

'I believe my lineage is as impeccable as yours.' Garrick moved closer to her as William's scowl deepened. 'Len, for God's sake, get inside before someone sees you.'

'It's too late,' she said, surprised how calm she sounded, how matter of fact, in the face of his rage.

Garrick's eyebrows shot up. He looked startled, even a little impressed. Had he expected her to lie?

William turned to Garrick. 'You'll meet me for this. In an hour in Green Park. It's all the time I have before I leave.'

Dread curdled her stomach. 'William, why are you in uniform?'

His lip curled. 'Because my country needs all the help she can get with traitors like this in our midst.'

'William, you can't. You have duties, responsibilities.'

His cheeks flamed. 'So do you, but you don't let them stop you.' He swung back to Garrick, his hand on his sabre hilt. 'Name your seconds, sir, or be named for a coward.'

Garrick looked down his nose. 'You've waited a

long time for this, haven't you, Castlefield? It's true what they say, then—revenge is best served cold.'

Eleanor grabbed her brother's arm. 'William, no! I went with him willingly.'

'Damn it, Len. Why?'

Garrick's smiled, cruel, taunting. 'Because she wanted some fun for a change.'

William lunged at him, fists flying. Garrick blocked his wild blows, captured his wrist.

Eleanor wormed her way between them.

'Stop it! It's bad enough that you might be killed by the French, but to risk death in a duel is nonsense. I have no virtue to defend.'

'A man who sends a woman to fight his battles is unlikely to fall victim to a French bullet,' Garrick said, releasing William's hand and stepping back.

William's face drained of colour. 'A traitor like you is more likely to shoot a man in the back.'

Eleanor had the hysterical urge to laugh. They were like male dogs, stiff-legged, hackles raised, circling each other. The two men that she loved most in the world hated each other.

William pushed her towards the door. 'You and Sissy are going home. Go inside and pack. I'll decide what to do when I return, but believe me, if this gets out, you will never again be accepted by the *ton*. Let us hope your behaviour hasn't ruined Sissy. As for you, you cur, damned well name your seconds.'

'It will be my pleasure,' Garrick said with a feral smile.

'No!' She clutched at William. 'I will not allow you to fight a duel over me.'

Garrick looked down at her, a glimmer of something strange in his eyes—yearning, or devilment? 'If you want to put a stop to this, marry me.'

She gaped at him.

'You will never come near this family again if you marry this murdering, traitorous cur,' William said.

Garrick stood silent, his face a mask.

William looked equally grim.

The painful truth kicked her in the stomach like a flying hoof, sending her heart into a runaway gallop. She couldn't breathe. She couldn't move. This was her last chance.

'Yes,' she said. 'I will.'

Face blank, Garrick stared at her. She'd called his bluff. He hadn't meant it. He was posturing, taunting William.

'Len.' William's voice was hoarse. 'Don't make it any worse, for God's sake.'

'I think it's best, William.'

He turned his back. 'Go, then, and be damned to the pair of you.'

'Garrick wants Piggot's letter,' she said.

His shoulders shook, but he did not turn around. 'He can go to hell.'

'Let me say goodbye to Sissy, then.'

'Leave, Eleanor. Now.'

Eleanor stumbled down the steps, held up by Garrick's strong arm.

'Ellie, don't let him see you cry,' he whispered fiercely in her ear. She pulled herself upright and held her head high.

'That's my brave Lady Moonlight,' he said softly as he handed her back into his coach.

Beside Garrick, in front of the altar of St Mary's in the City of London, Eleanor's heart seemed determined to make a quick escape. Was it fear or joy making it beat so hard? Perhaps both. Behind them stood Lieutenant Dan Smith, Joshua Nidd and Johnson the coachman, and rows of empty pews. Eleanor wore the gown she'd worn the previous evening.

The vicar perused the special licence. 'Everything seems in order.'

The sound of the church door opening interrupted the hushed solemnity. Garrick signalled impatiently for the man to go on, but Dan held up a restraining hand. Boot heels echoing, the young officer walked back to greet the latecomer.

Curious, Eleanor turned. A slight figure in a peach gown and green spencer hurried up the aisle on the Lieutenant's arm.

'Cecilia?'

'What the deuce?' Garrick said, looking beyond her, as if expecting someone else.

Cecilia brushed a dark curl off her shoulder. 'William forbade me to come. I left as soon as he went out.' She handed Eleanor a bouquet of silk flowers. 'I thought you might need these.' She looked accusingly at Garrick, who merely raised a dark arching eyebrow and turned back to the minister.

To Eleanor, the next few minutes passed in a blur, but throughout the ceremony she clung to Garrick, her lifeline in a storm-tossed sea while the necessary words were spoken.

He, on the other hand, seemed preoccupied, impatient for the conclusion, speaking his words crisply and clearly, tensing when she spoke hers. Considerate, and gentle when he kissed her, bland as he received the well wishes of those present, even generous as he hugged Cecilia and called her his *chère* sister, he clearly wished it over. Was he already regretting his hasty offer?

Eleanor had a strange sense of foreboding, when she should have been happy.

The moment the vicar sprinkled sand on their signatures in the register, Garrick hurried her down the aisle with his hand in the small of her back, almost pushing her into the carriage when she would have lingered with Sissy at the steps.

He turned to clasp the Lieutenant's hand. Garrick clapped a hand to the young man's shoulder. A look of regret passed between them. This was more than just a casual parting. The thought stuck her like a blow.

Garrick was leaving. Despite their marriage he was still going to France. And soon. Her stomach roiled as if the lifeline had snapped and all hope of rescue was disappearing into the distance. Somehow she had to stop him.

'Take Lady Cecelia home, Dan,' Garrick ordered, then climbed into the carriage.

Married. Garrick eyed his lovely wife on the opposite carriage seat. She smiled at him tentatively. He wanted to smile back, to pull her on to his lap, to bury his face in her hair and inhale her sweet perfume, when what he must do was get ready to leave. And he was going to have to tell her.

The carriage pulled up outside the door to Beauworth House. 'Here we are,' he said to fill the awkward silence when they'd never been short of conversation.

He handed his bride down. His bride? The beautiful English rose he'd thought he'd lost. But she'd married him to save her brother and her reputation. Would she constantly remind him of her sacrifice, or would she be content? If they never learned the truth about his mother's death, would she fear him? Hell, if she didn't she'd be a fool.

And yet she'd married him. Trusted him with her body and soul. He felt humbled and very afraid.

She peeked up at him, looking more nervous than she'd been last night, when she ought to have been terrified witless. A need to protect cut a swathe through his determination to remain uninvolved. He swept her up in his arms, bearing his burden with pride. It was what bridegrooms were supposed to do on their wedding day. He liked the way she clung around his neck, the weight of her, the curve of her waist, the bend of her knee, the glimpse of slender ankles when he glanced down to mount the steps to his open front door.

'This is your home now,' he said, putting her down when he wanted to keep her in his arms and run straight upstairs. 'Order it as you will.'

He stepped away while the butler relieved her of her outer raiment, the damned cloak she'd worn the night before, and beneath it the pale blue gown. He'd like to see her dressed in nothing but satins and silks in shades of gold and sapphire. Hell, he'd like to see her naked.

'Dinner is served, my lord,' the butler said.

'No point in waiting,' Garrick said. 'Unless you feel the need to freshen up.'

She shook her head.

'Good.' He held out his arm. He escorted her into the panelled dining room, with its twenty-foot table and two places set at one end.

'Will Lieutenant Smith not be joining us?' she asked, hesitantly.

The tiny hesitation scoured his heart. He could not allow her to wound him again, not with all that was at stake. 'Afraid to be alone with me, Ellie? Do you think I will devour you instead of the meal?'

At that she smiled, a glorious lightening of her beautiful face, and the band around his chest eased.

'Of course not,' she said. The butler placed several platters on the table, filled their glasses with red wine, then retreated to stand silent at the wall.

Garrick filled her plate with slices of roast duck, an assortment of vegetables and a slice of beef pie. They addressed themselves to the dinner. Or rather she pushed the food around on her plate, while he drank wine. After ten minutes of utter silence, he waved the butler away. The door closed softly behind him.

'What is the matter, Ellie?'

She bit her bottom lip, then raised her gaze to his face, her eyes swirling with shadows. 'I hope you don't regret...' she waved her fork as if words failed her '...this. Us.' A tinge of colour stained her cheekbones.

What had he hoped for? A declaration that her marriage to him was more than a saving of face? He leaned back, keeping his voice cool. 'To be honest with you, I had not thought of marriage at all. My life is already full.'

She responded with a lift of her chin. Proud and heartbreakingly vulnerable. He found himself wanting to kiss her. But he wasn't going to humble himself before the one woman with the power to bring him to his knees. Not again.

'Then I do hope I won't be in the way,' she said in bright, brittle tones. 'After all, it is no business of a wife's what a man does for entertainment.' She inspected the fruit centrepiece, as if expecting maggots to crawl out of it. 'I do not ask you to change.'

Bloody hell. So this is how she thought they would go on. 'How understanding, *ma belle mie.*'

Her eyes flashed, but she presented an innocent

smile. 'I assume, of course, that I shall have the same level of freedom.'

So, she would once more cross swords with him. This was more the Ellie he knew, rather than the crushed little figure who had stood at his side in church. But he didn't have time for games. 'Not at all.'

Her hand gripped her knife, as if she contemplated thrusting it into his anatomy. Then her shoulders relaxed and she smiled as if butter wouldn't melt in her mouth, the little witch. 'La, sir, shouldn't what is sauce for the gander be also sauce for the goose?'

His back teeth ground together. He knew her little games too well. She thought to keep him in England with threats of infidelity. God, he'd always admired her spirit, but in this she'd be disillusioned. He forced a smile and inclined his head. 'I see.'

Her disappointment, her hurt, flashed in her eyes, quickly hidden. It was wicked of him to be pleased, but then she should know better than to play her tricks off on him.

He pushed to his feet and moved to stand behind her. 'Perhaps I need to remind you that you are mine, *chérie*.' He placed his hands under her elbows, bringing her to her feet, unreasonably pleased when she didn't resist. He kicked the chair out of the way and spun her around to face him. Her gaze searched his face. Looking for what? His surrender? If he had any sense, he'd put her across his knee and spank her bottom. Lust flared at the thought.

Her eyes widened as if she had read his thoughts. He thought he might drown in their brilliant silver depths.

He had his orders. Dover tonight, France in the morning. In the time he had available, he wanted her settled and secure, even if he could not ease her fears.

He didn't want her throwing herself at another man in a fit of rebellion.

He bent his head and kissed her lips. She stiffened and he smiled. She would not resist him for long, she never did. He kissed her gently, a whispering brush of lips, a flicker of tongue. Her breathing shortened to little gasps, her hand came to his shoulder, she pressed her mouth against his and parted her lips. Oh, yes. His woman. His love.

He picked her up, so light, a creature of air and light and liquid silver who would slip through his fingers if he wasn't careful. He carried her upstairs to his bed. He did not know where his next meal was coming from once he left here, but the next hour would be food for his soul. And he would feast.

Overwhelmed by languor, Eleanor barely realised he was out of bed and dressing. Their lovemaking had been wild, almost desperate. Its intensity had left her limp and replete. Her eyes slid open as she heard movement beyond the bed.

He wore his usual black and his face looked bleak, as if he faced an unpleasant duty. Her heart sank. He was leaving. If the threat of her cuckolding him was not enough to keep him at her side, perhaps another weapon would work.

She smiled and reached out. 'It is too early. Come back to bed.'

'I didn't mean to disturb you.' He leaned over her and kissed her almost absently. 'I will return.' He moved towards the door.

'It is dark.' Panic laced her voice, but she didn't care. 'Stay until morning at least.'

'I'm sorry.' He turned the handle.

He did sound sorry. A small victory. 'You are going to France, aren't you?' she said, her voice rising, sounding shrill to her own ears. 'It is true what they say? You have changed your allegiance?'

He didn't look at her. Just opened the door. Finally he spoke in flat tones. 'I will not tolerate another man in your bed, Eleanor. If you so much as look at a man, I will kill him. You do understand, don't you?'

He shut the door behind him.

A hysterical laugh escaped her. She pressed the back of her hand to her mouth. As if she would ever want anyone else. How little he understood. Less than a day married and he'd left.

The tightness in her chest made it hard to breathe. If he really was a spy and he was caught, he would be shot.

A tear slipped over her lower lashes and made its way down her cheek. She swiped it away.

No, she would not believe such a thing of him. Betraying his country was dishonourable, and whatever Garrick was, he had never been that.

Wherever he was going, he had to return, because she hadn't said goodbye.

Waiting in the drawing room for Sissy to call as usual, Eleanor pressed her hand flat to her stomach. She still could not believe it. She and Garrick has made a baby on their final night together. After all the years of assuming she would never marry, she was going to be a mother. How she longed for Garrick to share her joy.

A contentment filled her, the thought of the future a bright shining horizon. Her and Garrick and their babe.

This news would bring him home now the war was over. Napoleon was finally defeated at Waterloo. All the reports spoke of a great victory.

Nidd knocked on the door. 'Lady Hadley,' he announced in solemn tones, as if Sissy did not arrive at the same time every day. Bless her, she'd ignored William's admonition to stay away and had visited almost daily these past few weeks.

'Have the papers arrived yet, Nidd?' Sissy asked with a jaunty smile.

Poor old Nidd could not resist her. 'I'll bring them directly, my lady.' He scuttled away.

'Len, don't think of getting up,' Sissy said, leaning over her. 'You need to be careful in your condition.'

'I'm not an invalid,' Eleanor said, kissing the soft cheek presented at her level.

A moment later, Nidd returned with a freshly ironed newspaper. '*The Times,* my lady,' Nidd said, offering it to Eleanor.

Sissy whisked it out of his hand. 'Thank you.'

'Will that be all, my lady?' Nidd asked.

'Tea, please, Nidd. And cake. And perhaps some of those cucumber sandwiches Cook makes.' The butler disappeared.

'Good Lord, Len, it is barely ten o'clock. You can't have finished breakfast more than an hour ago.'

'I feel nauseous if I don't eat,' Eleanor said.

'Oh, poor you. It must be simply dreadful.'

Eleanor smiled at her sister. 'No. It is wonderful.'

With much rattling and cursing, Sissy opened the paper. Everyone in London was doing it. Looking at the endless lists of the fallen. There was not a family among the *ton* who had not lost a brother, a son or a close friend.

Dark head bent over the paper, Sissy ran her finger down the columns of names. Her finger stopped its downward course a few lines down. She looked away, blinking, as if trying to clear her sight.

Eleanor snatched the sheet from her hand.

'Captain Lord Castlefield,' she read slowly. 'Missing.'

Sissy flung herself at Eleanor's chest, hugged her tight. 'Missing. It says missing, not dead.'

Eleanor took a deep breath, tried to keep the shake from her voice. 'He might well be wounded and not yet recognised.' Surely she would know if her twin was dead? A breath seemed to catch on a lump in her throat. So many of those listed as missing at the beginning of the week had more recently been reported among the dead. And what about Garrick? There had been no word. No information about those killed or wounded on the French side.

'I will write to Captain Smith,' Cecilia said, her eyes glistening with tears. 'He will search the hospitals.' She ran to the writing table.

Dan Smith, now a captain, had sent word immediately after the battle by way of a friend ordered to London with dispatches.

'Good idea,' Eleanor said, though why Captain Smith, so vilified by her brother, would feel obligated to seek him out wasn't clear. And what if he found him dead? She gulped a painful breath. 'Cecilia, we must prepare for the worst.'

Sissy looked up from sharpening her pen. 'No. William is all right. He has to be. And your Marquess, too.'

Eleanor swallowed what felt like a handful of pins. 'I am sure you are right.'

If that was so, why hadn't she heard? She held her hands to her waist for a second. Would his child ever see its father?

A week later, Sissy dashed into her drawing room, laughing and crying at once and waving a letter. 'He's safe! Oh, Len, William is safe. I received a letter from him this morning. He was unconscious for a while, but is recovered now. Captain Smith found him in a field hospital with other men from his regiment. They were at Hougoumont. Here, see for yourself.' She pressed the crumpled paper into Eleanor's hand.

Relief washed through her in a torrent. As Eleanor read William's letter, tears stole down her face, for his last lines touched her deeply.

Tell Len I send my love. I have had a great deal of time to think, lying here in hospital, with so many other good and brave fellows dying around me. I could not have borne it if I had left this world without a chance to beg her forgiveness. I have enclosed a letter for her eyes only.

'See,' Cecilia said triumphantly, 'I knew he could not be angry at you forever.' Four years had felt like a lifetime. 'Did you see where he mentioned Captain Smith? Not a word of censure. In fact, he says he's a good sort of chap and very brave. Oh, Len, everything is going to be all right.'

William sounded like a changed man. Eleanor smiled at her sister through her tears. 'I do hope so,' she whispered. 'Sissy, is there another letter for me?'

'Oh, yes, I'm so sorry, I almost forgot.' She pulled out a fold of paper from her reticule. While Sissy once more pored over the part of William's letter that spoke of Captain Smith, Eleanor went to the window where the light was better. Fingers trembling, she broke the seal. Her heart felt too large for her chest. William had forgiven her.

My Dearest Len,

I am sorry to be the bearer of bad tidings, but I feel it is my duty. One of the men who died here yesterday told me he saw Beauworth just before the battle started.

He had been captured by a company of Dutch. He was being held at their headquarters. No doubt, by now he has been executed.

A pain spasmed in her chest. She clutched her throat. Her vision blurred. She couldn't breathe. The paper shook so hard, she couldn't make out the words. She wiped her eyes with her handkerchief and forced herself to read on.

I am so sorry. But I feel obliged to unload my burdens and tell the truth at last. Beauworth was innocent of any crime against his mother. Le Clere was her murderer. I have Piggot's letter in my safe at Castlefield explaining it all. I picked it up and read it the day of the ransom and have kept it ever since. Dishonourable, I know.

When I read of his exoneration, I couldn't stand to think of him getting away with what he did to you. And, God help me, to me. Though I now know the truth of that, too, from young Smith. I can only blame it on some sort of madness. It has haunted me every day since. Part of the reason I returned to my regiment. A sort of atonement, I think.

To my shame, I believe my vengeful actions drove Beauworth into the arms of the French. I can only beg your forgiveness. I pray you will find it in your heart, though I cannot blame you if you turn away.

No matter what, I will take care of you always, if you will allow. Your loving brother, William.

Eleanor stared at the paper. Garrick. Dead. What William had done paled in comparison. The tears that had flowed so freely at the miraculous news of William's survival dried on her cheeks. Her mind seemed numb. The words *shot as a spy* reverberated like an echo in an empty vessel. He would never see his child.

Outside, the sun shone brightly on the garden in the centre of the square; inside, the house seemed to be full of fog. She couldn't see or feel, or hear. She wasn't even sure she was breathing. She didn't want to breathe.

Her eyes burned. She'd sent her man off to war and never once told him she loved him.

'What did William say?' Somehow Sissy's voice reached through the void. She held out the paper without looking at Sissy's face. If she saw sympathy, she might start to scream.

Her grip was so tight on the paper, Sissy had to force open her fingers.

'Oh, no!' Sissy's cry of anguish came from a great distance, then the floor shifted and a strange darkness descended. It was fitting that the world should be dark, she thought, as she watched the floor come up to meet her.

The months were passing and Eleanor moved through her life like a stranger. Only the child growing in her body held any real interest. This morning, as usual, she sat in her drawing room, waiting for Sissy to call and see how she did. No doubt Sissy would report on her progress to William, whose last letter had been full of news of Paris under the allied army of occupation. He had sounded cheerful and anxious to return home as soon as Wellington agreed to release him from his duties. While their reconciliation by letter had been wonderful, many things remained unsaid between them. It would be good to finally clear the air once he returned home.

Nidd knocked at the door. 'My lady?'

'Yes, Nidd, what is it?' She spoke gently. The old Yorkshire man looked thinner and more like a skeleton than ever. The loss of the Marquess had been difficult for all of the Beauworth servants.

'There's a man at the servants' door, said he was sent by Captain Smith to help Johnson in the stables. Is it all right if I give him your permission?'

This was the third unemployed soldier Dan Smith had sent. Starving men who had served with the Marquess in the Peninsula. Dan had insisted Garrick would want her to help them. Eleanor trusted Captain Smith, but she had found the other two men rather frightening. They were large and rough and clearly not used to serving in a gentleman's establishment. Once or twice she had found them lounging around in doorways or outside the stables with seemingly nothing to do.

'Perhaps I will speak to him first.' She followed him back to the kitchen.

Slouched against the doorpost, Garrick had to hold himself back when Ellie entered the kitchen. Would she know him, disguised as he was? He'd spent the last four days perfecting his disguise while his men, with Dan's help, infiltrated her house.

God, he'd missed her. She looked pale. Too thin, despite her blooming body. He longed to put his arms around her, hold her close, feel that soft body melding with his, run his hand over the soft swell of her belly full with their child. His child. Months he'd been without her, praying she'd wait for him. Thoughts of her had kept him alive during some of the worst days of his life.

Forcing himself to play his part, he pushed away from the wall. 'Look busy. 'Ere comes 'er ladyship,' he said in a hoarse voice straight from London's gutters.

'Let's have a little more respect from you, my lad,' Nidd said. 'This is the Marchioness of Beauworth. Bill Dodds, my lady.'

Garrick gave her a sloppy salute and kept his gaze fixed on the floor, his shoulders hunched. The patch he wore over one eye covered most of one side of his face and obscured his vision. The growth on his chin formed a straggling beard and his hair, cut short by Dan, he knew showed patches of white skin.

God, he hoped she wouldn't know him. It would ruin all his plans. He shambled across the room and made an awkward bow.

'Captain Smith suggests you help in the stables. What knowledge have you of horses?' She sounded tense, almost afraid. He didn't blame her. He cut a dreadful appearance.

He kept his one eye fixed on the cap he twisted in hands he'd roughened by working in the stables at Horse Guards. 'I looked after 'orses for the cavalry, yer ladyship.'

'You are fit enough for these tasks?' She gazed at his leg, which he favoured, giving an impression of an injury and reducing his height by leaning heavily on his hip.

'Aye, milady.'

She peered at his face, as if looking for someone she knew.

Dammit. For all his efforts, Ellie was going to see straight through the filth. God, he loved this woman.

He coughed, a harsh, chest-racking sound that bent him double. He hawked and looked around for somewhere to spit and decided on the sink.

With a grimace, she turned her face away. He hated that his ploy had succeeded so well she would not look at him. But he kept on coughing.

'Very well, report to Mr Johnson,' she said.

He breathed a sigh of relief. Le Clere might strike at any moment, but he would have to go through Garrick and his men to get to Ellie.

Without glancing at her face, he touched his forelock and shuffled out of the door. He sensed her staring at his back. He'd have to be very careful around his clever wife.

Chapter Twelve

A day or so later the weather turned fine and Eleanor decided to drive out in her carriage. She was a little surprised to see the scruffy Dodds on the driver's box when she stepped out of the door. She frowned. 'Where is Johnson?'

''E's got a touch of the rumytism, milady,' the shabby Bill Dodds explained.

Strangely, Johnson had spoken highly of Dodds's competence, despite her initial misgivings, and so she had left things alone. 'Well, Dodds, if you are going to drive my carriage, I would appreciate it if you would borrow Johnson's coat.'

'Er, yes, milady. Thing is, it don't fit.'

Eleanor grimaced. The man was far taller than Johnson, despite his slouch, and broader across the shoulders. 'Wait here.'

She returned with the oldest of Garrick's greatcoats. 'See if this fits.'

It could have been made for the man, she thought, as he shrugged himself into it.

'Thank you, milady. Right kind o' ye.' He grinned,

a flash of white teeth through the thick beard. A strange sense of recognition flooded through her. He turned away quickly, fiddling with the reins.

She was imagining things. Every tall man with dark hair on the street made her heart jump. She had stopped running after them, but her heart still gave a hopeful little lurch.

She stepped into the carriage. The horses trotted sedately through the traffic under the firm control of Bill Dodds and it wasn't long before they turned into Hyde Park. It was too early for the *ton* to be much in evidence. Some fresh air and a spot of exercise would do her good. Tired of the way everyone, from Sissy to Nidd, fussed because she was increasing, she longed for a rest from their anxious faces and solicitous words.

She tapped the overhead door with the handle of her parasol. It opened. 'Pull over, Dodds. I'm going to walk.'

'I don' know, milady. Better if'n you stay with the carriage.'

'Oh, for goodness' sake. Are you going to start now?'

He muttered an apology and stopped the carriage. He helped her down and stepped back quickly. There was something almost guilty about the way he refused to meet her gaze. She shook off her discomfort. The man was competent, that was all that mattered.

'I will be back within a half-hour. Feel free to walk the horses if needed.'

She was aware of the gleaming dark eye that followed her as she strolled away. She should not have been so fierce. It was their respect for the Marquess making them all so attentive. Given the rumours about Garrick, she was grateful for that respect.

Her spleen relieved by a brisk walk, she sat down on a stone seat beside the lake and watched the ducks dabble. She would bring the baby here. Garrick would have approved.

What would he have thought, had he known she was with child? Would he have left for France? She couldn't help a wry little smile, because she didn't doubt it for a moment. But she did wish she'd found the courage to tell him her true feelings. If they'd had more time, they might have rediscovered the joy they'd shared so briefly. In time, perhaps she would have found in him the handsome Marquess with warm brown eyes and wicked smile with whom she had fallen in love.

She would never know.

The pain in her chest rose into her throat in a hot, hard lump. Damn. She blinked back the watery veil obliterating the view.

''Scuse me, miss.' She gazed through the mist at the urchin standing in front of her. The boy seemed ill-at-ease and out of breath. 'You the Marchingness of Bosworth?'

She frowned. 'What of it, child?'

'I got a 'portant message. But yer gotta promise not to tell.' The ragamuffin shifted from foot to foot as if on the verge of flight.

Her heart picked up speed. She desperately tried to quell the rush of hope. It was foolish to hope. And yet she'd received no official confirmation of Garrick's death and it was always there, catching her unawares, like a candle that refused to be snuffed. 'I promise.'

''Ere.' The boy flung a dirty scrap of paper at her and dashed away.

Eleanor uncrumpled the paper. A bold scrawl emblazoned the page.

Meet me tonight after Midnight
at the corner of the Square.
B.

B. meaning Beauworth? It would be like Garrick to issue such a command. Who else could it be? Garrick was alive. Hands shaking, she stared at the note. She pressed it to her lips, inhaled the scent of ink. Her eyes burned and blurred. What? Crying? Now was not the time for tears. Think. He must be in danger if he couldn't come openly to his house. So she would go to him.

She tucked the note into her reticule. Alive. She leapt to her feet, her heart so light it could have carried her away on a breeze.

What would she wear? What would she say? Would he ask her to go with him? She headed back for her carriage and home. Would he be happy about their child? No matter what his circumstances, she would go with him this time. Even if it meant flight to the ends of the earth, if he asked. She pushed a surge of fear aside. When she reached the carriage, Dodds had a strange look on his face. If she'd hadn't known better, she might have thought it was utter relief.

The rest of the day passed far too slowly, the clock's hands creeping minute by minute until she thought her head would burst. After dinner, she went upstairs to her chamber, and after sending her maid away, changed into a practical walking gown, dressing her hair in a simple knot. If they were going to be on the run, the less fuss the better. Since he'd not asked her to bring anything, she decided not to pack a valise in case there wasn't room. On the other hand, he might be in need of money, so she stuffed her reticule with bills. What else? She paced in front of the hearth. A weapon?

She ran to the dressing room and opened her trunk to find the only thing she'd kept from her madcap youth in the bottom. Her sword.

She drew it part way from the scabbard. The blade caught the light of her candle with a wicked glint. As instructed by her father, she'd cleaned it and oiled it faithfully at regular intervals. Father had been right. You never knew when a sword might come in useful.

A woman with a sword wasn't exactly a common sight. She rummaged through her clothes' press and found a thick woollen cloak. She wrapped the sword and scabbard in the folds of the cloak and stood in front of her mirror. If she carried it like so, tucked under her arm parallel with her body beneath the cloak, it should pass unnoticed. After all, no one expected a woman to carry such a weapon.

Unable to think of anything else, she sat down to wait.

It was the most horrid hour she'd ever spent, but finally the clock on the mantel chimed twelve and she slipped downstairs and opened the front door, feeling a little bit like Cinderella. Garrick was waiting. She hugged the thought close.

What if he took her with him tonight? Sissy and William might never know what had become of her. It didn't bear thinking about. She took a deep breath.

Deal with one problem at a time. First she had to see Garrick. Find out what was happening. Her palms damp and her heart racing, she stepped out of the house and into the dark street.

Dark shadows loomed between the houses and beneath the trees in the middle of the square, but nothing seemed out of the ordinary. Her footsteps a light tap on the flagstones, the scent of coal fires in her nostrils, she stepped out briskly.

'Who's that?' Garrick, lounging against the side of the house, prodded his companion.

'I dunno. One the maids, I 'spose. The little saucy one, most likely. She slips out sometimes to visit her fella.'

'She ought to be careful, walking the streets at this time of night.' Garrick limped out on to the footpath, careful to avoid the light cast by the streetlamp. The maid paused at the curb, then crossed the street under a light. His breath hissed between his teeth. 'What the devil? Fetch my horse. Now.'

He dashed to the other side of the street, maintaining his halting gait and staying close to the park's iron railings where the shadows were deepest. He turned the corner of the square in time to see the woman step into a waiting hackney. The driver whipped up the horses as soon as the door closed.

Gut in a knot, he ran back. Abandoning stealth in favour of speed, he shouted orders as he ran for his horse. 'You, follow me. You, take this message to the Captain. Damn the woman. And damn Le Clere.'

The faces of his men looked tense as they hurried to do his bidding.

* * *

When the horses drew up at an inn somewhere near Hampstead Heath, Eleanor thought, she opened the door and jumped down.

The driver clambered down and waved her towards the entrance of a small, mean-looking place with moss-covered thatch and grimy windows. 'After you, my lady.'

The voice struck a chord of memory and she stared at his face. A face she only saw in her nightmares. 'Matthews?'

'I didn't think you would recognise me, my lady, after all this time.' He grinned.

A sick feeling churned in her stomach. Why would Matthews be helping Garrick? She hesitated. No. She would not turn away again. There must be some reasonable explanation.

'Where is my husband?'

'In there.' He jerked his head at the open door of the inn.

Eleanor strode into the taproom with Matthews close behind. The room was empty and Eleanor turned to him with raised brows, only to find the man holding a pistol. She stepped back. 'What does this mean?'

'It means, my lady,' said a hoarse voice from behind her, 'you have very kindly assisted me in my quest.'

She turned slowly and took stock of the man who had entered the room through another door. He was old and so bent over he was forced to look sideways up at her. Deep lines etched his heavily jowelled face below a shock of pure white hair.

Eleanor had never seen him before. 'Where is the Marquess?'

'Dead.'

Eleanor's knees weakened. The room seemed to

spin. She clung to the back of a chair. 'No! I received a note.'

'Oh, yes. A note. *Meet me tonight after Midnight at the corner of the Square.*' The old man cackled. The sound pierced her heart like knives.

'Really, my lady, do you think my traitorous nephew would be foolish enough to walk into England for you, even if he lived? British spies watch you every minute in case he returns. You didn't tell anyone where you were going, did you?' He glanced at the other man. 'Matthews, you are sure you were not followed?'

'No, sir, nary a sign or a peep.'

This twisted gnome was Duncan Le Clere. She recognised his cold eyes. Her heart beat became erratic. He'd tricked her. Garrick was dead. An ache spread through her chest. Cruel man to raise her hopes, then shatter them with a single word. She wanted to curl into a ball. To shut out the world. To let the darkness dancing at the edge of her vision descend. But she couldn't, for the sake of the child. Garrick's babe.

'Why?' she whispered, her voice breaking.

'Please be seated, my lady.' He waved towards one of the chairs. 'You carry his child, do you not?'

Eleanor put one hand protectively over her belly and held her ground. 'What concern is it of yours?'

'I want it. And I want a certain letter only you can get for me.'

The whole thing became clear. What a fool she'd been. She should have guessed. 'I see.'

His piercing dark eyes glittered like the eyes of a snake laid out on a rock watching a rabbit. She felt very much like a rabbit. 'You know, don't you?' he said.

She would not show her fear. 'That it proves you a

murderer? Yes.' He cocked his head on one side, his mouth twisting. Clearly the wrong thing to say. 'You cannot keep me against my will.'

'Can I not? You will be well looked after until the birth of the child. If you fail to produce an heir, there is a woman standing by with a male replacement. But you won't. Le Cleres always beget boys.'

His voice was so cold, so rational, she had no trouble believing he meant every word, mad as they sounded. She couldn't breathe. It was as if something was wrapped around her chest and was slowly squeezing all the air from her lungs. She felt dizzy. What a fool to walk into his trap. She had to do something. Her hand clenched around the scabbard hidden in the folds of her cloak. What could a sword do against a pistol? Perhaps something, if the right moment came along. She'd have to be patient. The safety of her babe depended on not making another mistake.

Le Clere grinned. 'Do what I tell you and who knows, I might let you live.' He withdrew a pistol from his pocket and cocked it. 'Matthews, have one of the men take the hackney back to London. There must be no trace. Then bring the coach around and let me know when you are ready. I will not be thwarted this time. I will have the heir in my control and this time he will be obedient.'

A shudder of horror crept down her back. Clenching the scabbard, she held herself rigid, aloof, waiting her moment.

Matthews left to do his bidding and Le Clere grinned up at Eleanor. 'You see, my lady, I amassed quite a fortune from Beauworth during the war, but Garrick managed to upset my plans.' His laugh was harsh and sounded more than a little crazed. 'I moved all my money to the Continent.' The old man's voice lowered to a mutter. 'France is ruined. I am ruined.'

The door opened with a soft click. He raised his voice, but didn't turn around. 'But what we did before, we can do again, isn't that right, Matthews?'

The door swung back. 'I'm afraid, Le Clere, that Matthews is otherwise detained.'

'Garrick.' Eleanor reeled at the sound of her husband's voice. It was really Garrick, looking like Dodds, without the patch and the limp. A sob of joy rose in her throat. She started forwards, wanting the feel of his arms around her, wanting to touch him to be certain it wasn't her imagination playing tricks.

'Hold,' Le Clere said, grabbing her. He hooked an arm around her throat. He pressed his pistol against her temple.

Garrick cursed.

Eleanor could not take her gaze from his dear face. Garrick had come home. Tears ran down her face. He was alive.

'Well, nephew,' Le Clere said with a sneer, 'I heard you were dead.'

Garrick nodded, his face grim, the lines beside his mouth deepening. 'I knew it would bring you out of whatever hole you had crawled into. I must say, though, I would never have recognised you.'

'An unlucky bullet the day you betrayed me. It hit my spine. I have not walked upright since. I should never have let you take her across the field.'

From the wild look in the old man's eye, Garrick judged him capable of anything, even the murder of an innocent woman. There was no doubt in his mind. Le Clere was quite mad.

'Drop your weapon and kneel down, Garrick.'

He should have waited for Dan, but his fears for Ellie had scrambled his wits. 'Go to hell.'

Le Clere's lips drew back in the grimace of a smile and he jammed the pistol harder against Eleanor's temple. Her repressed gasp told Garrick he'd hurt her. No more. He'd done her far too much ill already. He threw the pistol to one side and, with one hand on the arm of the chair, sank to his knees, praying his men would arrive soon.

'That's so much better.' Le Clere's grin was sly. 'I hate looking up at anyone.'

'Let her go. Your quarrel is with me.'

'But you don't understand, Garrick, she is with child. Your heir.'

He kept his face blank, despite the roar of blood in his ears. 'I know. So?'

'Sadly, you were spoiled by the time you came under my authority. I had thought that without your mother's influence, you would settle down. Hence, I disposed of her. But you proved uncontrollable. This newest addition to the Beauworth family will learn obedience. This one will know his master.'

By his own admission, this man had killed his mother. Anger raged inside him like a beast that refused to be chained. His vision narrowed. All he could see was Le Clere's leering face. He clenched his fists, ready to launch himself forwards.

Ellie. He was pointing the pistol at Ellie. Garrick took a deep breath. Then another until the beast subsided. He would not risk Ellie's life to satisfy his lust for blood.

Le Clere, watching him closely, nodded. 'Thought better of it, eh, Garrick? You always were a coward.' He shifted his aim to Garrick. 'You always tried to save your own neck. Well, it won't work this time, dear boy.'

Garrick gritted his teeth and fought for control. If he could just get Le Clere further away from Ellie, he could give the signal to his men. 'I'm not your dear boy. I never was.'

'True.' The old man grimaced. 'I must say I was shocked when I heard of your activities in France.'

Ellie fiddled with her cloak, as if looking for somewhere to lay it down.

Garrick's hackles rose. He kept his face blank and glared at his uncle. 'You know nothing of my activities.'

'No? I heard secrets exchanged hands. I sold a few myself. Had to recoup my losses somehow. Not that the bastards paid me very much.'

Ellie leaned against the back of a sofa, her free hand fussing with the cloak's folds, which looked strangely stiff. A long, dark object fell to the floor. Oh, no. She couldn't have.

'I, on the other hand, made a fortune,' Garrick said, watching his wife from the corner of his eye.

The old man leered. 'And it will all be mine.'

As Ellie shifted, Garrick blinked at the flash of steel she let him see. Blood buzzed in his ears. Damn her. If she missed, someone was going to die.

There was no stopping her, he could see it in her face. And she trusted him to follow her lead. He glared at Le Clere and made as if to rise.

The old man tightened his grip on the pistol. 'Are you so ready to die?'

Ellie let the cloak drop, the blade clutched in her fist behind the sofa. A sword against a pistol. Utter madness. But she'd done it before.

He needed to keep Le Clere looking his way. 'You whoreson. You won't get away with this.'

Le Clere took aim. 'Now then, Garrick, such language in the presence of a lady.' He sounded almost jocular.

Garrick got a firm grip on the chair. 'She is not the lady you think her.' His voice was hoarse, hating the thought of the pain she'd endure.

Le Clere grinned. 'I guessed as much.'

One quick step. Her arm came up. The hilt arced. The pistol discharged into the ceiling with a puff of smoke, a deafening roar and a rain of plaster. She threw the sword, hilt first, to Garrick.

He plucked the weapon from the air. 'She's Lady Moonlight.' He pricked Le Clere's throat before he could so much as blink, watching the trickle of blood run down his neck with supreme satisfaction.

The door sprang open. His men charged through. Ellie looked terrified. She backed against the wall, her gaze fixed on him. She must think they were Le Clere's men.

Dan clambered in through the window, pistol at the ready, his expression furious. He pointed his pistol at Le Clere and the old man put up an arm to shield his face.

'Why the hell didn't you wait?' Dan said.

'Give me a moment.' Garrick crossed the room to where Ellie stood rigid, unsure whether to kiss her or to shake her for taking such a risk. Neither seemed appropriate from the fearful expression on her face.

'You idiot,' he said instead. He lifted her hand, pulled off her cotton glove and looked at her bloody palm. 'You were lucky. I don't think you will need stitches.' He tied it up with his handkerchief.

'I'm all right, or I will be, when you tell me what is going on,' she croaked. 'Who are these men?'

Some of the men were speaking French. After what his uncle had said, no wonder she looked horrified.

'Not all Frenchmen are loyal to Napoleon. I'm sorry, *chérie,* I can't talk now. Some of Le Clere's henchmen are still on the loose. Captain Smith will see you get home.'

He turned to survey the room. Le Clere was already handcuffed. Matthews had been dragged in. But until he saw Le Clere safely to prison he would not feel easy.

'Dan,' he called out, 'take Lady Beauworth home.'

And that was it. Numb, reeling, not sure what to make of what was happening, Eleanor watched him stride coldly away. It was as if what was happening in the room gave him the excuse he needed to pull away, to keep her at a distance.

A moment later, Dan was at her side. 'I have a carriage waiting outside, my lady.'

Eleanor glanced across the room to where Garrick was issuing orders in French.

Not Napoleon's men. Was this the truth, or had Le Clere been right? Was it simply a smokescreen to ensure her compliance? And how did Captain Smith come to be involved?

The captain urged her forwards, supporting her around her shoulders, leading her to the waiting carriage. One of the recent additions to her stables jumped down from the box and opened the door. Now Garrick had accomplished his goal, heard Le Clere's admission of guilt, would he regret being trapped into marriage? He must have known about their child and yet he'd stayed away.

Which would be worse? Finding out he was a traitor, or losing him?

Captain Smith handed her into the coach and gave orders to the driver in a low voice, then he returned to speak to her through the window.

'You are quite safe now, my lady. You will be taken home.'

'But what about Garrick?' She sounded pathetic, she knew she did, but she did not care.

'He will come to you as soon as he can, he gives his word.'

His word. He gives his word. It was all that sustained her on the long drive home.

Chapter Thirteen

The case clock announced five in the morning and Eleanor pulled back the edge of the drawing-room drapes. No word from Garrick. She rubbed her arms, trying to maintain some warmth in her limbs. The fire in the hearth had died long ago.

If he was not a traitor to England, he would have revealed his presence instead of skulking in her stables for weeks on end. Or would he? She still found it hard to believe he would betray his country. Nevertheless, she had sent the scullery maid back to bed when she had come to light the fire just a few minutes ago. She didn't want the servants seeing him and talking.

If he came.

She heard a noise in the entrance hall and ran to see. Garrick was already climbing the stairs. He turned when he heard the drawing-room door open.

He had changed his clothes. His hair was still impossibly short, but the scruffy beard was gone and she had no trouble recognising her husband.

'Ellie, I didn't expect to find you awake.' He spoke

softly and came back down to her, putting his hands on her shoulders.

'You expected me to sleep?' She pushed him away.

'I thought we would talk tomorrow.' A gentle smile curved his lips, his gaze dropping to her stomach. 'You need your rest.'

'Will you be here tomorrow? For months, you let me think you were dead.' Her voice caught in her throat and she swallowed hard. 'I have to know why.'

His expression filled with doubt, then he nodded. He took her hand and led her back into the drawing room.

'It's cold in here,' he said, looking at the empty grate. 'No wonder your hands are like ice.' He sat opposite her and leaned back negligently. 'What would you like to know?'

There it was again, the withdrawal. The feeling he didn't want her involved in his life. 'Everything. Start with tonight.'

He made a sound of disgust. 'Tonight was almost a disaster. I had sworn to bring Le Clere to justice for his part in what he did to you. He admitted it all to the magistrate just now. How he made me believe I killed my mother. How he drained the estate year by year after her death.'

'The man was evil.'

He looked up as if surprised at her vehemence, then returned his gaze to the empty fire.

'I knew Le Clere would never give up, not once he heard you were with child and I was dead. I used you as bait.' He paused, as if expecting a reaction. When she said nothing, he went on.

'I persuaded Dan to get me and my men into this house so I could be close to you.' He chuckled slightly. 'I thought you had recognised me that first day, and I thanked my lucky stars for that evil cough left over from the Dutch prison. I have never seen such a look of disgust as on your face.'

He glowered. 'I almost missed you when you slipped out tonight. We had no idea you'd had contact with him. It must have been during that damnable walk in the park. I couldn't leave the horses.' He looked at her for confirmation and she nodded. 'If I hadn't known that walk of yours, the determined tilt of your chin, I might not have guessed who you were tonight.'

He frowned. 'You risked my child.' He brushed his knuckles down the line of her jaw. 'I would have been at *pointe non plus* right now if you had not stopped under the light.'

Guilt clenched her stomach. He was right. She had risked their child. She hadn't given it a thought. All she could think of was Garrick. She should have known something was wrong. Impetuosity always had been her downfall. 'Thank God you did know it was me.'

His eyebrow flew up.

'But Garrick, Le Clere said you sold secrets to the French. And those men?' The catch in her voice betrayed her efforts to appear calm. 'Who were they?'

'The two men Dan placed here are from my old regiment. Known as "sweeps", they do all of the army's dirty work. Reconnoitring, spying, cleaning up the messes left by the redcoats. The Frenchmen are friends of mine. They followed Le Clere from France and had the inn surrounded before we arrived. I thought I could handle Le Clere alone. They were waiting outside for a signal from me.'

His mouth quirked up in the cynical smile she had realised he used to hide his feelings. 'It was very nearly a bullet in my brain that brought them in on us.'

She couldn't prevent a shudder.

He looked at her as if surprised. 'Would you have cared, *mignonette?*'

'How can you ask? How did you come to be involved with these men? Frenchmen, Garrick.'

He hesitated, his eyes shuttered against her. Her heart sank. What web of lies would he spin?

'*Chérie,*' he answered, soft and low, 'these are not my secrets to tell.'

'I am your wife. If you can't trust me, there is no more to be said.' She started to rise.

'What then, *ma perle*? Will you send me away again?' He sounded bitter.

It was hopeless. She began to move away, but his low voice continued and she sank back down. He was staring at the hearth as if seeing events unfolding in the cold ashes.

'I bought a commission in a regiment after I saw you at Castlefield, as you probably know. The Ninety-Fifth. It's not one of the most glamorous regiments and the work is dangerous. It suited my mood.'

He leaned forwards, elbows on his knees. 'You know what I feared I had done.'

'You are innocent. William has the letter. I'm so sorry.'

'I know. Sissy told Dan and he told me.'

She thought he'd be pleased, but it seemed to make him sadder, more remote as if he was already lost to her. Could she blame him? After all, she had trapped him in a marriage he didn't want. She wanted to reached out, but didn't dare, kept her hands clenched in her lap.

'You saw Le Clere. That blood runs in my veins.' He looked sickened. 'I hoped I would be killed and end the damned curse. Indeed, when I first joined the regiment I cared so little for my own safety, men called me the mad Marquess.' He smiled, but there was no joy in it, just bleak satisfaction.

She shivered.

'I liked army life. The danger kept my mind off other things.'

'What things?' It was foolish to ask, and she couldn't keep the hope out of her voice.

He glanced up. 'You.' It was said so simply, without anger or accusation, that she felt his pain. She forced herself to remain still, much as she wanted to kneel at his feet and beg forgiveness.

Once more he sat silent and gathered his thoughts, staring into the past. Finally, he continued in the same low tone.

'Then the rumours started. I'd ruined a virtuous lady. Beaten a youth to within an inch of his life. They were muttered behind my back, and sometimes hinted at to my face. Slowly, my friends among my brother officers dwindled away. They believed it. No smoke without fire, eh, *chérie*?'

She winced. He would never forgive William for starting those rumours or her for believing them. How could he? If only she'd trusted her heart. 'Go on.'

'During that time my French background came to the attention of a certain man on the general's staff. You will forgive me if I do not give you his name. The fact that I had little care for my own personal safety also suited his plans. Briefly, I was recruited as a spy, but not by the French.' He smiled grimly. 'For England. I was honoured to be chosen. It was, and is, a very important task. But it has some drawbacks.' He laughed softly.

Wishing she could comfort him, Eleanor reached out. He saw her hand, but didn't take it, keeping his gaze fixed on the fireplace as if he couldn't bear to look at her face.

'It was the hardest thing I ever had to do...almost.' He gave her a look of such raw agony, she knew instinctively he was referring to the day he had walked away from Castlefield Hall. Her heart shrank painfully small. She felt his hurt with pain of her own. The pain of regret.

'I sold out. Complained I'd been passed over for promotion.' He shook his head. 'My fellow officers suspected me of more cowardice. All but Dan, poor lad, cut me dead.' This time his smile was warm.

'I became a malcontent. Half-French, bitter at England and highly placed. The perfect material for use by England's enemy. Unfortunately, I was seen in France by a captured English officer. More rumours made the rounds. Not a bad thing as a smokescreen, but if I became a pariah, I would lose my usefulness to the French. We arranged for the Prince of Wales to befriend me—after all, who would speak out against Prinny's closest companion without proof? The French were delighted with the development. The Prince thought it a great joke. Able to move freely in France, I rallied the few remaining loyalists. Some of whom you saw tonight. I still hold the rank of Major in the British army. Not that it will ever be acknowledged.'

That hurt him. She could hear it in his voice. 'Garrick, I—'

He winced and held up his hand, his face stark, his eyes clouded by inner storms. 'As a spy, I had access to many resources, here and abroad. I discovered your brother was the source of the rumours about what I had done to you. It didn't come as a surprise. I was just glad he never let fall your name. For that I would have been forced to take his life.'

The chill determination in his face sent a shiver down her back.

He took a deep breath, as if forcing himself to go on. 'Over the years, I thought about the letter's disappearance.' He laughed, a bitter, self-disparaging sound. 'I'm such a bloody romantic, I thought you'd tried to save my worthless skin by hiding it.'

She should have trusted him as her heart had demanded. Her vision blurred. 'I wish I'd thought of it.' Her voice caught.

He looked up. 'Ellie, don't, please. Let me finish. With Napoleon imprisoned on Elba, I thought the war was over. It was time to put my personal affairs in order.'

'But why were you so set on recovering the letter, if you thought it proved your guilt?'

This was the moment Garrick had feared most. He could not draw back. He had committed to telling her everything.

He hung his head. He'd thought revenge would ease the pain. All it had done was make things worse between him and Ellie.

'I sought you out with the express purpose of finding the letter and accusing your brother of protecting a murderer.' He could not stay his short, hard laugh. 'I would get my punishment, and he'd go to jail. The perfect Le Clere revenge. I knew your brother would accept the blame rather than see you punished.' Bile rose in his throat as he heard himself utter the words. He forced himself to continue.

'Everything William did, he did to protect his

family. But that wasn't good enough for me. I wanted him to suffer because he took you from me, even if it hurt you, too.'

She laid her hand on his. He stared at her small bandaged fingers resting on his large tanned hand. He had almost been the cause of her death tonight, her and the babe. Only her courage and wit had saved the day.

He put a hand on top of hers, encasing the cold, icy skin. Thank God she didn't pull away in disgust. Somehow feeling her hand beneath his gave him the courage to go on. He smoothed it gently.

'I even went so far as to involve your sister, pretending I would ruin her, to lure you in. I used you. When you agreed to marry me, I couldn't believe it.' He closed his eyes and shook his head. 'It was hell on earth. I had my orders. I had to be back in France the next day. Yet I couldn't resist. It was all I ever wanted. You. A family…' His voice broke. 'I never meant to give you a child. Before I met you, I intended never to marry. To never pass on the Le Clere curse. You trusted me and I let you down.' A lump in his throat made further speech impossible.

The truth lay between them, ugly and raw. Now she knew he was just as bad as Le Clere. Worse. She knew he'd planned her beloved twin's downfall.

She didn't move or speak, just stared at him with her grey eyes huge in her pale oval face. The face he saw every night in his dreams.

'I'm sorry,' he said softly. 'I'll not force you to stay with me. I am not fit for human company. All I ask is a role with our child. That somehow we find a way not to destroy another life with bitterness and hate.'

He could not look at her. He heard her get up. She would leave now. He would not beg her to stay. He'd begged once before and she had sent him away. And rightly so. It was for the best.

The silence between them seemed endless.

The rustle of silks as she knelt beside him whispered of hope. 'I don't believe in curses.'

Ah, Ellie—even now she would try to take his part. He could not let her be fooled. '*Chérie*, the Le Clere tempers are legendary, it shows up in history books.'

Ellie couldn't bear the sorrow-edged guilt in his voice, the defeated slump of his shoulders. 'Name one person you have hurt in a rage. Yes, you have a temper. But so do I. And like everyone else you control it.'

He lifted his gaze to her face, his eyes wide. 'Don't be blind, Ellie. Look what Le Clere did to your older brother, to my mother. Looked what I planned for your brother.'

'Le Clere is a bad man. But he did nothing in a rage. He planned it. All of it. And he made you, a small boy, believe you were evil.' She shook her head. 'You had every right to be angry at William, but you never followed through with your plans. Think back, Garrick. Even when you had me at your mercy, when you discovered I was Lady Moonlight, you were furious. But you did nothing but help me. You were kind to me.'

'That was different, *chérie*. I had other plans for you.'

The words struck a chord low in her belly and with it came flutters of desire, sparks of heat. She thought she might go up in flames. She fought to keep her voice full of reason, not passion. 'People get angry and they do exactly what you do. They control it.'

The crease between his brows deepened. 'Not always. I once came very close to murdering a man.' His fists clenched. 'I don't know what would have happened if I hadn't been stopped. It was what decided me to join the army.'

The starkness in his expression cut her to the quick. She had the feeling that if she showed the slightest doubt, he would leave, that she would never see him again. She had never feared him. Not for one moment. 'Tell me what happened.'

His lips thinned. 'I caught him beating a child. I lost all reason and attacked in a blind rage.'

'This man, he was a scrawny fellow, begging for mercy while you attacked him, I suppose.'

'God, no. He was a bruiser. Could have killed the boy with one blow. It took two fellows to hold him down after Harry pulled me off.'

'Fisticuffs, then, between two equals. It sounds as if he deserved a taste of his own medicine. And yet you didn't kill him.'

'Don't make light of it, Ellie. What if I hurt you? Or our child? How can I know for certain? You are better off without me.'

Her heart gave a little hop. Was this the reason for his withdrawal? Not his anger at being forced into marriage?

'I know,' she said firmly. She put a hand under his chin, drew his gaze up to meet hers. 'I know you. I trust you.'

A smile dawned slowly. A smile full of hope as well as love. A smile that made her stomach tumble and her heart leap. 'So, you are willing to take a chance on me?'

'Of course.' She put her heart and her soul into the words. 'I love you.'

He leaned forwards and nibbled her neck. 'Are you sure?'

The flutters tightened into yearning and arousal.

'Absolutely certain.' She punched his shoulder. 'Take me to bed.'

'Ouch!' He leapt up. 'No more of this abuse, beloved. And no more sitting in this freezing room. You have a child to consider. My child.' The pride in his voice, and the joy in his face, sent a sweet pang to her heart.

He gazed into her eyes. 'I know a place where you and I could be warm together. Will you come with me, my one and only love?' He held out his hand and stood, hesitant, waiting for her reply.

Eleanor's eyes misted. His love. At last he had called her his love.

'Oh, Garrick. If only I had said yes, instead of sending you away, none of this would have happened.' She blinked and swallowed the sob that threatened to choke her. 'I was a coward. Afraid of making another mistake.'

He reached out and touched her cheek, catching, with his finger, one of the wayward tears. 'You are the most courageous woman I know.'

So many things had got in the way of their love, her pride as well as his, but even as that regretful thought saddened her, a new enlightenment followed.

He would never be the wicked careless young man she had fallen for that summer so long ago, but it was this man, this battle-weary, hard man who now had the courage to bare his heart whom she loved. He was her own true love and the man she and her child needed, and in this man she was truly blessed.

She opened her arms. 'Oh, Garrick, I love you so much, I always have. When I thought you were dead, if it hadn't been for the child I would have died, too.'

'Thank God for that, then,' he said hoarsely. 'Come with me, Ellie, wherever life takes us from this day forth.' He enfolded her in his arms.

'Yes, my love,' she whispered against his lips.

He crushed her to him and kissed her mouth, the beat of his heart a rapid tattoo against her ribs. She melted against him and heard his deep sigh of relief as he picked her up and started for the staircase.

'Welcome home, my wicked Marquess,' she whispered.

* * * * *

Kay Young returned to woozy consciousness to find that she was lying on a soft sofa beneath a heap of quilts near a cheerfully burning fire. When she tried to move, however, everything hurt, and she groaned.

At once she heard a sound, then a stranger with a hard, harsh face was squatting beside her. "Shh," he said softly. "You're safe here. I promise."

"I have to go," she said weakly, struggling against pain. "He'll find me. He can't find me."

"Easy, lady," he said quietly. "You're hurt. No one's going to find you here."

"He will," she said desperately, terror clutching at her insides. "He always finds me!"

"Easy," he said again. "There's a blizzard outside. No one's getting here tonight, not even the doctor. I know, because I tried."

"Doctor? I don't need a doctor! I've got to get away."

"There's nowhere to go tonight," he said levelly. "And if I thought you could stand, I'd take you to a window and show you."

But even as she tried once more to pull away the quilts, she remembered something else: this man had been gentle when he'd found her beside the road, even when she had kicked and clawed. He hadn't hurt her.

Terror receded just a bit. She looked at him and detected signs of true concern there.

The terror eased another notch and she let her head sag on the pillow. "He always finds me," she whispered.

"Not here. Not tonight. That much I can guarantee."

*Will Kay's mysterious rescuer protect her
from her worst fears?*
Find out in HER HERO IN HIDING by New York
Times *bestselling author Rachel Lee.*
*Available June 2010, only from Silhouette®
Romantic Suspense.*

HARLEQUIN® *Romance*®

Four friends, four dream weddings!

On a girly weekend in Las Vegas, best friends Alex, Molly,
Serena and Jayne are supposed to just have fun and forget
men, but they end up meeting their perfect matches!
Will the love they find in Vegas stay in Vegas?

Find out in this sassy, fun and wildly romantic miniseries
all about love and friendship!

Saving Cinderella! by MYRNA MACKENZIE
Available June

Vegas Pregnancy Surprise by SHIRLEY JUMP
Available July

Inconveniently Wed! by JACKIE BRAUN
Available August

Wedding Date with the Best Man
by MELISSA McCLONE
Available September

www.eHarlequin.com

HRI7663